THE ANSWER CAME TO HER—
FROM DEEP INSIDE HER HEART . . .

He watched her sitting passively on the elegant brocade settee, her red-gold curls catching the reflections of the firelight. Only her tightly clasped fingers betrayed the tension she was under.

He cleared his throat. "Is that what you wish me to do, my dear? Do you honestly want that promise to be kept?"

Samantha raised her eyes from her lap and fixed her wide amber gaze on his sun-tanned face. His question had surprised her, forcing her to confront her own feelings . . . As Samantha gazed into the dark depths of his eyes, she felt a wave of longing sweep through her body. And then he smiled, his generous mouth curving up at the corners in secret amusement, and Samantha suddenly knew, without a shadow of a doubt, that yes, she did indeed wish most desperately for that promise to be kept . . .

Lady Samantha's Choice

Olivia Fontayne

JOVE BOOKS, NEW YORK

LADY SAMANTHA'S CHOICE

A Jove Book / published by arrangement with
the author

PRINTING HISTORY
Jove edition / April 1993

ISBN: 0-515-11081-7

Jove Books are published by The Berkley Publishing Group,
200 Madison Avenue, New York, New York 10016.
The name "JOVE" and the "J" logo
are trademarks belonging to Jove Publications, Inc.

PRINTED IN THE UNITED STATES OF AMERICA

10 9 8 7 6 5 4 3 2 1

Prologue

MR. ARCHIBALD MACINTYRE, SENIOR PARTNER OF THE FIRM OF London solicitors MacIntyre and Hamilton, paused to clear his throat and glance uneasily at the assembled family and dependents of his former patron, Lord Edward James Montegue Ashley, the fifth Earl of Midland. He fervently wished, not for the first time since his arrival at Ashley Hall the previous winter afternoon, that he had sent his junior partner, Mr. Matthew Hamilton, to read the earl's last will and testament to his bereaved and unsuspecting family.

With an imperceptible sigh of resignation, Mr. MacIntyre looked down at the offending passage he was about to read. In the fifty-odd years he had been a solicitor, he had encountered many oddities among his noble clients when it came time for them to dictate their wills, and the particular condition Lord Midland had insisted most adamantly on inserting in the present document was by no means the most eccentric Mr. MacIntyre had been privileged to witness. If truth were told, the stolid solicitor rather favoured the old-fashioned stand the earl had adopted regarding the future well-being of his eldest daughter. Knowing Lady Samantha Ashley as well as he did, however, Mr. MacIntyre was understandably nervous about her reaction to the clause he was about to read.

He had good cause for his misgivings. No sooner had his voice died away than a perceptible chill invaded the subdued yet congenial atmosphere which had reigned among those seated around the blazing log fire in the open hearth of the library at Ashley Hall.

The awkward silence was broken almost immediately by an incredulous exclamation from Lady Samantha herself.

"I beg your pardon, Mr. MacIntyre." Her clear voice held that precise note of calm authority which the old solicitor had come to know well in the four years since Lady Samantha had taken over the running of the Ashley estates while her father spent his time in India. "Are you quite certain that you have read that correctly? I cannot conceive of anything so gothic coming from my dear Papa."

"Hush, my love," Lady Midland interjected soothingly, anxious to forestall her eldest daughter's notorious habit of speaking her mind without considering the restrained demeanour expected of young ladies of her birth and fortune. "Your Papa only wanted what was best for you, dearest."

"You knew about this . . . this . . . atrocity?" Samantha turned to her mother and regarded her accusingly, her amber eyes flashing dangerously in a face pale with suppressed hostility and shock.

"Oh, no, my love. Of course not." Lady Midland glanced appealingly at the solicitor.

This portly gentleman cleared his throat again and, for want of a better solution to the uncomfortable situation, reread the offending passage in his ponderous voice.

The remainder of my estate, including all monies, goods, and chattels not expressly entailed to my legal heir or distributed in the above bequests, shall go to my eldest daughter, Lady Samantha Lucia Abigail Ashley, on the condition that, within a year to the day after my death, she be joined in marriage to the son of my lifelong friend, James Arthur Silverdale, Fourth Marquess of Carrington, of Silverdale Grange in Hampshire, in accordance with an agreement between us entered into on the day of her birth, September 20, 1793. In the event that this marriage has not taken place as stipulated above, the portion of my estate intended for my daughter Lady Samantha shall go to my legal heir, Gerald Bartholomew Ashley, with the understanding that he will provide for both my daughters until such time as they are wed.

"Happy to do so, my dear Cousin. Very happy to oblige." The new Earl of Midland forced his thin lips into a slight smile to cover the bitter disappointment he had just suffered at the hands of his deceased uncle. Ever since receiving notice of the untimely demise of his predecessor during one of the earl's lengthy sojourns in India, Gerald Ashley had managed to convince himself that, as heir to the title and the new head of the family, he was entitled to and would undoubtedly receive the lion's share of his uncle's enormous fortune. On these expectations, he had immediately spent a goodly sum on setting himself up in a style befitting an Ashley of Ashley Hall.

Samantha threw a withering glance at her father's heir, the new Earl of Midland, ill concealing her dislike for this ubiquitous, dandified fop who had so unexpectedly acquired an unpleasant degree of power over her future.

"You would like that, wouldn't you," she hissed angrily. "And within the year Ashley Hall would be sold off to pay your gambling debts, no doubt. But you can stop gloating in that odious way, Cousin, because I do not expect to require your charity."

Lady Midland again intervened to divert what experience had taught her could easily develop into a shouting match between her impetuous eldest daughter and her only nephew, son of her dear Edward's late brother George.

"If that is all, Mr. MacIntyre," she said hastily, "perhaps you would like to join us for refreshments in the dining room?"

The solicitor wiped his brow with a damp handkerchief, thankful to have slid through a deucedly uncomfortable moment with relative ease.

Later that afternoon Lady Samantha confronted her anxious parent in Lady Midland's sitting-room, and loudly derided her Papa's inconsiderate and arbitrary disposition of her future.

"Try to be philosophical about it, dear," her mother begged. "After all, Gerald has been dangling after you for years now." She glanced uneasily at the unladylike scowl on her daughter's face and added rather helplessly, "Perhaps things will work out after all."

"If by that you mean that I might accept an offer from Gerald and remain as mistress of Ashley Hall, you have windmills in your head, Mama. Nothing, and I mean nothing, could induce me to marry that grasping toad. I would rather starve than accept that fate. So pray do not mention it again."

Samantha turned back to the window and gazed resentfully out at the huge expanse of park still covered with yesterday's light snow. Her heart constricted at the thought of Ashley Hall and its surrounding estate and farms falling into the hands of her mercenary cousin. This was her home, the place where all her sweetest and dearest memories were rooted. She had roamed, first on her pony and then on the most mettlesome horses in her father's stables, over every inch of the rambling estate. She knew the life history of every tenant on the numerous farms belonging to the Ashleys and could tell within a shilling the market value of every crop grown on the Home Farm. This was hers for another year. She would not give it up easily.

Lady Midland regarded her daughter's rigid back and sighed. "Do not fly off the handle, love. I would not dream of asking you to do anything that is repugnant to you. Gerald might well let us live in the Dower House at the Hall. He is not a monster, after all."

Samantha turned to look at her mother pityingly. "You do not know him, Mama. He is no longer the docile lad who used to spend his summers with us at Ashley Hall. Have you forgotten what Aunt Eliza wrote only last month about his mother having to mortgage her house in London to keep him out of Newgate?"

"Anyone can suffer a small *contretemps,* my love. You are too harsh on the lad."

This attempt at mollification was greeted by an unladylike, derisive snort. "You are far too good, Mama. Believe me, Gerald is a Captain Sharp of the worst kind. And woe betide us if we must throw ourselves on his mercy. Do you realize that, unentailed as it is, Ashley Hall could be sold out from under us and we would be homeless and penniless?"

"There you go again, dearest, exaggerating everything. Even if Gerald does behave in such a shabby manner—which I don't for a moment believe he would—we still have the lifetime use of the Dower House at Midland Grange, and my portion is quite sufficient for us to live reasonably well."

"Well, reasonably well is not good enough, Mama. What about Felicity's come-out? Surely you would wish her to have a Season in London when the time comes?"

"You did without one, dearest," murmured Lady Midland.

"Yes. Because I preferred to stay here and manage the estate while Papa was in India."

"Miles could have taken care of everything, you know," her ladyship interrupted gently. "It's not as though the estate were abandoned."

"You know as well as I do that Miles is getting too old to supervise such a big place; besides, his rheumatism is worse than ever. Papa really should have pensioned the old man off before his last trip abroad."

Her ladyship sighed again. She loved Samantha dearly, but she did wish that her handsome, headstrong daughter would find her amusements in the social whirl of London's *beau monde* where an eligible son-in-law might be found, rather than in riding out with Miles, the steward, or trudging through the Home Wood with Harper, the head game warden.

"Well, perhaps life in Northumberland will not be as dreadful as you picture it, dearest," she murmured optimistically, hoping to chase the blue-deviled expression from her daughter's lovely face.

"No," came the caustic reply. "It will be infinitely worse, Mama. Can you really contemplate taking up residence in that musty, damp cavern of a place, miles from anywhere? Furthermore, it is bound to be in catastrophic disrepair. Papa has not been near the place in ten years. Are you prepared to spend a small fortune putting it in habitable shape?"

Samantha took an agitated turn about the comfortable room and returned to gaze out at the first snowflakes of a new storm that floated effortlessly past the window. Her mind was full of trepidation at the unpleasant array of choices which lay before her. Why, oh why, had her dearest Papa, a man usually blessed with the ultimate of good sense, seen fit to place her in such an impossible situation? Must she indeed choose between her obnoxious cousin and a total stranger? The alternative— removal of her Mama and her young sister Felicity to the dreary moors of Northumberland—was unthinkable.

She turned from the window and gazed lovingly at her gentle, impractical mother, tranquilly absorbed in setting neat, tiny stitches in a fine linen handkerchief, apparently oblivious that the world had suddenly fallen in upon them. Clearly it behooved her to make the best choice to get them out of the present tangle.

"No! I will not accept any offer from our rackety cousin

Gerald," she exclaimed with more confidence than she felt. "At least until I have exhausted every other possibility," she added under her breath.

Lady Midland looked up from her needlework, a faint smile on her youthful face. "As you wish, dear," she murmured gently.

"Neither will we be exiled to the wilds of Northumberland, Mama. So do not vex yourself."

"We will manage somehow, dearest, never fear," her ladyship said with conviction.

"Yes, you can count on it, Mama," replied her more practical daughter. "Even if this means that the Marquess of Carrington must be brought to see his duty, love."

She paused, then added softly, "When the time comes, I shall see to it."

1 * The Reluctant Marquess

TEN MONTHS LATER, ON A CRISP AFTERNOON IN LATE OCTOBER, LADY Samantha descended from the Ashley travelling chaise in front of Fathington House in London. As soon as the front door opened, Jaspers, her uncle's ancient butler, greeted her with a warm smile and ushered her into the hall with discreet inquiries about the health and well-being of Lady Felicity, one of his favourite young ladies.

"All is well at Ashley Hall, Jaspers, thank you," Samantha replied with a smile. "And Felicity asked me particularly to inquire after you and Mrs. Jaspers. I believe she also mentioned something about those lemon tarts Mrs. Jaspers plied her with so generously last time we visited Lady Fathington. They seem to have made a lasting impression on her."

Leaving Jaspers and her abigail to supervise the unloading of her trunk and bandboxes from the chaise and their unpacking upstairs in the room reserved exclusively for her use by her doting aunt, Samantha announced herself to Lady Fathington in the Green Drawing-room.

The Fathingtons were childless, a state they had come, not without a considerable amount of sorrow, to accept over the years. As a result, Lady Fathington had lavished all her thwarted motherly love on her two nieces and treated them as if they were her own daughters. Never was she happier than when one or other of her sister's girls came up to London for a visit.

It was, therefore, with genuine pleasure that she threw down her needlework and rushed to embrace Lady Samantha when her niece walked into her drawing-room on that autumn afternoon.

"Samantha, my love," she carolled happily as she hugged that elegantly clad young lady to her ample bosom. "I am delighted that you are to spend a month or two with us. I have implored your dear Mama a hundred times to send you to me for a Season, love. But would she heed me? No, of course not.

Until it is almost too late to find you an eligible parti, my dear. Fie on it! But trust me, dearest. I will—''

"Weeks, dear Aunt. Weeks, not months," Samantha broke into her aunt's happy flow of chatter ruthlessly.

"Weeks?" Her ladyship looked blank.

"I distinctly wrote that I could only spend at the most two weeks with you, Aunt Eliza." She smiled regretfully at the disappointment which momentarily clouded Lady Fathington's handsome face.

"But how can I be expected to find you a husband in two weeks, my love? That is unreasonable, even for me."

Samantha laughed and hugged her aunt again.

"I didn't come to Town to catch a husband, Aunt, but to refurbish my wardrobe and attend Georgina Beauchamp's wedding. She is to marry Sir Edward Haviland on November fourth at St. George's, you know. She has asked me to be one of her bride's maids."

Although Samantha was genuinely looking forward to attending her childhood friend's marriage, the autumn wedding had provided her with a timely excuse for coming to London on an entirely different matter. She had procrastinated as long as possible about taking this trip, but the time had come for her to see that the unwelcome conditions of her father's will were honoured.

"There is absolutely no need for you to sacrifice yourself to a marriage of convenience, my love," Lady Midland had pointed out once again, as she had innumerable times during the past ten months. "Your Papa has been most generous with my portion, and I still have that small legacy from my great-aunt Mathilda. We could all live very comfortably on that until either you or Felicity marries."

"And no doubt Northumberland is swarming with eligible gentlemen anxiously waiting to offer for two penniless girls," she answered with an edge of impatience in her voice. She was weary of trying to convince her beloved yet sadly scatterbrained parent that although an income of five thousand pounds was certainly generous, it would require the severest economies for them to maintain even a pale semblance of the style they now enjoyed on a revenue in excess of fifty thousand.

"I shall apply for a post as a governess, Mama," Felicity insisted for the twentieth time. "Then you would not have to buy me any more pretty gowns. Remember how poor Miss Featherby always wore the same dreary brown bombazine every day except on Sundays?"

"And would you enjoy wearing one dreary brown dress every day for weeks, dearest?" enquired her elder sister caustically.

"No, but I would if it might help you and Mama."

"Thank you, darling," her mother said warmly. "But I am sure we will manage somehow. Samantha will know just what to do, so don't worry your pretty head, love." Her ladyship cast an appealing glance at her eldest daughter and added anxiously, "You will, won't you, dear?"

Unwilling to continue the argument and sensing, as she had so often in the past few years, that her mother had unconsciously placed the whole burden of managing their affairs squarely on her daughter's shoulders, Samantha sighed and rang for the tea-tray to be brought in.

"Yes, of course," she said with all the confidence she could muster. "I shall go up to London next week and bring the marquess up to scratch. I am sure I will be married long before the anniversary of dear Papa's death. Then there will be nothing to worry your head about, dearest."

I will have to be, she thought to herself as she returned her Aunt Eliza's motherly embrace the following Wednesday afternoon in Lady Fathington's elegant London drawing-room. If I am not . . . but she refused to contemplate the painful alternatives to achieving the unknown marquess's compliance with the conditions of her father's will.

Samantha dragged her thoughts back to the immediate present and smiled affectionately as she realized that Lady Fathington was in the middle of describing a small soirée she had planned for the coming Friday in her niece's honour.

"You should not go to such trouble, Aunt," Samantha protested mildly. "I did not plan on going about much in society."

"Nonsense, love. It will only be a small, select group of friends. And besides, you will want an opportunity to show off your new gowns."

Before Samantha could argue that she had no intention of showing off her gowns, Lady Fathington had moved on to another topic dear to her heart.

"Speaking of which, there is a new French modiste in Town, dear. A Madame Lucille, who is all the crack. She made this little walking dress for me," her ladyship continued, indicating with an offhand gesture the elegant creation of spruce-green figured silk she wore. "And I am quite pleased with it. I am told the colour suits me. What do you think, dear?"

Samantha considered the question to be superfluous since it was obvious that her aunt was in prime twig, exuding her usual elegance from the tips of her soft kid half-boots to the top of her modishly coiffed head.

Nevertheless, Samantha smiled and agreed that she did indeed find the gown vastly flattering. "I am relying on you to give me your expert advice, Aunt. And by all means, let us visit this Madame Lucille as soon as possible as I am not to be completely cast into the shade by the elegant Lady Fathington on Friday evening," she added playfully.

Lady Fathington gleefully took up the challenge, and by midmorning on the following day the two ladies were ushered into the smart salon on Harley Street where Madame Lucille, an aristocratic-looking Frenchwoman of indeterminate age and well-preserved appearance, held sway. The modiste greeted her visitors with every possible attention and soon had both ladies engrossed in the rival merits of a deep blue velvet with ivory Brussels lace at the low neckline and a heavy apricot silk, so simply cut as to be almost severe, relieved by a single deep orange rose in the daring décolletage.

Madame was enthusiastic about the effect of the blue velvet with Samantha's clear complexion and red-gold hair. "It is good on you, milady. You have a natural poise which few women of your height achieve. The blue velvet gives you a regal air which will set you apart from the crowd."

"Yes, I think you are right," Lady Fathington agreed. "But the apricot silk is so very chic. I love that simplicity, and it does wonders for your figure, my dear."

She turned to Madame with a pleased smile. "We will take both gowns; but we will need one of them ready for my soirée tomorrow evening. Can that be arranged?"

Madame declared that such a feat was indeed within her power and was gratified when the ladies proceeded to order a selection of morning, afternoon, and walking-gowns in the latest fashions.

Samantha resisted her aunt's entreaties to order a riding habit in a new shade of green with dashing military epaulettes and silver buttons. She doubted that, if indeed her mission failed and she was forced to remove to the wilds of Northumberland, she would stand in need of such an extravagant garment.

The following morning, seated in Georgina Beauchamp's private sitting-room, Samantha shared some of her misgivings over the choice she had made with her friend and confidante.

"You cannot approach a strange man and tell him he must marry you, Samantha," Georgina protested after she had heard her friend's story and read over a copy of the offending clause in Lord Midland's will. "Are you quite sure you have never met him?"

"Not that I recall. Our solicitor tells me that the old Marquess of Carrington spent most of his time abroad, like Papa. It seems that they were partners in several ventures that were immensely profitable."

"Are you telling me they were in Trade?" Georgina's voice showed her amazement that a man like Lord Midland, whose family traced its lineage back to the Norman conquest, could so far forget himself.

"I'm afraid so." Samantha laughed ruefully. "Mr. MacIntyre told me all about my Papa's passion for commerce after he read the will last year. I knew the non-entailed fortune was considerable, but I had no idea how extensive it was until poor old MacIntyre confided the approximate sum to me. In hushed tones, I might add."

"It all sounds very romantic and intriguing," Georgina confessed, her initial disapproval giving way to curiosity.

"Yes, that's what I thought at first. But then it occurred to me that Papa was really living a secret life out there in India or wherever else he went that we know nothing of. And of course, the marquess shared much of that life with Papa. It makes me wonder what else there is we know nothing of."

"Whatever can you mean, Sam?" Georgina burst out impetuously, reverting to the pet name the two girls had used in their childhood. "Do you suppose your Papa had . . . ?" She hesitated, reluctant to offend her dear Samantha, but incapable of hiding the speculation in her dancing eyes.

"A mistress, do you mean?" Samantha laughed. If truth were

told, she had often wondered the same thing herself. Her dear Papa had been a kind, affectionate, and generous parent and—as far as she knew—husband. At least Lady Midland had never complained about her lord's frequent and often lengthy absences.

"I don't really know," she replied after a slight pause. "It might well be that he did and that I have a whole slew of little brothers and sisters in Bombay," she added with a mischievous twinkle.

"Samantha! How can you talk so?" Georgina chided with an embarrassed giggle.

"Well, I didn't come here to talk about my Papa's amorous pursuits, my love. I had hoped you would be able to tell me something about the marquess and this son of his who is promised to me."

"I know less than you about them, Sam. Although I have heard that their title is not as solid as yours, it is still respectable, and they are rumoured to be full of juice."

Samantha grinned at her friend's lapse into stableyard cant. She had often begrudged Georgina the possession of two elder brothers and three younger ones, from whom she had acquired an enviable facility with inelegant language.

"If by that you mean they are plump in the pocket, then I have heard that same information from Mr. MacIntyre," Samantha pointed out. "What I had hoped you could tell me, Georgie, is whether they are in residence for the Season. My aunt is slightly acquainted with the marquess but has not seen him for several months, she tells me."

"I cannot help you there," her friend replied. "But I do know that somebody is in residence. Edward drove me through the mews last week to see a new hunter he has acquired, and we noticed the Carrington travelling chaise in the stable yard."

"How did you know it was theirs?"

"It had their crest on it, you peagoose. How else? Two rampant azure lions in a field of argent drooling over what looks like a moribund doe. Quite gruesome, I've always thought, but perhaps it suits them."

Samantha felt a return of her uneasiness about confronting the marquess. "What do you mean, exactly?" she demanded.

"I was only joking, silly," Georgina said soothingly. "I'm just glad that Edward's crest is less aggressively male, if you know what I mean. I have only caught one glimpse of Carrington's son two Seasons ago, but I remember at the time he reminded me of those lions, aloof but dangerous.''

Samantha was remembering her friend's words as she mounted the marble steps to Carrington Court in Berkeley Square later that morning, accompanied by her stalwart abigail Sally, who, at a sign from her mistress, pulled the bell smartly. She had decided on impulse after her visit with Georgina to take her Uncle Henry's advice, oft repeated during her frequent sojourns on the Fathington estate during the hunting season, to get over heavy ground as lightly as possible.

If only it were as simple as her uncle made it seem, she thought as she waited before the great carved door, her heart beating uncomfortably fast and her mouth dry.

She was surprised that her voice did not betray the least sign of trepidation when she gave her name and card to the Carrington butler and demanded to see the Marquess of Carrington on a matter concerning her late father, the Earl of Midland.

After relieving Samantha of her fur-lined cloak and settling the abigail on one of the straight-backed chairs in the hall, the butler led the young lady, whom he had immediately recognized as Quality, into an adjoining saloon. The room was warm and richly furnished with delicate French satinwood sofas and spindle-legged chairs. Samantha particularly appreciated the healthy fire that blazed in the hearth and, casting aside her gloves and reticule, bent to warm her chilled hands.

An ornate ormolu clock on the green marble mantelpiece marked the quarter hour with brief silvery chimes, and Samantha wondered fleetingly if quarter past eleven was perhaps too early to call on a fashionable London gentleman. Used to rising early herself, she had given little thought to the different tempo of life as lived in the city. Therefore, when she heard the door open behind her, it was with a feeling of relief that she turned to greet her host.

What she saw made her pause, a small frown of impatience gathering on her brow. The man who stood in the doorway was too young to be her Papa's childhood playmate. Obviously he was not the man she sought. The marquess must be around her Papa's age, in his late fifties. This gentleman could not be more than thirty-two or three. From his clothes, buckskin breeches and topboots, a well-cut coat of dark blue superfine which seemed to be smoothly welded to his tall muscular frame, and a Belcher handkerchief knotted carelessly around his throat, she judged he had but this instant returned from a gallop in the Park.

Samantha realized she was staring rather rudely when a flicker of a smile passed over the gentleman's thin lips.

"I have business with the Marquess of Carrington, sir," she said with the same cool authority that brought her respect and obedience from the various gentlemen of her acquaintance.

The gentleman before her bowed slightly.

"So Turner tells me," he said laconically, his dark eyes never leaving her face.

With a start, Samantha realized who he must be. This must be Lord Philip Silverdale, the marquess's only son; this then was the man her father had destined to be her husband. She felt her courage drain out of her. The man was impossibly uncivil and arrogant. Handsome, perhaps, in a harsh, unbending sort of way, but he would have to dispense with the cynical glint in his penetrating gaze and learn to relax the grim line of those thin lips to earn any approval from her. And too tall by half. Being tall herself, Samantha appreciated a tall man, but this one was a giant. She would get a crick in her neck if she . . . Abruptly she collected herself. What nonsense was she indulging in, for heaven's sake?

She dropped her eyes in confusion at the track her unwary thoughts had taken and strove to control the faint blush that threatened to suffuse her cheeks. She was not used to being put out of countenance by members of the opposite sex and deeply resented the awkwardness of the present situation. She refused to tolerate it any longer.

"If it is not convenient for the marquess to receive me at this early hour, perhaps you will be so kind as to tell me when he might receive me." Her voice was icily polite, and she met Lord Carrington's enigmatic gaze without flinching.

Receiving no immediately reply, Samantha gave a shrug and walked over to the green settee to gather up her gloves and reticule. The poor man was a fool on top of everything else.

"Oh, but it is convenient, my dear. Please take a seat, and I will get Turner to send in some refreshments."

Without another word, Lord Carrington strode over to the hearth and jerked the bellpull, leaving Samantha seething over the familiarity of his address.

Turner must have anticipated his master's summons, for he appeared instantly with a large silver tray containing an assortment of pastries and small cakes. From the sideboard he brought a bottle of sherry and two crystal glasses.

Lord Carrington took the sherry from the butler and glanced enquiringly in Samantha's direction. "Will you have sherry, ma'am, or shall I ask Turner to bring you a glass of ratafia?"

"Neither, thank you, sir. What I would like is to talk to the Marquess of Carrington about a matter that concerns him most closely. I understood you to say that this is a convenient time to do so. Well, my lord, I am waiting."

Samantha had the distinct impression that Turner shot her a startled glance before leaving the room. She was more certain of Lord Carrington's reaction because she was looking directly at him.

He smiled. Only slightly, to be sure, but he actually smiled. Samantha was not at all sure she liked his smile.

Then he laughed, and that was infinitely worse. A short, world-weary bark of a laugh that gave Samantha goose pimples.

"I don't know what your game is, my dear," he drawled, raking her slowly with his dark eyes, whose colour Samantha could not determine, for it seemed to change with his changing moods. "But whatever it is, you can abandon it this instant. I have heard more than my share of Banbury tales, and yours will be no more successful than a hundred others from ambitious young women with marriage on their minds."

Samantha stared at him in amazement. He must already know the conditions of her father's will, she thought. And is letting her know in no uncertain terms that he will have none of it. Her case indeed appeared hopeless, but the thought of her dear Mama striving to cope with the wilderness in Northumberland gave her the courage to swallow her pride and continue.

"This is no game, I can assure you, my lord," she said after a pause, striving to keep her voice calm and reasonable in the face of this unexpected attack. "If I may only speak with your father, I am sure the situation will become perfectly clear."

"You are too late," he replied shortly.

"Too late?" The interview was becoming increasingly strange. Samantha wondered fleetingly if his lordship was not perhaps one of those unfortunates who was born with less than full mental capacities.

"Too late for what, my lord?"

He looked at her for several moments, eyebrows slightly raised in a rakish expression of sardonic amusement.

"Too late to speak with my father, naturally."

It was Samantha's turn to stare again. She did so for a full minute before she began to lose her patience.

"I do not follow you, my lord. You have just finished telling me that I can see your father, and now you tell me I am too late to see him. What is it to be?" she added with more sharpness than was her wont.

"You certainly cannot see him here, my dear," Lord Carrington said softly, an unreadable expression in his dark eyes.

"Where is he, then?" Samantha demanded bluntly.

"In heaven I am told, although I seriously doubt it." His eyes had lost their intense expression and now regarded her with a gleam of amusement.

Samantha's temper snapped. "Botheration!" she exclaimed before stopping to consider the shocking nature of her words. "Why didn't you say so in the first place?"

Lord Carrington's brows shot up, and he regarded her coolly. "I hate to be so obvious, my dear, but you never asked me, that's why."

"Oh, but I did," she shot back sharply. "I specifically asked for the Marquess of Carrington, and . . ." She stopped abruptly, her anger evaporating as the truth dawned on her. "Oh, no. Of course. How stupid of me." Her hands flew to her warm cheeks. "You must be the . . ." She strove to control her mortification and frustration at seeing her plans disintegrate before her eyes. "You are the Marquess of Carrington," she finished miserably.

"At your service, my dear," drawled the marquess, a note of mockery in his voice.

2 * The White Knight

THE MARQUESS OF CARRINGTON GENTLY SIPPED HIS SHERRY AND wondered if perhaps he had not misjudged the regal young lady who stood staring angrily at him as if she wished he would disappear in a cloud of smoke. The experience was a novel one, and it intrigued him to know that there was at least one marriageable female in London who regarded him with obvious distaste.

Accustomed as he was to the tongue-tied, simpering adulation of nervous young ladies eager to make a suitable connection during their first Season on the Marriage Mart, he found Lady Samantha Ashley's forthright approach rather refreshing. She did not flinch under his lazy scrutiny; in fact, her haughty expression and the cold disdain in her curiously compelling amber eyes told him more clearly than any words that she held him in utter contempt.

He wondered why. And for the first time since he had walked into the room, he seriously considered the possibility that the alleged business she claimed to have with his father, the late marquess, might have some foundation of truth. It might be amusing to find out. His cousin, Anthony Dalton, with whom he was engaged to drive over to Tattersalls that afternoon, would certainly not put in an appearance before noon, so he could afford to spend a few idle moments of what had started out as a very boring day in discovering what Lady Samantha had wanted with his father.

He unbent, both mentally and physically. Picking up her untouched glass of sherry, he advanced across the room and, bowing gracefully, offered it with a conciliatory smile.

"I fear I have been rather abrupt, ma'am," he murmured smoothly. "I trust you will be generous enough to overlook my rudeness and share a glass of sherry with me?"

Although Lady Samantha did not return his smile, she did

accept the glass and allow herself to be persuaded to take a seat on the green settee, where she sat regarding him warily.

"I understand you had some personal business with my late father," he began, deciding it best to come straight to the point with this direct young lady. "If it is within my power to assist you in his regrettable absence, I can assure you I will be most happy to do so." It occurred to him belatedly that he was being incautious to the extreme in making this blanket offer, but he could hardly withdraw it now.

Lady Samantha regarded him in silence. He could see skepticism and disbelief in her eyes. "You might easily do so, my lord," she said dryly. "But if I read your character correctly, you will wash your hands of the whole affair."

For some inexplicable reason, it annoyed him that she had come so close to recognizing the lack of sincerity in his offer. "I trust you will allow me to be the judge of that, ma'am," he replied rather stiffly. He'd be damned if he would permit this chit to predict his actions for him.

"You were well acquainted with my late father, Lord Midland, I believe, my lord?"

The question did not surprise him. If anything, he probably knew Lord Midland, whom he had called Uncle Edward for as long as he could remember, as well as Lady Samantha herself.

"Were you there when . . . when he . . ." Lady Samantha hesitated slightly, then repeated in a firmer voice. "Were you with him when he died, my lord?"

"Yes," he answered simply. "My father and he had just finished their usual game of piquet after dinner. Most partial to a game of piquet was your father. He asked me to pour him another glass of claret, but when I came back with the bottle, he was slumped over the table. He never regained consciousness except for a few moments after we got him upstairs and into bed."

"Did he say anything?"

"He called out 'Bella' twice, quite distinctly, I remember. Your mother, I understand."

"Yes, that's my mother's name, Annabella."

Samantha had been quite overcome by the obvious affection in the marquess's voice as he retold the events of her father's sudden death. She was unaccountably comforted to know that he was capable of feeling such an emotion for her father.

"You loved him, didn't you?" she ventured to ask almost shyly.

He stared at her for a long moment before replying briefly, "Yes, I did. He was like a second father to me."

Samantha sighed. "He loved you too, you know. He talked about you all the time when he was at Ashley Hall. My sister and I were quite jealous of you at one time, even though we had never met you. But I can see now that you were the son he could never have here in England. He must have hated the thought of the title going to our Cousin Gerald, a loose screw if ever I saw one. Felicity and I must have been a terrible disappointment to him," she added ruefully.

"If you believe that, you are sadly mistaken, my dear," he said. "Over there in India, your father talked about his two girls, as he always called you, all the time. I know more about you than you could possibly imagine, Samantha."

She gazed at him in confusion and was surprised to see a fleeting grin flash across his saturnine features. Somehow it seemed right that he should use her given name. It created an atmosphere of intimacy which she knew to be false but which prompted her to broach the subject that had brought her to seek him out.

"Since you were so close to my father, perhaps you already know about the preposterous conditions of his will?"

She saw a flicker of surprise and wariness in his eyes.

"You did know he included you, did you not?" she added quickly.

"No. I was not aware that I figured in Lord Midland's will at all," he said coolly. "He certainly gave me no indication that I would be." He seemed to consider the implications for a moment, then added hastily, "And I have no intention of accepting anything that will disinherit either you or your sister. You may be completely easy on that account."

"You are to have everything," she replied quietly, watching his face closely for any sign of his reaction to this astounding news. "Everything, that is, except the official residence of the Earls of Midland in Northumberland. That goes to Gerald with the title. My mother, Felicity, and I are most anxious to know whether you will accept it, my lord.''

Lord Carrington stared at her in amazement. After a long moment, during which Samantha felt his dark gaze trying to penetrate the most secret recesses of her mind, he rose and stood looking down into the fire, one elegantly booted foot resting on the brass rail.

''He was mad,'' she heard him mutter half to himself, and a reluctant smile brightened her face.

''I couldn't agree more, my lord, but this is how the will reads. We have known it ever since last December.''

''And why am I only now being informed of it, may I ask?'' He rounded on her accusingly.

''We were given a year's grace period, to come to terms with my father's last wishes, I suppose,'' she replied. ''If we cannot do so, the entire non-entailed estate falls into the hands of his heir, Gerald Ashley. My despicable cousin, now the impecunious sixth Earl of Midland, is counting the days. It is a sorry state of affairs, my lord.''

''I understood you to say that Lord Midland named me heir to his non-entailed estate?''

''Oh, he did. But there's a condition, you see.'' She hesitated, unwilling, even now, to put the embarrassing stipulation into words.

''What condition?'' he demanded brusquely.

''One that you will find totally incongruous, as I do myself, my lord. If it were not for the sake of my dear Mama and Felicity who are depending on me to extract them from this onerous situation, I would not be here.''

''What is the condition?'' He spoke softly, but the softness barely concealed a note of steel which made Samantha shudder.

She glared at him helplessly. Their former ephemeral closeness had evaporated, leaving her more vulnerable to the impending humiliation she felt was inevitable.

''Here.'' She groped in her reticule and pulled out a folded sheet of paper. ''This is a copy of the clause concerning you. Read it and see for yourself the impossible position in which I find myself.''

She had risen to hand him the paper, and now she retired to

the window overlooking Berkeley Square, to watch with unseeing eyes the midday activity in that elegant thoroughfare.

The silence in the room lasted for perhaps two minutes, but to Samantha it felt like an eternity. She struggled to control a rising tide of emotion that threatened to overflow into tears, a display of missishness she heartily despised.

When it came, the marquess's reaction was not at all as she had expected and steeled herself to endure.

"Why is it that at twenty-two you are not already married with a family of your own, Samantha?"

"Twenty-three, my lord," she corrected automatically. "I'll be twenty-three next month, on the twentieth."

"Then you have been out quite long enough to have found a suitable husband, I should imagine. Although I understand that fair beauties are now in vogue, I would hardly call you an antidote." The grin she had glimpsed once made another quick sortie across his face.

"You are too kind, sir," she replied with a trace of sarcasm.

"And you certainly are a notable heiress, which almost always guarantees catching a willing victim during a first Season. Even for an antidote," he added with another faint smile. "What did you do to scare off all the young bucks, my dear?"

Samantha felt her anger rising. Even the knowledge that he was deliberately baiting her failed to check her sharp retort.

"I have not had an official Season, if you must know, my lord." His raised eyebrows prompted her to explain this unusual situation.

"I prefer country life to the pointless rounds of frivolous amusements society has decreed as *de rigueur* for a successful London Season, my lord. Aside from a few weeks spent here with my aunt, Lady Fathington, over the years, I have chosen to stay in Hampshire. Besides, since Papa has been gone for such extended periods, someone had to take charge of running the estate."

The marquess looked amused. "Are you telling me that you, single-handedly, have managed your father's estates all these years? Forgive me, but isn't that a rather unusual occupation for a young lady of Quality?"

"I have lived at Ashley Hall all my life," she said quietly. "I know everything there is to know about running an estate.

Naturally, we have a competent steward, but in Papa's absence someone had to make the decisions. For over five years now, that someone has been me.''

When his lordship made no reply, Samantha became impatient again. ''Can you understand now why I have had no time for frivolous excursions to Town, my lord?''

''Am I expected to believe that you have received no offers for marriage at all?''

Again, his reaction surprised her. ''Of course I have received offers,'' she snapped, unaccountably annoyed that he would think her totally devoid of attraction for the opposite sex. ''Far too many of them have been either from Bond Street Beaux who consider the tying of their cravats more worthy of their attention than the running of an estate, or from blatant fortune-hunters who expect me to save them from debtors' prison.''

Samantha seated herself on the settee again and tried to regain her composure. ''None of them would help matters now anyway,'' she remarked. ''It is too late for that.''

''What about this cousin of yours, the new earl? If he gets the fortune by default, he is obligated to provide for you until you do wed. Wouldn't this answer?''

''No, never!'' Samantha curled her lip in disgust. ''You cannot have met him, my lord, or you would not suggest it. He is by far the worst of the fortune-hunters. A Captain Sharp of the worst kind.'' She paused, reluctant to reveal such personally distasteful information to a stranger.

''I gamble myself occasionally,'' Carrington said mildly. ''Most gentlemen do, I believe.''

''In moderation, perhaps. But Gerald is obsessed by it and never has a feather to fly with. He has even tried to borrow money from me.''

''Am I to understand that your cousin is one of your suitors?'' the marquess asked softly.

''Of course he is,'' Samantha burst out angrily. ''For as long as I can remember, he has pestered me with his unwelcome attentions. He gulled my father into believing that marriage to me would reform him, but since Papa died, he has made no secret of his intention to have both me and the Ashley fortune.''

"He can hardly marry you without your consent, my dear girl," the marquess said shortly.

Samantha looked at him pityingly. "Gerald has threatened to turn us out of Ashley Hall and deny us the use of the Dower House there if I refuse him. He will do it, too, once it becomes legally his on the anniversary of Papa's death. In less than two months' time," she added in a subdued voice. "That is unless . . ." Again, she could not bring herself to utter the ultimatum.

The marquess had no such reservations. "Unless I marry you myself, is that it?" he demanded flatly.

Before Samantha could think of a suitable reply to this blunt question, the saloon doors burst open and a tall, startlingly handsome young man, dressed in impeccable riding clothes and carrying an ornate malacca cane, strode into the room.

He stopped abruptly when he perceived that his cousin was not alone. "I do beg your pardon, coz," he said jovially, eyeing Samantha with every evidence of approval. "Had no idea you were entertaining such a charming young lady, or I would have been here much sooner."

"My cousin Anthony Dalton," the marquess said in a resigned voice, indicating the newcomer with a brief wave of his hand. "I might as well apologize right away for his deplorable manners and the outrageous things he is bound to say to you, ma'am."

"Nonsense. Pay no attention to old Philip, ma'am, he's too top-lofty by half," the newcomer remarked with a friendly wink. "Tony Dalton at your service," he added, taking Samantha's hand and carrying it to his lips with an exaggerated bow, his eyes brimming with laughter as he met her startled gaze.

"Lady Samantha Ashley," the marquess said formally. "And I would thank you not to make a cake of yourself, Tony. At least not in front of my guest."

Dalton's face took on a look of mock horror, and he focussed his attractive blue eyes on Samantha, whose hand he still held tenderly in his. "And I must ask you, dear coz, not to embarrass me in front of Lady Samantha by insinuating that my conduct is anything but strictly *comme il faut*."

"I am sure your conduct is above reproach, Mr. Dalton," Samantha told him pleasantly, gently withdrawing her hand from his grasp. "And now, my lord, I shall leave you, our business being concluded."

"Business?" Dalton ejaculated in horrified tones. "Do you mean to tell me, coz, that you waste a perfectly wonderful assignation with a beautiful woman talking about business? Shame on you, old man. Now, if I had been in your shoes, Phil—"

"Well, you are not, Tony," Carrington said sharply. "And as for our business, Lady Samantha, I do not consider it finished at all."

Samantha glanced uneasily from the marquess to his cousin. Tony Dalton grinned mischievously, then tried to look woebegone. "I see I am sadly *de trop,*" he said with a sigh. "I shall take myself off to drink a bottle of Blue Ruin with Turner," he whispered *sotto voce* to Samantha.

"Oh, don't be ridiculous, Tony," his cousin said affectionately. "Lady Samantha, perhaps I shall see you at the Devereaux's ball tonight?"

"Oh, no, my lord," Samantha protested. "My aunt is giving a small soirée this evening which I must attend since it is in my honour." She regarded him uncertainly. "If you would not find such simple amusements insipid, I'm sure she would be more than happy to receive you, my lord."

"An excellent idea, coz, upon my word it is," Dalton cut in happily. "We accept with pleasure, my dear. And if there is to be dancing, I insist that you save the first one for me," he added with such a charming smile that Samantha had to laugh at his impudence.

"We shall certainly look forward to seeing you this evening, then, Mr. Dalton," she said, laughing, as she pulled on her gloves and moved towards the door.

"I wouldn't miss it for the world, my dear," Dalton murmured as he closed the door gently behind her.

As soon as they were alone, Dalton turned a quizzical expression on his cousin. "I declare, Phil, you are a sly dog. Wherever did you find the delectable Samantha? And who is she? Any relation to the Earl of Midland by any chance?"

"His daughter," came the short reply.

Dalton regarded his big cousin speculatively. Although almost six years separated them, the cousins had always been as close as brothers. Anthony had spent considerable time with his uncle and cousin in India and was well aware of the long-standing friendship that had existed between Lord Midland and his uncle.

Dropping his banter, he poured himself a glass of sherry and remarked seriously, "There is something here that is bothering you, coz. Care to talk about it?"

From his position before the fire, the marquess regarded his cousin for a moment, then shrugged. "You may as well know the worst, Tony," he replied with an ironic smile. "Lady Samantha came to claim me as a husband."

For once Tony Dalton was bereft of speech, a situation which provided his cousin with a certain amount of grim satisfaction.

"You're quizzing me, Phil. I don't believe a word of it."

"Here, read this," the marquess said. "A clause from Midland's will." He handed over the paper Samantha had given him. "Perhaps you can tell me what I should do under the circumstances."

After reading through the clause twice, Dalton raised an amused pair of eyes to his cousin. "Are you sure this is not a page out of the latest romantic novel?" he inquired. "I had no idea this kind of Gothic secret pact was still being practised. Do you know what this means, old man? You have been betrothed since you were ten years old and never knew it. I wonder what the Incomparable Miss Caroline Summers will have to say to this? I'd give a monkey to see her face when she finds out the biggest catch of her life has been snatched from under her nose."

The marquess smiled. He had no real interest in Miss Summers, or in any other lady of his acquaintance, for that matter. His partiality to her had been vastly exaggerated; mainly by her hopeful Mama. He dismissed her from his mind.

"I am not yet in the parson's mousetrap," he pointed out. "Do you see a way out of this contract, Tony?"

"Not unless you wish to call Lord Midland a liar, old man," Tony replied bluntly. "I take it your father did not remember to mention this little verbal agreement to you? No, I thought as much," he said in answer to his cousin's negative response. "And Midland never so much as hinted at what was in the wind, I suppose?"

Carrington shrugged his broad shoulders. "No, this took me completely by surprise. He used to talk about her all the time, of course, and perhaps I should have seen it coming; but you know how it is. Marriage?"

"Yes, I know, coz. You never even gave it a thought. Neither have I, to tell the truth."

This remark was greeted by a snort from his lordship.

"But the old man cast you in the role of the White Knight," Dalton continued, warming to his subject. "Riding to rescue the lady from the evil new earl. He is bound to be evil, don't you think, coz?"

"As a matter of fact, he does seem to be a pretty sleazy character," his cousin agreed, beginning to see a glimmer of humour in the situation that had been thrust so unexpectedly upon him. "I expect we will find out for certain this evening at Lady Fathington's soirée."

"Well, then, I don't see how you can, in good conscience, fail to throw yourself into the breach, old man. Unless you want to be the real villain of the piece. Do you?"

The marquess did not know what his answer to that question might be since he did not, as yet, know his own mind on the subject of Lady Samantha Ashley.

3 * The Waltz

SAMANTHA WAS TROUBLED WITH SIMILAR THOUGHTS AS SHE DRESSED for Lady Fathington's soirée that evening. She was not at all sure that she liked the Marquess of Carrington; yet neither could she bring herself to admit that she actually disliked him. He was an enigma to her. Undoubtedly attractive in a severe, imposing way, but with a smile that suggested a softer side to him, he was all too clearly accustomed to more than his fair share of female adulation and homage.

Well, he would soon learn that she was not one of those feather-headed females who hung, starry-eyed, on his every word, she told herself firmly. Neither was she accustomed to taking orders from anyone, and she had more than a sneaking suspicion that Philip Silverdale was one of those top-lofty individuals who spent their entire lives giving orders and expecting them to be obeyed.

She was more than a little annoyed with herself for allowing the marquess to upset her normal tranquillity of mind. And she partially blamed her well-meaning Aunt Eliza for some of the unsettling thoughts that now plagued her.

"My love, what a splendid coup," her ladyship had cooed in a fit of near ecstasy when Samantha had begged her indulgence for adding two new guests to the evening's list. "Of course I don't mind, you silly goose. I had no idea Carrington was in residence. He comes and goes so often that I gave up long ago trying to keep up with him. Quite elusive, you know; but certainly the most eligible bachelor in London now that he has inherited the title, that is, if one could but pin him down."

"Do you know him well, Aunt?" Samantha asked casually, thankful that Lady Fathington had not asked her how she had met Carrington. She had decided that it would be best, at least for the moment, not to worry her aunt and uncle with the unfortunate conditions of her Papa's will.

"No, dear. But I used to know the old marquess back when I first married Fathington. He was a handsome devil, I can tell you, but like your father, he spent too much of his time abroad in those unhealthy climates. His son, Philip Silverdale, is just as bad they say, but he would make an excellent match, my love. I still cannot believe that he actually promised to come tonight."

Samantha wondered what her aunt would say if she knew that the elusive marquess was actually promised to her niece in marriage. *If only I can persuade him to keep that promise,* she mused, smoothing down the apricot silk gown Madame Lucille had delivered shortly before tea-time that afternoon. To make matters worse, she could not make up her own mind whether she really wanted him to keep his father's promise.

"You'll make the other young ladies weep with envy, Miss Samantha," declared Sally, who had just put the finishing touches to her mistress's gleaming red-gold curls, as she stood back to regard her handiwork. "Will you wear the pearls, miss? Or shall I unpack the diamond pendant?"

"The pearls, Sally. And I had better take the new silver gauze shawl downstairs with me. I feel rather undressed in this gown."

"Nonsense, love." Her ladyship laughed as she swept into her niece's bedchamber to survey the effects of the new gown. "Actually it is quite modest by the most recent French standards."

Samantha peered down at her exposed bosom and grimaced. "I am glad you did not allow Madame Lucille to follow that fad too closely, Aunt. I fear I have not much more to reveal." She tucked the gauze orange rose more snugly in her décolletage.

"You are refining too much, dear." Lady Fathington examined Samantha with approval. "You look simply magnificent. I was right to order that gown for you; it is truly elegant. Come now, child, don't dawdle. Our first guests will soon be arriving."

In spite of herself, Samantha was looking forward to an evening of renewing old friendships, meeting her aunt's latest bosom-bows, and spending as much time as possible with Georgina Beauchamp and her fiancé, Sir Edward Haviland.

The only sour note she anticipated was the ubiquitous presence of her cousin Gerald Ashley, who had followed her into Town and was staying with his widowed mother in her little house on Jermyn Street.

"I wish you didn't have to invite that tiresome coxcomb, Aunt," Samantha had complained over tea that afternoon. "I know I shouldn't say so, but he is a disgrace to the family, and I'm glad Papa is not alive to see the spectacle he is making of himself in Ashley, parading his title all over the village and running up bills at both posting inns that he is unable to pay."

Lady Fathington looked at her niece in surprise. "Unable to pay? You cannot be serious, love. Your mother told me that you received the bulk of the unentailed estates, of course, but I assumed that your Papa had provided for his heir as well."

"Oh no. Gerald only got the official seat in Northumberland, which has practically no income at all, and it made him furious. It is forever pockets to let with him, you know. And now that he has the title, it irks him all the more not to be able to live up to his own expectations."

"He sounds like a loose screw indeed, my dear. But he is the head of the family, and I could hardly not invite him to a party in your honour, now could I?"

Samantha had to agree with her aunt, but the prospect of spending a whole evening listening to Gerald's snide simperings and suggestive remarks put a damper on her spirits.

Nevertheless, she brightened visibly when she remembered that the charming Mr. Anthony Dalton would also be present. Samantha suspected that beneath the outrageous flow of flirtatious chatter, Mr. Dalton was a good deal more serious than he seemed. As for his famous cousin, she seriously doubted that the Marquess of Carrington would come at all, but she hadn't the heart to say as much to her aunt.

These doubts became a certainty when, after the first hour of mingling with her aunt's guests, Samantha realized that neither gentleman had put in an appearance.

Georgina was even more put out by their absence. "I think it is too bad of the marquess to keep us in suspense like this," she complained to her friend over a glass of iced champagne. "I have not yet had a chance to see him at close range, you know. They say he is devastatingly handsome. I declare it is too provoking of him.''

''Who is this villain who is provoking you, my dears?'' enquired Lord Henry Fathington in his jovial manner, stopping on his way to the card room to tease his favourite niece and her friend. ''Not Sir Edward, I trust?'' He cocked a bushy eyebrow at Georgina, who blushed prettily and assured his lordship that her fiancé was never provoking.

''Wait until after the wedding, my dear,'' Lord Fathington said with a twinkle in his eyes. ''Then we shall hear a different story. Shan't we, my love?'' he asked his elegant wife, who came up in time to hear this exchange.

''Don't believe a word of it,'' her ladyship protested calmly. ''Marriage has a sedative effect on most gentlemen, and they soon settle down to a respectable, staid existence. As indeed you have, my lord.'' She smiled as she moved on to see the card-room properly set up.

''Your aunt is right, of course,'' Lord Fathington said. ''Nothing like a good marriage to settle a man down.'' After delivering this piece of homely wisdom, he took himself off to the card-room after his wife.

When the music struck up half an hour later, Samantha had quite given up on her two capricious guests and was wondering how she could escape dancing the first dance—which she had dutifully saved for Mr. Dalton—with her persistent cousin Gerald. Even now he was heading across the room in her direction and she was looking desperately around for a substitute partner when a pleasant voice said at her elbow: ''I believe this is my dance, Lady Samantha?''

She swung round and could not keep the relief out of her voice as she greeted Mr. Dalton and allowed him to lead her out onto the floor.

''I did not see you arrive, sir,'' she said politely.

Dalton groaned audibly. ''What a terrible set-down, my lady. I am crushed. Here I am, exhausted with the effort of getting myself rigged out in all my finery and expecting to see you waiting with bated breath in the front hall for my belated arrival, and what do I hear? You are totally unconcerned about my presence. How can you be so cruel?'' He grinned at her so charmingly that Samantha forgave him this blatant attempt at flirtation.

"Quite the contrary, sir," she said, amused at his brash nonsense. "You arrived in the nick of time to save me from a most terrible and excruciating fate. I am, quite frankly, much obliged to you and delighted to see you."

Dalton carried the hand he was holding at that moment to his lips and kissed it gravely. "Those words are balm to my poor heart, Lady Samantha. I shall forgive you for ignoring my arrival."

They joined the set of a country dance just forming, and when he had a chance, Dalton enquired as to the exact nature of the fate his hostess had escaped.

"Oh, I really shouldn't tell you, sir," Samantha answered ruefully. "It was rash of me even to mention it. Pray forget I said it. I am not usually so muddle-headed."

Samantha concentrated on the steps and made a deliberate effort not to scan the room for a particular tall gentleman with dark brooding eyes. She told herself firmly that she did not care a button if he had come or not, and gave Mr. Dalton such a saucy smile when next they came together that he was quite overcome and came close to missing a step.

When the music came to a close, he escorted her to the buffet set up in the dining-room, where he procured a cool glass of champagne for her.

"I don't suppose that terrible and excruciating fate has anything to do with an overdressed jackanapes in a tight violent puce coat and a yellow-striped satin waistcoat who is glaring at us as though he would like to cut my liver out and eat it, does it?" he enquired lazily, smiling down at her with a twinkle lurking in his blue eyes.

Seeing her face cloud with annoyance, he added apologetically, "Dash it! There goes my stupid tongue again. Doubtless he is some relative or other of yours and I have sunk myself beyond reproach with that careless remark."

He looked so chagrined that Samantha had to laugh. "As a matter of fact he is my cousin, the head of the family, no less."

"Do you mean to tell me that Bond Street Beau is the new Earl of Midland?" Dalton asked in genuine astonishment. "No wonder you were anxious to escape his company, my dear.

Can't blame you. I wouldn't want to claim him myself, come to that. Not at all the thing, your cousin. Puce and yellow! Great Scot!''

Samantha was so diverted by this exaggerated display of revulsion that she let a bubble of laughter escape her.

Dalton grinned down at her. ''What has this miserable rasher-o'wind done to distress you, my dear? Would you like me to go over and darken his daylights for him? Happy to do so, you know. Just say the word.''

''Not brawling again, are you, Tony?'' came a drawling, faintly bored voice from behind them.

Samantha turned to find the Marquess of Carrington gazing down at her in amusement, his dark eyes as inscrutable as ever.

''I have come to rescue you from my impetuous cousin and to claim the next dance, which I believe is a waltz,'' he announced calmly, bowing over her fingers, which he then placed on his sleeve preparatory to leading her out onto the floor.

Samantha did not know whether to be amused or annoyed at this cavalier behaviour. ''I believe this dance is already promised, my lord,'' she observed coolly, glancing at her card.

Carrington twitched the offending card from her fingers, scratched out her cousin's name, and calmly wrote in his own.

''So I see,'' he remarked. ''It is promised to me.''

By the time Samantha had recovered from her astonishment at such high-handed behaviour, she was being guided round the dance floor to the strains of the latest Strauss waltz, the marquess's hand firmly planted on her slim waist. The sensation of this closeness was strangely exhilarating, and it was not until they had circled the room twice that she dared to tear her eyes away from her partner's pale grey waistcoat.

''Are you always so . . . so . . .'' She fumbled for a word that would describe his behaviour with just the right hint of censure.

''So what?'' He was so obviously laughing at her that Samantha felt some of her annoyance evaporate.

''So impetuous?'' she finished somewhat lamely.

''That is hardly a word I would choose to describe myself. No, I cannot think myself impetuous, my dear.''

"What I meant was, do you always ride roughshod over everybody as you did just now?"

"Did I indeed ride roughshod over anybody?" He sounded amused, and his lips had relaxed into a faint smile.

"You certainly did, sir," Samantha said severely. "Did you stop to ask yourself if I wanted to dance with you or not? No, of course it never even occurred to you. And what about the poor gentleman whose place you so ruthlessly usurped, my lord? Does your conscience not bother you on that score?"

"Since that 'poor gentleman,' as you choose to call him, was that same jackstraw cousin of yours, the fellow you told me only this morning is a confirmed rum touch and fortune-hunter—Captain Sharp, I believe is the term you used—then I can honestly say that my conscience is clear." He paused for a moment, and Samantha thought she discerned a glimmer of devilry in those dark eyes.

"And you do not think you were slightly high-handed, my lord?" she enquired sweetly.

"Certainly not. And I fail to see that you can be anything but grateful to me for fobbing him off, my dear. Especially so if that so-called poor gentleman is the one glowering at us from the doorway over there. If his sartorial tastes are any indication of his character, I strongly suggest that you disassociate yourself from him entirely. Bad *ton* is written all over him, no doubt about it."

"Oh, you are right, of course, my lord. And after December the tenth, I hope I never have to see him again."

"What is so special about December the tenth?"

Samantha glanced up at him uneasily, then replied calmly, "It is the anniversary of my Papa's death. The day Gerald will come into possession of the Ashley fortune."

Despite her efforts to control it, her voice quavered slightly at the end of this speech. She dropped her eyes to the grey waistcoat again and swallowed the lump that suddenly seemed to obstruct her throat.

The silence between them stretched out for so long that Samantha finally ventured to look up at him. His face had taken on a bleak expression, and he was gazing out over her head, his lips drawn into a hard line.

Samantha was immediately filled with remorse. She had

promised herself that, in the unlikely event that Carrington did attend her aunt's soirée, she would avoid any mention of the will. And here she had already broken her promise and reminded the marquess of his uncomfortable role in the future of the Ashleys.

She sighed faintly and set herself to correct her error.

"There is no earthly reason to look so thunderous, my lord," she said with an attempt at levity. "It is not the end of the world, as you said yourself this morning. Perhaps if I did marry Gerald, he would not be so obnoxious after all."

"I forbid you even to consider anything so hare-brained," came the unexpectedly sharp reply. He was looking down at her now, and there was no mistaking the seriousness in his voice. Samantha realized that her previous evaluation of the marquess had been all too correct; he had given a command and expected to be obeyed without question.

Something in her rebelled.

"It is hardly your concern, my lord," she said stiffly in her best authoritarian manner.

"Nonsense, my girl. Your father obviously intended me to make it my concern since he placed both you and the Ashley estates at my disposal. And if I have anything at all to say in the matter, you will not marry Gerald Ashley. Take my word for it."

Samantha suddenly became conscious that the music had stopped and that they stood glaring at each other in the middle of the dance floor.

"We are making a spectacle of ourselves, my lord," she said with some acerbity. "I think we could both use a cooling drink."

Silently the marquess took her by the elbow and guided her to the buffet. Over the rim of a fluted champagne glass, Samantha observed him cautiously. "I gather you are determined to interfere in my affairs, my lord?"

He sketched a grim smile. "I would not call it interfering, my girl. But I do intend to see to it that you and your sister are provided for, one way or another."

Samantha had a definite feeling that this impossible man was dictating to her again. She was not used to being dictated to, and the sooner he discovered that she had no intention of letting him get away with it, the sooner they could begin to deal comfortably with each other again.

"I think you should realize, my lord," she began in a carefully controlled voice, "that I am not accustomed to being told what to do, especially when it concerns my choice of a husband."

"Any fool can see that, my girl," he replied with a brusque laugh. "But you will learn. Believe me, you will learn."

Paralyzed at this effrontery, Samantha was unable to find a suitable set-down for this arrogant coxcomb.

"We cannot talk here," the marquess continued, as though they had been engaged in an amiable conversation. "I shall call for you tomorrow afternoon at two o'clock and take you driving in the Park. We can continue our discussion then."

"Are you asking me or ordering me, my lord?" Samantha enquired with icy politeness.

Carrington raised his eyebrows in mock amazement. "Your wits have gone begging, my dear girl. Wherever did you get the impression that I am so lacking in address?"

Before she could think up a suitably crushing snub, he had raised her hand to his lips and begged her to give his congés to Lady Fathington. The next minute he was gone, his broad shoulders clearly visible as he disappeared into the crowd.

In the small hours of the next morning, the Marquess of Carrington sat up before the cheerful fire in his library and wondered aloud if he should not perhaps have washed his hands of the whole Ashley business.

"Oh, fiddle!" exclaimed his cousin rather more mildly than was his wont. He sat slouched in a leather easy chair opposite Carrington, his booted feet propped negligently on the brass guard-rail.

"You are thrust willy-nilly into the most romantic sort of adventure imaginable, and all you can say is: 'I wonder if I should have washed my hands of it?' Fie on you, coz, you're a dull dog if ever I saw one."

"What would you have me do, Tony?" his lordship queried morosely. The numerous glasses of his father's excellent brandy he had imbibed over the past three hours had not helped to make his involvement in the Ashley affair, as he called it, any clearer.

"Well, I would consider my options, if I were you," Dalton replied. "That Ashley chit is not something to turn your nose up at, if you ask me. Not an accredited Beauty like the Summers girl, of course, but undoubtedly a female of the first consequence. Birth, breeding, fortune. Make someone a first-class wife, coz. Has that kind of beauty that'll last past her thirtieth year. Intelligent and witty, too, which is not something you could say about the Summers chit."

"You seem to have given her a very thorough scrutiny, my lad," his cousin drawled, his dark eyes fixed speculatively on Dalton's face.

Tony laughed good-naturedly. "Don't get on your high ropes with me, coz. It won't fadge. I knew you would want the benefit of my extensive experience with the fairer sex in making your decision, so of course I made an effort to draw her out."

"Looked more like ordinary flirtation to me, Tony. One of these days you'll go too far and find yourself leg-shackled, my lad. Serve you right, too. Don't tell me you have been bowled over by the fair Samantha?"

Although Tony loudly denied having anything but a friendly interest in what he chose to call his cousin's promised bride, Carrington caught himself experiencing an unfamiliar stab of envy at the ease with which his fair, blue-eyed cousin had conversed so uninhibitedly with Lady Samantha during the previous evening.

"You should relax more with the lady," Dalton said in his teasing voice. "I noticed you already had her nattered at you before you were halfway into the dance. Why you must needs come to points with a beautiful woman while you are holding her in your arms is beyond me, coz."

When his cousin only grunted in response, Dalton continued in a more serious tone. "This one will not be easy to win, if my instincts serve me well, Phil. You'll need light hands on the ribbons if you intend to get into this race, old man. Remember what I say."

4 * Unwelcome Proposal

THE MORNING AFTER LADY FATHINGTON'S SOIRÉE DAWNED BRIGHT and crisp and inviting. Samantha had intended to sleep late for a change, but an errant ray of sunlight, slipping into her bedchamber through a crack in the curtains, woke her before eight. After trying unsuccessfully to go back to sleep, she gave up and rang the bell for her hot chocolate.

At ten o'clock, bathed and dressed in an elegant morning gown of lilac twilled silk, embroidered with ivory lace around the hem, Samantha tapped gently on the door of her aunt's boudoir. She found her ladyship sitting comfortably before the fire, drinking a cup of strong tea and having her luxurious brown hair brushed vigorously by Pennington, her dresser.

"You may go, Penny," her ladyship said when she saw her niece come in. "I shall ring when I'm ready to get dressed."

"Come, my love!" she exclaimed, turning to her niece. "Sit down with me and tell me everything those delightful gentlemen talked about last night. I swear it caused no end of speculation when the marquess arrived, danced one waltz with you, and then left without so much as looking at another female. I am positively agog with curiosity, dear. Do tell."

Samantha laughed at her aunt's enthusiasm. "There's really nothing to tell, Aunt." She could not very well tell her ladyship that Mr. Dalton had offered to darken Gerald's daylights, as he called it, and that the marquess had discussed her father's will.

"Oh, nonsense, girl. Do not, I beg you, be so provoking. Did they not compliment you on your gown, at the very least?"

"No, neither gentleman seemed to notice that I had anything on at all," she murmured, a mischievous twinkle in her amber eyes. "I could have saved myself the exorbitant bill I am sure Madame Lucille will present in due course. Any old gown would have done just as well."

"You cannot mean it? What a terrible lack of address in both gentlemen not to notice the lengths we go to in order to dazzle them.''

Samantha looked at her aunt with amusement. ''I do not recall going to any lengths at all to dazzle any gentleman, Aunt,'' she replied.

''Well, from what I could see, Mr. Dalton appeared to be quite taken with you, love. You'll not deny that, I hope.''

''Mr. Dalton is an accomplished flirt, ma'am, and a perfectly charming one, too. That I will admit. I find him most entertaining,'' she added, hoping to provoke her aunt into providing some crumbs of information on this particular gentleman.

''He takes after his father in that. Old Arthur Dalton was a recognized Tulip of fashion in his youth; always had an eye for the fairer sex, too. They say he kept a string of high-flyers in his time that must have cost him a pretty penny. Fortunately, Amelia Silverdale caught his eye before he had dissipated all his fortune, and marriage made a new man of him. I would hardly have believed it if I hadn't seen it with my own eyes.''

''Does his son also keep a string of ladybirds?'' Samantha asked innocently.

Lady Fathington looked at her reprovingly. ''Those are things that a well-bred young lady does not need to know,'' she said severely. ''I should not even have mentioned it myself, dear. Not the thing at all, although everybody knew, of course.'' She eyed her niece roguishly.

''If left to their own devices, most gentlemen tend to be rakish, quarrelsome, gamblers, or spendthrifts,'' she continued in a more serious tone. ''It is up to us ladies to keep them in line, as you will discover soon enough when you enter the married state yourself, my dear.''

''I see no sign of that happening in the immediate future,'' Samantha remarked unwisely.

''You are full of nonsense this morning!'' her ladyship exclaimed crossly. ''How can you talk like that, dear, when you had two highly eligible bachelors dancing attendance on you last night?''

Samantha was spared the necessity of answering by the appearance of Pennington, followed by a footman carrying an enormous bouquet of roses in the palest shade of apricot.

''For Lady Samantha, ma'am,'' the dresser explained. ''Shall I have them put in your room, my lady?''

"Oh, no, thank you, Penny. Why don't you leave them in here so that my aunt and I can both enjoy them?"

After the servants had retired, Samantha opened the gilt-edged card that came with the roses.

"Well?" demanded Lady Fathington impatiently. "Don't keep me in suspense, girl. Who is the thoughtful gentleman?"

A faint blush invaded Samantha's cheeks as she perused the note written in Mr. Dalton's florid hand. Then the audacity of his message hit her, and she burst out laughing.

"Listen to this, Aunt, and tell me if this is not evidence enough that Mr. Dalton is an irredeemable flirt." She cleared her throat and read in a theatrical voice: " 'These lovely flowers are but the shadow of an apricot vision I carry in my heart.' "

"Pshaw!" Lady Fathington exclaimed loudly. "And you tried to bamboozle me into believing that neither gentlemen noticed what you were wearing last night, my love. The man is a shameless rogue, of course, but at least you seem to have bowled him over. We will have you leg-shackled yet, dear. But you must alter your plans immediately to stay at least until mid-December."

Her aunt's mention of December brought a tremor to Samantha's fingers as she laid Mr. Dalton's missive on the spindle-legged table next to her chair. By December tenth, the anniversary of her father's death, Gerald Ashley would be in possession of her beloved home and she would be banished with her dearest Mama and Felicity to the cold Northumberland Dower House.

She sighed unhappily. "I wish I could, dearest Aunt. You and Uncle Henry are always so good to me." Impulsively she rose and hugged Lady Fathington fiercely. "I cannot thank you enough for all you have done for me," she exclaimed huskily as her ladyship stared at her in amazement.

"I forbid you to go all mawkish on me, love. You know that both you and Felicity have a home here with me whenever you want it. I just wish you would make more frequent use of it," her ladyship remarked, trying to suppress a desire to be mawkish herself.

"Perhaps I can persuade Mama to bring us both up to London to spend Christmas with you, if you care to have us?" At least they might spend one last holiday season in comfort before embarking on their Northern journey.

"Need you ask, dear? Although I have never known you to spend Christmas anywhere but at Ashley Hall, Samantha. I cannot begin to count the times I have invited you all to come to us here in London."

"This year it might well be different," Samantha replied with forced cheerfulness. Her aunt would find out soon enough just how different this Christmas season would be for Lady Midland and her two daughters.

She saw a quizzical expression in her ladyship's eyes, but any awkward question her aunt may have formulated in her mind was interrupted by Jaspers, who scratched discreetly at the door to announce that the Earl of Midland had arrived to call on Lady Samantha.

"I have put him in the Blue Saloon, m'lady."

"Thank you, Jaspers," Samantha said quietly, casting a pleading look at her aunt as the butler softly closed the door. "I trust you will not leave me alone too long with that addle-headed clodpole, ma'am. Because I cannot answer for my actions if he pesters me with his advances again."

Lady Fathington sighed at her niece's unladylike language and reached out to ring for her dresser.

To say that the new Earl of Midland was upset with his cousin would be to misrepresent the intensity of his displeasure. He was barely able to control his seething fury at the perversity of the wayward chit. The discovery the previous evening that his chosen bride was actually acquainted with the Marquess of Carrington had given him a severe jolt, but the sight of Samantha blithely circling the dance-floor in the arms of that highly dangerous rival caused Gerald Ashley to grind his teeth in frustration.

He had spent considerable time and effort over the past ten months trying to convince his unsympathetic and highly intractable, independent cousin that to apprise Lord Carrington of the conditions of the late earl's will would be the height of folly and impropriety. He had thought to dissuade her by concocting wild stories of Philip Silverdale's rakish and dissolute reputation. As the anniversary of his uncle's death drew nearer, he had resorted to dropping sly hints regarding the nature of the relationship between Carrington and the renowned London Beauty, Lady Sylvia Towers, a widow of exceptional grace and elegance rumoured to be the gentleman's latest *chère amie*.

Lady Samantha had disconcerted him by showing not the slightest discomposure upon learning this tasty bit of gossip.

"It shows he has the most discerning good taste," she had remarked coolly. "I hear that Lady Towers is ravishingly handsome. I heartily commend his choice."

Nevertheless, Gerald Ashley had quite convinced himself that he had succeeded in giving Lady Samantha a healthy dislike for the philandering marquess. And then last night his plans to acquire both the lady and the Ashley fortune on December tenth had suffered a severe setback. Not only had he been thwarted in his attempt to claim the first dance with Samantha, thanks to that interfering coxcomb Dalton, but the callous chit had actually allowed the marquess to usurp his own promised waltz with her.

By the time Lord Midland had been shown into the Blue Saloon at Fathington House that morning, he was fit to be tied. It did his self-consequence little good to be kept kicking his heels for nearly twenty minutes before the door opened and his cousin entered, followed closely by the butler bearing a tray of refreshments.

"Good morning, Cousin." As Samantha greeted him with her usual cool reserve, Gerald felt a stab of real fear at the hitherto suppressed possibility of losing both the lady and his uncle's immense wealth. He cared nought for the estate. His memories of summers spent at Ashley Hall with his two younger cousins were coloured by the intense envy he had always felt because so much had been denied him. He had always been treated kindly by his uncle, but he could never forget that he was the poor relative, living in borrowed splendour at his uncle's expense.

"Good morning, my dear," he murmured as he caught her limp fingers and raised them to his thin lips. "You are looking in high gig this morning, Cousin, if I may say so." His avid gaze ran over her slim form approvingly. "That colour suits you, Cousin. Your taste is exquisite, as always." He accepted a glass of sherry from Jaspers and took a proprietary stand in front of the fireplace, sipping it eagerly.

"Good stuff, this," he remarked in condescending tones. "Though it can hardly compare to the vintage Spanish sherry in the cellars of Ashley Hall, eh, my dear? Which, I should add, we will soon be enjoying together, Cousin. Could be enjoying at this very moment if you would only put aside this coyness you insist on affecting, my dear, and set a date for our nuptials.''

Samantha had delayed entering the Blue Saloon as long as she dared and now sat on the blue embroidered silk settee, as far removed as possible from her cousin's thin, angular presence, listening calmly to his flippant reference to Ashley Hall as if he already were master there.

At his renewed insistence on assuming that their eventual marriage was a foregone conclusion, Samantha's thoughts flew to the deliberately provoking remarks she had made last night to Lord Carrington. A marriage of convenience was certainly nothing new in their world; and perhaps, as she had suggested to the marquess, if she could bring herself to marry Gerald, he might not be quite so obnoxious as he seemed now.

Lord Carrington's reply had surprised her, and she examined the man before her, debating the possible gratification to be derived from disobeying the marquess's order not to do anything so hare-brained.

The new Earl of Midland was tall and sparse, his slightly stooped shoulders defying his tailor's efforts to pad his lordship's coats convincingly with buckram. Samantha had always thought that her cousin might have been, if not handsome, at least pleasant-featured if only his eyes were less shifty and his mouth less unrelentingly grim. And always providing he could control his temper and learn not to sneer.

No, she thought ruefully, all thoughts of defying Lord Carrington's command evaporating at this close observation of her cousin. She could not do it. She would rather live in Northumberland than marry Gerald Ashley.

The small smile that had softened her face at the memory of Carrington's overbearing ways quickly disappeared as her cousin, perhaps taking her silence for acquiescence, suddenly threw himself on his knees beside her and grasped her hands in his.

"My dearest girl," he muttered hoarsely. "Do not, I beg you, keep me any longer from my heart's desire." To Samantha's dismay, he proceeded to smother her cringing fingers with damp kisses in spite of her strenuous efforts to pull them away.

"Oh, do stop it, Gerald," she expostulated, unsure whether to laugh or cry at the ungainly spectacle he presented. "This is ridiculous."

"How can you be so heartless, my love?" he moaned, clutching her hands more firmly. "All I ask is a chance to show you what true love is like. Only say the word and you will make me the happiest man in all England."

"Also one of the richest, or had you forgotten that?" Samantha remarked tonelessly.

He glanced up at her, his eyes unreadable. "I do not want the Ashley fortune without you, my love," he murmured softly. "You are the fortune I covet much more than any mere wealth. And fortunate indeed will I be the day I call you mine, sweetling."

Thoroughly revolted by this whole scene, Samantha tried to rise, but the earl, his face flushed with desire and the conviction that he had his victim cornered at last, threw an arm around his cousin's rigid shoulders and tried to draw her down to receive his kiss.

"Stop making a cake of yourself, Gerald," Samantha cried breathlessly, struggling to escape from this highly distasteful embrace, her eyes tightly closed and her head turned away from her cousin's hot breath.

Neither of them heard the door open or the quick strides across the Axminster carpet. The first indication that they were not alone came when the enamoured earl found himself violently jerked to his feet.

"Didn't you hear the lady?" Anthony Dalton said in a dangerously calm voice as he relinquished his grip on Ashley's coat collar. "She told you not to make a cake of yourself. And I suggest you take her advice and try to behave like a gentleman in the future."

"Keep out of this," Gerald snarled, a dark flush of anger suffusing his cheeks. "When I want your advice, Dalton, I'll ask for it. This is a family matter which does not concern you, and I'll thank you to keep that in mind."

"And I'll thank you to be more civil to my guests, Gerald," Lady Fathington demanded sharply as she swept into the room, a frown of displeasure on her usually placid countenance.

"Mr. Dalton"—she turned a smiling face to this gentleman—"a pleasure to welcome you, I'm sure. And I apologize most sincerely for Gerald's rudeness; he always did take after his poor Papa, who was more at home in the stables than in

a lady's drawing-room.'' She gave the unfortunate earl a
withering glance that quickly silenced any protest he may have
wanted to make.

''Please sit down and take a glass of sherry with us, sir.''
She nodded to Jaspers, who had followed her into the room,
and the butler, his face frozen in acute disapproval, stepped
forward to serve Dalton with the wine.

''What family matter is this you were shouting about,
Gerald?'' she enquired, riveting the earl with her coolest
stare.

''I was not shouting, ma'am,'' Gerald responded sullenly,
his face still red with hostility and embarrassment.

''I could hear you out in the hall,'' her ladyship remarked
acidly. ''Well, never mind. I do believe your half-hour is up,
sir, so we won't keep you from these pressing family matters,
shall we?'' she added, looking pointedly at the clock on the
marble mantelpiece.

After the door had closed behind a cowed Lord Midland,
Lady Fathington turned to her niece and enquired mildly,
''And what was that all about, my dear?''

''I warned you how it would be, Aunt, if you left me too
long alone with that pretentious gapeseed.'' She turned with a
grateful smile to Mr. Dalton. ''I am doubly in your debt, sir.
First for the beautiful roses, and now for saving me from an
exceedingly unpleasant scene. I cannot thank you enough.''

''I am most happy to be able to perform this small service for
you, my lady. Indeed, it is my pleasure entirely. I trust you will
not be inconvenienced again by Midland's unwelcome attentions.''

''I only wish that would be the case, Mr. Dalton, but my
cousin is sadly lacking in common sense and refuses to
concede that his case is hopeless.''

''He is also sadly lacking in funds, my love, as you have told
me yourself,'' her ladyship remarked, anger depriving her of
her usual reserve. ''I shall certainly refuse his escort to the
theatre on Wednesday evening, which he hinted at last night,
my dear. Lord Fathington will be happy to take his place, so
you will not be deprived of that enjoyment.''

Mr. Dalton was not slow to take the hint that her ladyship
had so subtly thrown in his direction. ''There is no need for his

lordship to inconvenience himself, my lady,'' he said glibly. ''I am partial to the theatre myself, and it would afford me the greatest pleasure to escort you both to the new play next week. I am entirely at your service, ma'am.'' He bestowed his most charming smile on Lady Fathington, which caused her ladyship's heart to flutter quite alarmingly.

''It is quite clear to me,'' remarked her ladyship as she sat in the small dining-room with her niece, partaking of a light luncheon, ''that Mr. Dalton is one of the most charming men I have ever met and that he is obviously much taken with you, dear. I think we should encourage that connexion, don't you? Do you feel any partiality towards him at all?''

Samantha laughed. ''How could I not, dear Aunt, when he is blessed with such charm and good looks? But I doubt he is the man I shall marry.''

Lady Fathington looked cast down by this pronouncement. ''How can you be so sure, love?'' she wanted to know. '' 'Tis true he has not come into his title yet and his father is only a baron; but his fortune is considerable. The old Dowager Countess of Almsbury was telling me last night that he has over twenty thousand a year, and the Dalton estates are extensive.''

''You are wool-gathering, Aunt. For all his charm, and I'll admit he has an abundance of it, Mr. Dalton does not strike me as being anxious to settle down. He has five younger brothers, I understand, so there can be no pressure on him to set up his nursery.''

''Well, perhaps you are right, dear. But it would do no harm to cultivate the connexion. He is, after all, first cousin to the Marquess of Carrington, a vastly superior catch if we can achieve it.''

''If by that you mean that I should throw my cap at Lord Carrington, then you cannot have studied his character very closely, Aunt. I assure you that no one pushes his lordship into doing anything he has not already decided to do. And furthermore, I do not intend to try, even if I wished to do so, which I don't.''

Lady Fathington was familiar enough with her niece to know that when Samantha set her mind to something, there was no use arguing with her. So her ladyship served herself some more wafer-thin slices of Yorkshire ham and, after a prudent pause, returned to the topic with deceptive mildness.

"I wouldn't dream of encouraging you to do anything so brass-faced, my love. It's bad enough that there is already one rag-mannered jackstraw in the family. But it can do no harm for us to attend those gatherings at which the marquess is most likely to be found, wouldn't you agree?"

Samantha regarded her aunt's match-making ploys with amusement. "And precisely how are we to determine which those gatherings are, ma'am?" she enquired sweetly.

"Oh, I will ask around discreetly," her ladyship replied. "It shouldn't be too difficult to find out."

"If you prefer, I shall ask the marquess himself this afternoon," her niece offered in a deliberately casual voice.

Her aunt stared at her in astonishment, her usually placid countenance frozen with shock. "What?" she exclaimed in agitation. "Does his lordship plan to call on us?"

"He is taking me driving in Hyde Park," Samantha confessed, highly gratified at her aunt's reaction to this piece of news.

"Never say that Carrington has offered to drive you out in his curricle, Samantha? I do declare, girl, you must tell me these things sooner. Now I have missed a whole morning's worth of gloating. You are a minx to keep this triumph a secret from me, my love."

"I would hardly call it that, Aunt." Samantha laughed at her ladyship's propensity for melodrama. "After all, I have ridden in a hundred curricles before, and I am sure Lord Carrington has taken that many females out driving."

"What a gentleman has done in the past is no sure indication of what he will do in the future, dear," came the sententious reply. Lady Fathington's optimism would not be vanquished, and Samantha's news had given fresh impetus to her vivid imagination and match-making proclivities.

"That makes two highly eligible gentlemen dangling after you, my love," she crowed, clapping her hands in sheer delight at the prospect. "Who knows what may happen now?"

Samantha asked herself the same question an hour later when she went up to change for her drive in the park. Who could tell what the marquess had in store for her? For some odd reason her heart hoped for one solution to her problems which her head told her quite emphatically was highly improbable.

5 * The Promise

As the Marquess of Carrington assisted Samantha into his smart yellow-wheeled curricle shortly after two o'clock that afternoon, she was glad she had decided to wear one of the fashionable new walking dresses Madame Lucille had delivered that morning. She knew that the green French cambric, dashingly striped with ivory and frilled round the high neck with scalloped ivory lace, was highly flattering to her tall, slim figure. And when she caught the warm look of approval in his lordship's eyes, Samantha silently thanked Lady Fathington's insistence on purchasing the extravagantly expensive green poke-bonnet, embellished with two saucy ivory roses and tied with green velvet ribands.

Springing up beside her, his lordship gathered the ribbons and called to his Tiger to stand away from the heads of the four magnificent greys who fretted to be gone. Any apprehension Samantha may have felt at riding in an open carriage obviously built for speed rather than leisurely travel evaporated as she watched the dexterity with which his lordship manoeuvred his nervous team through the afternoon traffic of hackneys and heavy trade waggons.

They were silent until they reached the Park, when Samantha could no longer resist the urge to comment on the superb performance of the greys.

"I pride myself on knowing something about horses, my lord. The Ashley stables have been famous for their blood cattle every since my great-grandfather's time."

"So I have heard," the marquess remarked pleasantly. "And the late earl certainly continued that tradition, I believe. Many a time have I heard him wax eloquent on the quality and performance of his horses."

"Yes, he was proud of the Ashley hunters," she agreed. "When I was a girl, he used to take me to all the meets in the neighbourhood during the hunting season, and although it is not Cotswold country, of course, we can offer superior hunting for all but the most fastidious riders.''

''You no longer hunt, then?'' he enquired as they slowed to a sedate trot, the prescribed style for driving in the Park.

She looked at him in surprise. ''Oh, indeed I do, my lord. I rarely miss a day during the season every year. We Ashleys are all hunting mad, you know,'' she added with a brief smile. ''Even Mama was a famous equestrienne when she met Papa. I have always believed that her fame as a horsewoman was what brought them together.''

''Your father did not accompany you in more recent years, I take it?''

''He could hardly have done so, my lord,'' she replied with more asperity than she had intended. ''Since he spent so much of his time in India with you and the late marquess.''

There was an awkward pause during which Samantha wished she had not betrayed her feelings about her father's frequent and extended absences from Ashley Hall.

''You resented Lord Midland's sojourns in India, I take it,'' Carrington remarked quietly, and Samantha felt his quizzical gaze on her face.

''No, not exactly,'' she replied hesitantly. ''That is to say, yes, I suppose I did,'' she corrected herself, turning to meet his dark gaze. ''I missed him, you see. I used to accompany him everywhere, either to look at a promising horse or entertain visiting buyers; to settle disputes among the tenants, or help with the harvests, and determine the crops to be planted. He even taught me to shoot so that I could hunt with him when there were no shooting parties at Ashley Hall. And I beat him so often at cards that he refused to wager anything, for he was sure to lose it.''

Samantha smiled wistfully at the memory of so many good times that were gone forever. Her companion could think she was being mawkish if he cared to, but the truth was she begrudged him every single moment he had shared with her father, moments that might have been hers to treasure, instead of this vast emptiness which occasionally threatened to engulf her as it was doing now.

Luckily for her composure, which was on the brink of disintegrating into a fit of the dismals, Samantha was recalled to her surroundings by a cheerful greeting from a passing phaeton driven rather recklessly by an acquaintance of the marquess.

Samantha gazed after the departing carriage disapprovingly. "That's too good a team to be driven at so reckless a pace on these narrow streets," she declared heatedly. Then, realizing that she had perhaps criticized one of the marquess's friends, she glanced at him apologetically. "I did not mean to be critical of your friends, my lord, but a more cow-handed whipster I have rarely seen."

Carrington looked down at her, and an engaging smile softened his rather stern features, transforming his countenance so dramatically that Samantha caught her breath in astonishment. The man is really extraordinarily handsome when he smiles, she thought, looking away quickly and smoothing the beaver muff on her lap with nervous fingers.

"No particular friend of mine, my lady. A mere acquaintance, I assure you. And you are perfectly correct in your assessment of his driving skills; they are non-existent."

Her composure restored, Samantha looked at him and smiled warmly. "Papa always used to say that I was too quick to speak my mind, my lord. It is one of my great failings, I fear."

"You have more than one, my dear? I fear you are being too hard on yourself. I confess I can detect none at all."

This was clearly a compliment, and Samantha, who would normally have given the offender a crushing set-down, felt an unexpected glow of pleasure, which she hastened to suppress.

"Now you are trying to bamboozle me, sir," she said with a laugh. "My Mama could give you a whole list of my failings. And speaking from such short acquaintance, how can you possibly tell?"

"Lady Midland must be wrong, my dear," came the amused reply. "Your Papa assured me any number of times that you were flawless. A trifle headstrong, perhaps, but otherwise flawless. I see no reason to disagree with him. At least, not yet," he added softly.

If the marquess had hoped to unsettle her with his last remark, he was disappointed. Samantha regarded him with a cool smile. "You have put me on my mettle, sir," she exclaimed. "I see I shall have to watch my behaviour here in London to avoid ruining this glowing reputation I seem to have acquired, thanks to a doting parent. I admit it will be rather exhausting to be such a pattern card of respectability, but for two weeks I should be able to manage.''

''Two weeks?'' he asked in a surprised voice. ''I understood from Lady Fathington that you had come up for the Season?''

''My aunt would like me to, that is true. Having no daughters of her own, she takes a personal interest in my well-fare and is fired with match-making fervour where I am concerned. She claims it will take her more than two weeks to find me a suitable parti.'' Samantha laughed softly. ''Poor Aunt, she is doomed to fail, I'm afraid. She believes I am still an heiress, you see.''

''She knows nothing of your father's will, then?'' He sounded surprised.

''Only that I inherited everything that was not entailed. But Mama and I agreed that it was better not to tell her the actual conditions my father imposed on the final possession of the inheritance. She is such a dear and is bound to insist that we all stay with her here in London. And I couldn't bear to place my dear Mama in the uncomfortable role of poor relative.''

Although she had tried to answer his question dispassionately in a cool, level voice, Samantha could not control the emotion that added a slight quaver to her last exclamation.

The marquess pulled his team to a walk and sat looking ahead, his firm lips twisted into a slightly ironic smile.

''So you came to London to remind my father of his twenty-year-old promise?'' It sounded more like a statement than a question, and his voice was devoid of expression.

''Twenty-two, actually,'' Samantha amended automatically. ''And no, I came to attend Georgina Beauchamp's wedding. We have been best friends since our nursery days. The Beauchamps are neighbours of ours in Hampshire, and Georgina and I grew up together.''

The marquess regarded her quizzically. ''Yet you did come to Carrington Court looking for my father,'' he pointed out. ''Am I to assume your business with him did *not* concern that clause in the will?''

''Of course it did,'' Samantha replied impatiently. ''I wanted to see if he remembered the promise he had made and . . .'' She hesitated then plunged ahead recklessly. ''If you must know, I wanted to see for myself the kind of man who would commit his own son to such an outrageous agreement. How could he possibly know that I would not grow up to be squint-eyed, pimply, and stunted?''

Carrington threw his dark head back in a crack of laughter that attracted the attention of a group of strollers and two passing riders, and convinced Samantha that there was a side to his nature that might be well worth cultivating. She smiled at that intriguing thought.

"Thank goodness we do not have that to worry about, my dear,'' he observed with amusement, ''since it is obvious to everyone that you are happily free of such defects.''

"By pure coincidence, my lord,'' Samantha pointed out smoothly, unreasonably pleased at the marquess's compliment. "But what gives a father the right to coerce an offspring into a life-long contract on such a whim? Unfortunately, I could not ask my father that question, since he did not think it important enough to inform me of this agreement. So I was determined to ask Lord Carrington. I have been thwarted there too, of course.''

"Are you telling me that you had no intention of holding my father to his promise?'' His lordship's tone clearly indicated how absurd he considered this notion to be.

Her pride stung, Samantha answered without thinking. "How could I have done so, my lord? I had no idea whether you were suitable or not.''

"You mean, I presume, that you feared I might be squint-eyed, pimply, or stunted?'' he enquired, an unexpected twinkle in his eyes.

It was Samantha's turn to dissolve into laughter.

"I hope those fears have been laid to rest,'' he remarked before she could regain her composure. "I have been called many things in my time, but never squinty, pimply, or stunted. Particularly not stunted, I am happy to say.''

"That I can well believe,'' Samantha managed to say, glancing up through her lashes at his lordship's broad shoulders. "But there are worse defects than physical ones, you know. You could have been unbearably top-lofty, a veritable Captain Sharp, a sleazy fortune-hunter, or a confirmed libertine. How was I to know?''

"And do you know now?'' he asked softly, his dark eyes regarding her steadily.

"The only thing I know for certain," Samantha responded coolly, "is that you are not a fortune-hunter. I also doubt that you cheat at cards. That is something in your favour, at least."

The marquess inclined his head in amused acknowledgement.

"As for the rest, I have personally experienced your high-handed dealings, but that may not be entirely your fault. I expect few people care to stand up to you because you are so . . . well, so large," she added dryly, unable to prevent her mouth from twitching into a smile. "So you have naturally acquired the habit of browbeating them."

After a slight pause, during which the marquess seemed to be considering the distance between his lead horse's ears, he turned his dark stare on his companion.

"Am I to assume that you are prepared to stand up to me, my dear?" he said in an amused voice that nevertheless carried a hint of a challenge in it.

"Oh, no, my lord," Samantha replied with a bright smile. "You are altogether too quick to assume things about me, sir. If you knew me better, you would know that I am, in fact, looking forward to my return to Ashley Hall."

If her reply surprised him, he did not show it, his attention taken up for several minutes in threading a path through the thickening cluster of carriages congregating in the Park.

"You plan to retire from the field without firing a shot?" he asked as soon as they were clear of the mob and trotting sedately again. "You disappoint me, Samantha."

Sensing derision in his tone, Samantha bristled. "I resent your bellicose imagery, my lord. This is not a game, and I find nothing amusing in my situation. But if you expect me to badger you into keeping your father's rash promise, you are sadly mistaken, sir. The prospect of acquiring a husband under such circumstances is abhorrent to me, and the idea of bribing a man to marry me is even worse. Besides, that ruse would never work with you, my lord, so it's a moot point."

During this speech an angry flush had suffused Samantha's cheeks, and her eyes fairly blazed with indignation and embarrassment at having to speak her mind so clearly to this man who seemed to treat the whole episode as a joke.

"Bribery?" His dark eyebrows rose in surprise. "Did you indeed contemplate such a step, my lady?"

"No, I did not," she retorted contemptuously. "But our London agent, Mr. MacIntyre, reminded me that money is often more appealing to a gentleman than filial duty. The will sets aside the sum of ten thousand pounds a year to make the contract more palatable. I did not intend to insult you by bringing it up at all, and after I met you, of course, I realized that you are . . . that you would . . . that it would not serve," she finished lamely. Drat the man, she thought furiously, he has me stuttering like a schoolroom chit.

"I see." His tone was noncommittal, and when Samantha stole a glance at him from under her long lashes, she noticed his jaw had hardened and his lips were compressed into a grim line.

Shortly afterwards the curricle swung out of the Park and within minutes had pulled up before Fathington House on Brook Street. The ride back had been accomplished in complete silence. Samantha felt too emotionally drained to attempt idle conversation, and her companion obviously felt no desire to break the silence between them.

As Samantha moved to descend from the curricle, the marquess laid a restraining hand on her arm.

"I shall speak to MacIntyre and see what can be done," he said shortly, his dark eyes enigmatic and distant.

Surprised at this sudden change in his mood, Samantha protested. "There is absolutely no need for that, my lord," she said stiffly. "It is no longer any concern of yours. And I would prefer to have the matter closed, if you please."

"Well, I don't please." A suggestion of a perverse smile lurked in his eyes as they held hers in a challenging stare, as if daring her to argue with him.

Inwardly seething, Samantha regarded him in stony silence. She would at least refuse him the satisfaction of giving her another set-down. With cool deliberation, she shook off his hand and descended from the curricle without waiting for the Fathington footman who ran down the steps to assist her.

"I shall inform you as soon as I have reached a decision," he added in what Samantha considered an abominably offhand and overbearing manner.

"Thank you for a delightful drive, my lord," she said icily, then swept up the steps and into the house without a backward glance.

* * *

And that was the last Samantha saw of the elusive Marquess
of Carrington until the following Wednesday evening when she
accompanied her aunt and Mr. Dalton to the theatre.

She had spent the intervening days oscillating between relief
at not having to tolerate Lord Carrington's calm assumption
that she would accept any decision he chose to make regarding
her future and a totally inexplicable desire to watch his
well-shaped mouth relax into that slow, faintly caressing smile
that made her breath catch in her throat. When she was in
the latter mood, she looked forward eagerly to his possible
appearance with his cousin on their doorstep that Wednesday
evening. When she remembered his cavalier assumptions about
her, however, she fervently wished she might be spared any
further aggravation from this particular gentleman.

When Jaspers ushered Mr. Dalton into the drawing-room
that evening, and Samantha realized that he was not accompanied by his cousin, her initial reaction was a sense of relief.
This was short-lived, however. Before the carriage had traversed
half the way to Covent Garden Theatre, where Kemp was
playing his inimitable Macbeth, Samantha found herself wondering what the marquess was doing and whether he had come
to any decision about their possible alliance.

As she watched Anthony Dalton settle her aunt's chair more
comfortably in the Fathington box and then seat himself between
the two ladies to entertain them with a flow of delightful small
talk, Samantha felt a warm glow of appreciation. She noticed the
attention their escort was attracting from several young ladies in
the adjoining box and made up her mind that if it was a light
flirtation the charming Mr. Dalton wanted during her short stay in
London, she was not at all averse to the notion.

"You are dazzling tonight, Lady Samantha," he was even now
murmuring, his deep blue eyes glinting roguishly. "But what is
this I hear from Lady Fathington that you intend to return to
Hampshire immediately after Georgina Beauchamp's wedding?"

Samantha smiled. "That is true, sir. I am not overly fond of
Town life. My heart is in the country, and particularly at
Ashley Hall, my beloved home."

Dalton eyed her thoughtfully before saying what was uppermost on his mind. "Philip has confided your dilemma to me,
my dear. I hope you do not mind."

At Samantha's startled expression, he continued gently. "I was also well known to your father, you see. Believe me, I sympathize with you, but you can trust Philip. He's a high stickler at times, I'll admit, but sound as a rock when it comes to family and friends."

"I can hardly count myself as either," she pointed out ruefully.

"You must know that Lord Midland became Uncle Ned to both of us over in India, my dear. And Philip, in particular, doted on him. So I can assure you that, in his mind, you can be nothing less than family."

When Samantha looked skeptical, he added in a bracing tone: "He is bound to find a way out of this business, never fear."

"You are very kind, Mr. Dalton, but—"

"Please call me Tony," he interrupted with a grin. "And I will be only too happy to call you Samantha. That is," he rushed on as her eyebrows shot up reprovingly, "if you have no objection. After all, we are practically family, you know."

Samantha could not resist this charming argument, although she had serious doubts that the marquess would concur with Tony Dalton's assessment of her claims on him. She had to admit, however, that his words had eased her mind a little, and she smiled at him gratefully.

"You cannot possibly be so cruel as to deprive us of your company so soon, my dear Samantha," Tony said with mock severity. "You have no idea how many hearts you will break if you insist on leaving Town."

"Including yours, no doubt?" she teased him.

"Of course, my dear," he replied quickly. "Mine most of all, perhaps, because I have the distinction of being counted as a particular friend, or at least, I hope so." He eyed her speculatively.

"Besides being family, of course," she could not help adding. "Or practically so."

"Touché." He laughed. "Has anyone ever told you that you have the most enchanting smile, Samantha? No doubt hundreds of country beaux are even now languishing for lack of it."

"Not hundreds, my dear sir. You exaggerate. Merely dozens at most. And I do believe you are flirting with me, Mr. Dalton," she replied, her severe tone belied by the amusement in her eyes.

"Nothing was further from my thoughts," Tony lied smoothly.

"But if a little innocent dalliance would amuse you, my dear, I'd be happy to oblige."

Samantha had to laugh at his audacity. "You are a rogue, sir. And need I remind you that I am promised to your cousin. At least, according to my Papa's will."

"I shall endeavour to keep that thought in mind during the rest of the evening," he said with a laugh. "Although I confess I would much rather forget all about my noble cousin and talk about you." He smiled at her so charmingly and with such clear admiration in his eyes that Samantha felt constrained to remind him that they were in a very public place.

This agreeable exchange was cut short as the curtain went up to reveal the three witches muttering their suggestive verses into the bubbling cauldron.

So entranced did she become with the performance on stage that Samantha sat through the intermission impatient for the play to continue. She absentmindedly thanked Tony for the refreshment he had procured for them, and took only a minor part in the flow of small talk between her aunt and the several visitors who came by their box to exchange pleasantries.

Once the play resumed, Samantha's attention was entirely caught up in the tragic unfolding of a king's downfall.

At some point near the end of the fourth act, a subdued murmur of voices and an obtrusive rustling of movement from the audience interrupted her concentration. She turned an enquiring gaze to her escort to discover the cause of the commotion and found his eyes fixed on a box directly across from their own.

A latecomer, she thought irritably. Some Pink-of-the-Ton more concerned with attracting attention by a fashionably late entry than in enjoying the superb performance of the Shakespearean actors.

Idly she glanced at the offending couple and caught her breath. She felt her face go rigid and quickly turned her eyes back to the stage. But her enjoyment of the play was at an end.

For some inexplicable reason, the sight of the Marquess of Carrington leaning forward to whisper intimately into the ear of the much celebrated Beauty, Lady Sylvia Towers, caused her to lose interest in Macbeth's downfall at the hands of a man not born of woman.

6 * Samantha's Choice

LADY MIDLAND REGARDED HER ELDER DAUGHTER WITH A WORRIED frown on her normally unperturbed countenance.

"If we are to be ready to leave Ashley Hall for London in two days, my love, you should really pack your clothes. Felicity has packed hers, and my own things are almost done. And those two trunks have been standing in the hall outside your room for over a week now, Samantha dear."

She went over to the library window, where Samantha had been standing motionless for all of fifteen minutes, staring blindly out at the light snow drifting down onto the shrubbery outside. Wordlessly, she put an arm around her tall daughter's drooping shoulders and squeezed her affectionately.

"Don't dwell on it, dearest. What's done is done, as they say. No use moping about it. We will manage somehow, never fear. And please don't blame your poor Papa for our predicament, love. He only did what he felt was right for us, after all. How could he know that . . ." She hesitated, unwilling to mention the name of the gentleman appointed by the late Lord Midland to protect his family and fortune.

"That his precious Carrington would choose to ignore his own father's promise? Is that what you mean, Mama?"

"Hush, dear," that lady replied gently. "We should not blame a young man for not wishing to saddle himself with such a responsibility."

"Fiddle!" snorted her daughter rather rudely. "He is not young. He must be thirty-two or three, if he's a day. And why shouldn't we blame him, pray? A promise is a promise, isn't it?"

"Yes, but one made by his father, dear."

Samantha was unmoved by her mother's attempt to find excuses for the gentleman so conspicuous by his absence. She herself was far less inclined to forgive the elusive marquess for his failure to keep not merely his father's promise to Lord

Midland, but particularly the promise he had made to her that late October afternoon during their drive in the Park. *"I shall inform you as soon as I reach a decision,"* he had said. And although at the time she had taken umbrage at his high-handed manner, she had felt relieved that the dilemma of her future had been transferred to his capable hands.

And here it was, already December seventh, just three days short of the anniversary of her Papa's death and their departure forever from Ashley Hall. And still no decision had been made, at least on his part. She had waited in vain for the marquess to broach the subject to her during the various soirées and dinners he and Anthony Dalton had attended at Fathington House that past October. But Georgina Beauchamp's wedding had come and gone, and Lord Carrington had shown no sign of committing himself to the liaison prescribed by his late parent.

In a fit of pique and exasperation, Samantha had left her aunt's house two days earlier than planned and returned to Hampshire to spend her last month in the beloved home of her childhood.

Her own choice had been made. She would not accept Gerald's offer, reiterated almost daily for the past month. To give him credit, she thought, he had tried to be pleasant. But as the days passed and December tenth—the day he would assume possession of his uncle's estates and fortune—grew ever closer, Gerald Ashley had been unable to contain his smug anticipation. Less and less had Samantha been able to tolerate his ubiquitous reminders that, if she would only say the word, she could stay on at Ashley Hall as his countess. The increasingly proprietary tone of these reminders and the sly references to the delights she would enjoy as his bride finally snapped her patience and provoked her into banishing the sixth earl from Ashley Hall until December the tenth.

By that time we will be gone, she thought morosely, watching the snowflakes gather on the lilac bushes outside the window. They had decided on a December ninth departure because Samantha was reluctant to ask any favours of her cousin, who, on the tenth, would become the sole owner of all the carriages in her father's stables. And all the hunters, too.

She gave an involuntary shudder at the thought of her beautiful horses being sold off, as they undoubtedly would be, to settle her cousin's gambling debts.

"You are taking a chill, dear, standing by the window like this," her mother murmured, giving her another squeeze. "Come over to the fire, and I'll ring for some tea."

For once, Samantha allowed her mother to fuss over her, pouring her a cup of steaming tea and tempting her with a plate of Cook's famous raspberry tarts.

Under Lady Midland's soothing influence, Samantha's melancholy mood dissipated and she began to feel more herself.

"I wouldn't have him now, even if he crawled all the way from London on his hands and knees," she remarked forcefully, her mouth full of raspberry tart.

"Who won't you have, Sam?" Felicity demanded, bursting into the library in time to catch her sister's odd remark.

"Come and have your tea, darling," her mother interjected. "Cook has sent up your favorite tarts, too."

"I want to know what sapskull is going to crawl here from London on his hands and knees," Felicity insisted. "Sounds like another romantical Banbury story to me. Who is he, Sam? One of your Town flirts?"

"Watch your language, Felicity," her mother interrupted again. "I've told you not to bring stable-talk into the drawing-room."

Felicity did not look at all put out by this reprimand. She helped herself to a raspberry tart and grinned at her sister knowingly.

"I know already," she announced with her mouth full, an action which incurred a frown from Lady Midland.

"It can't be that pudding-faced cousin of ours, because I know he's racking up at the Black Boar Inn over in Twyford," she announced with a grin. "Besides, he must be still blue-deviled after the dust-up you had with him last time he called on us, and furthermore—"

"Felicity!" her mother cried in horror. "You will oblige me by not using those cant terms in my presence. If you cannot behave like a lady, you may have your tea upstairs in the schoolroom, my girl."

Felicity had the grace to look penitent at Lady Midland's rebuke but Samantha knew her sister too well to imagine she would let the matter drop.

After a prudent pause, during which she demolished three more tarts, Felicity returned to the subject.

"It's that marquess fellow, isn't it, Sam? I don't believe he would really crawl all the way from London. It stands to reason he wouldn't want to ruin his clothes if he's trying to fix his interest with you, now would he?"

"He is not trying to fix his interest with me, Felicity," Samantha replied patiently. "Wherever did you get that scandal-broth?"

Felicity pondered this for a moment, while she reached for another tart. "If I were you, Samantha, I wouldn't say no to a gentleman just because he won't crawl in the mud and snow for you, especially since he has not even arrived yet. How can you refuse a man who hasn't offered for you, can you tell me?"

"He is not going to offer for me, you peagoose. Haven't you guessed as much by now? We are all going to move to Northumberland and live among the sheep."

"It's you who's the goose, Sam. You're just miffed because this marquess has not come posting down to Ashley Hall to throw himself at your feet. Miss Morgan is right," she added, referring to the amiable dragon who served as governess and companion to both Ashley girls. "You always did read too many of those silly novels which portray girls swooning away at the least thing and generally behaving like ninnies."

She regarded her sister speculatively. "If you ask me, Sam, I think you have a tendre for this White Knight who is supposed to come prancing up to your door and drive off the dragon."

Lady Midland was somewhat startled by this notion and glanced at Samantha. She had difficulty imagining her level-headed daughter in the role of love-sick damsel. In fact, she had attributed that rosy flush which had suffused Samantha's pale cheeks to justifiable annoyance at Felicity's impertinent suggestion. On the other hand . . . Her ladyship cast back in her memory at the countless times her outspoken younger daughter had revealed a perceptiveness quite unusually acute for a seventeen-year-old miss just out of the schoolroom.

Samantha had been equally startled at her sister's absurd suggestion. And of course, it was absurd. She had been frankly attracted by Lord Carrington's rare, seductive smile and relieved that he had not shown her the door when she called to acquaint him with that unfortunate condition in her father's will. But not for a moment had she imagined he would agree to become her husband.

No, she corrected herself quickly. She had indeed imagined herself as his bride, which was not quite the same thing. But to suggest, as Felicity had done, that she was falling into a decline because he had not appeared to save Ashley Hall for her was ridiculous. Quite beneath her, in fact, she told herself resolutely.

Suddenly she became aware that both Felicity and her Mama were regarding her intently; her little sister with one of her disturbingly knowing grins, and Lady Midland with considerable alarm.

"You are being quite nonsensical, Felicity," Samantha said crossly. "It is true that I like to read the latest novels, and so does Mama for that matter, but I have never imagined myself in one of them." She got up to pour them all a second cup of tea, the flush slowly fading from her cheeks.

"More's the pity, Sam," Felicity announced dryly. "Because I have a distinct premonition that your White Knight will prove to have no more sense than one of those romantical gentlemen in novels who arrive on their lady-love's doorstep in the middle of a wild snowstorm, catch a near fatal case of pneumonia, and have to be nursed back to health by the simpering heroine herself. And in this intimate setting their secret passion will, of course, burst into flame. They will discover their hopeless love is not so hopeless as they had imagined. Sick as he is, this gentleman will fling himself on his knees, declare his love, steal a passionate kiss, and—"

"Felicity!" her mother interrupted, torn between annoyance and amusement. "Wherever do you get all these wild ideas? And let me tell you, young lady, a gently bred miss should know nothing of such matters."

"Novels are full of equally maudlin scenes, Mama," Felicity answered disgustedly. "As you must know, since you read them. But don't worry, my dears. I don't believe a word of it. No self-respecting gentleman—at least not one I would care to marry—would be such a nod-cock as to risk taking his cattle out in a snowstorm."

This unflattering assessment of Lord Carrington's character made Samantha laugh outright. Felicity's sense of humour was contagious, and she appreciated her little sister's attempt to cheer her up.

"I'm afraid your powers of premonition have misled you

this time, dearest. I cannot imagine the marquess braving a snowstorm on my account. And if there is any snowstorm in the forecast for the next few days, I have not heard of it. So he is quite out of luck, isn't he?'' She smiled.

"Don't be too sure of that, Sam," Felicity remarked. "If you'll take a look out of that window behind you, you'll see what looks to me like the beginning of a fair to middling blizzard. Just the kind of weather novelists use to test the devotion of a lovesick swain.''

As the two ladies turned towards the window in alarm, Felicity cocked her head at a sudden commotion from the front hall. She smiled a small, complacent smile. "And speaking of the White Knight," she murmured smugly, "I believe he has arrived just in time to slay the evil dragon and carry off the princess to live happily ever after.''

"Don't be ridiculous, Felicity," Samantha snapped. "That is probably the vicar come to commiserate with us and enjoy Cook's raspberry tarts for the last time.''

Further argument was obviated by Biddle, the long-time Ashley butler, who opened the library door and announced in his rich, well-modulated voice: "Lord Carrington to see Lady Samantha, milady.''

The silence which greeted this announcement did not seem to cause the gentleman who stood in the doorway any discomfort. After a cursory glance around the room, a small smile twitched the corner of his well-shaped mouth. When his dark eyes came to rest on Samantha's face and one eyebrow rose quizzically, she realized she had been staring at the visitor open-mouthed. Appalled at her breech in manners, she jumped to her feet, her cheeks glowing with embarrassment.

Advancing towards him as he stepped into the room, Samantha forced a smile to her lips and held out her hand.

"Welcome to Ashley Hall, my lord," she murmured disjointedly, wondering if this were all a dream.

Lord Carrington took her proffered hand and raised it smoothly to his lips. "I trust I find you well, Samantha, and that you had not yet given me up as lost in the snowstorm," he said politely, his eyes filled with an amusement Samantha was far from sharing.

Not knowing quite what to reply to this comment, Samantha

ignored it and proceeded to make the Marquess of Carrington known to her mother and sister.

Lady Midland was barely able to conceal her astonishment and pleasure at the sight of this devastatingly attractive giant who had so unexpectedly invaded her library. Much of her daughter's moodiness after her precipitous return from London now became clear to her. Perhaps, she mused as she watched the grace with which the marquess inclined his head over her hand, Felicity was right again.

After the conventional greetings, she insisted on drawing Lord Carrington closer to the hearth. "You must be chilled to the bone, my dear boy," she exclaimed, her motherly instincts rising to the occasion. "Samantha, love, ring for another cup and a fresh pot of tea, there's a dear."

Felicity, who had been examining the new arrival with considerable disappointment, felt impelled to remark on his healthy appearance.

"At least you don't seem to have caught pneumonia, my lord," she said with a sigh.

Detecting what he took to be a note of regret in her voice, Carrington looked at her in surprise. "I should hope not," he replied. "Was I supposed to have done so?"

"Oh, no," Felicity grinned. "How could you do so since it is obvious from the state of your . . . of your . . ." She did not quite dare mention the gentleman's impeccable buckskin breeches, which molded his muscular thighs enticingly. "That is, your clothes," she amended quickly, "that you did not crawl here on your hands and knees, my lord."

The marquess looked startled, but before he could reply, Samantha broke in sharply.

"Pay no heed to Felicity, my lord. She is forever coming up with these odd starts." She frowned at the culprit, who countered with a cherub-like smile that made Samantha long to shake her sister until her teeth rattled.

Lady Midland threw herself into the breach. "Isn't it time you went up to change for dinner, my love?" she asked her younger daughter in a tone which Felicity immediately recognized as brooking no argument.

Turning to the marquess, she continued, "I will personally see that a room is prepared for you, my lord. The Hall is rather topsy-turvy at present because we planned to travel up to my sister's in London for the Christmas season.''

"It was not my intention to impose upon you, my lady," the marquess replied at once. "I understand the Black Boar in Twyford is highly regarded. I should be tolerably comfortable there.''

Lady Midland would not hear of such a ramshackle arrangement. "Nonsense," she said to Carrington's suggestion. "You will stay here at the Hall with us, my dear boy," she declared. "Inns are all very well in their way, but there is nothing like a well-aired feather bed to make you feel really at home. Come along, Felicity.'' She gestured imperiously at her younger daughter as she bustled out.

"And besides, you wouldn't want to stay at the Black Boar, sir,'' Felicity whispered from the doorway, her eyes widened for effect. "The dragon is racked up there," she added and slipped out of the room after her mother, leaving the bewildered marquess to gaze after her and wonder if perhaps he had made a serious mistake in coming down to Hampshire.

"Dragon?" he repeated, turning to Samantha for enlightenment.

"That's another of Felicity's odd starts," Samantha explained, wishing her sister had a less vivid imagination. "She came up with the bird-witted notion that you would arrive, covered with snow, and beset by an acute case of pneumonia, my lord. Quite the White Knight, I believe she dubbed you, but somewhat the worse for wear.'' She could not help smiling at the absurdity of the picture this description conjured up.

The marquess, who had positioned himself before the comforting warmth of the hearth, looked down at her in amusement. Although she appeared rather paler than he remembered, she was definitely a delectable armful, as his cousin had pointed out to him on more than one occasion during the preceding month. Dalton had also reminded him that, at thirty-two, he was at an age to think seriously about setting up his succession.

"Don't count on me to fill your shoes, coz," he had warned. "I do not aspire to such exalted heights. Not my style, old boy. Besides, I have a mind to remain single myself and play the benevolent uncle to your brats when they come along. And the Ashley chit is a superior parti in every way.''

He was right, Carrington admitted grudgingly. Tony usually

was in matters of females and social niceties. His smile broadened as he met the amused amber gaze which held his unself-consciously.

"The worse for wear having crawled here on my hands and knees, I suppose?" he murmured. "And let's not forget the severe case of pneumonia, shall we? I presume I was to be nursed back to health by the damsel in distress?" he queried, dredging up memories of his own childhood fantasies.

"Felicity has always been one for nursing the sick," Samantha answered quickly. "She is forever running off to sit with tenants' children with the measles, or bringing home stray and wounded animals. At present she is tending a badger with three legs, a duck mauled by a fox, and a hare with some as yet unidentified ailment."

"And she had thought to include me among these sick animals, no doubt?"

Samantha laughed. "Oh, I imagine she would have brought you into the house rather than put you out in the shed with the other animals," she said innocently.

"That certainly takes a load off my mind." He grinned. "But what about that dragon? What did your inventive sister mean when she said a dragon was staying at the Black Boar?"

The smile disappeared from Samantha's face. "Our cousin Gerald is staying there, my lord," she said ruefully. "Felicity calls him the Dragon; actually the Green Dragon, because he affects brilliant green waistcoats. It is very naughty of her, I know. But I cannot bring myself to blame her."

Seeing the surprise in her guest's eyes, Samantha continued. "You would expect him to put up here at the Hall, I know. But he made such a spectacle of himself that I had his trunk removed to the Inn. We had quite a dust-up over that, I can tell you. He got very hot in the spur and threatened all kinds of dire consequences if I did not immediately restore him to what he considers his rightful place in this house. Of course, I did no such thing. I wanted our last days here to be peaceful, if not happy. So I gave Biddle strict instructions not to admit him."

Although there was no bitterness in her voice, Samantha's smile was so sad that it wrenched at Lord Carrington's heart.

"I see I should have come sooner," he remarked tersely.

"Perhaps," came her soft reply. Then after a pause, "But

only if you intended to keep your father's promise, my lord."

The marquess stood in silence for several minutes, his dark gaze on her averted face. The moment had come to commit himself to a lifetime alliance with a female he knew more by hearsay than in person, and he was uncharacteristically nervous. Of course, he could always offer monetary assistance and retreat to his carefree bachelor existence in London. But something told him that Lady Samantha Ashley would reject such a cowhearted offer out of hand. No, he would honour his father's promise. The decision was made before he left London, and he had a special license in his pocket. He would marry the damsel in distress, but only with the lady's free consent.

He watched her sitting passively on the elegant brocade settee, her red-gold curls catching the reflections of the firelight. Only her tightly clasped fingers betrayed the tension she was under.

He cleared his throat. "Is that what you wish me to do, my dear? Do you honestly want that promise to be kept?"

Samantha raised her eyes from her lap and fixed her wide amber gaze on his sun-tanned face. His question had surprised her, forcing her to confront her own feelings about the man her father had picked for her. Dispassionately she examined him. She had been wrong about his height; he was not too tall for her at all, she decided. His angular face was handsome, but not in a foppish, dandified way. There was strength there, especially in the set of his jaw. His nose was straight and slightly flared, a nose undoubtedly made for looking down, she recognized. But she could live with that; she had a nose like that, too. His hair was a riot of dark curls falling carelessly onto his wide brow. And his eyes . . . As Samantha gazed into their depths, she felt a wave of longing sweep through her body, a tremour of excitement such as she had never experienced before. And then he smiled, his generous mouth curving up at the corners in secret amusement, and Samantha suddenly knew, without a shadow of a doubt, that yes, she did indeed wish most desperately for that promise to be kept.

"Yes," she said simply, an answering smile on her own lips.

The marquess took her hand and raised her to her feet. "Then that is all settled between us, my love," he said, his smile broadening into a grin. "I shall speak to Lady Midland after dinner."

He put a finger gently under her chin and bent to place a lingering kiss on her upturned lips.

7 * A Shot in the Wood

THE FOLLOWING MORNING DAWNED CLEAR AND CRISP. THE SNOWSTORM
had not developed into a major blizzard overnight, but petered
out before midnight after depositing a bare inch of snow on the
ground. The temperature had risen, and the mantle of new
snow already showed signs of thawing in the shelter of the
rhododendrons lining the main driveway.

Lord Carrington entered the breakfast-room shortly after
eight o'clock to find Felicity already helping herself to a
generous plate of scrambled eggs and bacon.

"Good morning, Philip," she said cordially, placing her
heaping plate on the table and reaching for the silver teapot. "I
have decided to call you Philip, since we are to be related. And
you must call me Felicity, please." She smiled at him
unself-consciously. "And not, I beg of you, any of the other
names my sister occasionally uses when she is suffering from
a fit of the blue devils."

The marquess was not accustomed to young ladies address-
ing him so casually by his given name. His mere presence
usually threw the Season's debutantes into nervous twitters and
incoherent starts. This young lady was obviously made of
sterner stuff, for she showed no sign whatsoever of being
impressed by his rank or good looks. After his initial surprise,
he found Lady Felicity's frankness refreshing.

"Does she often do so?" he enquired with an amused grin.
"Fall into a fit of the blue devils, I mean."

"Not as a rule. Usually she's in high fettle, the very best of
sisters. But these last few weeks have been a trial to her and put
her sadly in the dumps. She was really cut up at having to leave
the Hall, you know." She paused to take a bite of toast.

Carrington served himself from the various chafing dishes
on the sideboard and allowed Felicity to pour him a cup of
strong tea.

She regarded him silently for a few minutes as he sampled the excellent York ham and buttered eggs.

"You seem to me to be pretty much up to snuff, Philip," she remarked candidly, apparently satisfied with her scrutiny. "A real downy one if you know what I mean." She grinned impishly at Carrington's raised eyebrow. "Yes. I know that's stable-talk, but you'll not pull caps with me over that, will you, Philip?"

"I don't guarantee that I'll countenance such language when you visit Carrington Court, young lady," he warned.

"Oh, I promise to be the very pattern card of respectability when I visit London," she said, laughing. "Although I find that a great bore.

"But speaking of Samantha," she continued more seriously. "What I meant was that you look as though you could take care of her, and that is precisely what my dear sister needs."

Carrington was so taken aback by this piece of information that he suspended a forkful of ham above his plate and looked across at Felicity in astonishment. "I would never have thought that Lady Samantha needed mollycoddling, my dear. She strikes me as being very much up to snuff herself."

"There you are glaringly off the mark, sir," Felicity corrected him. "But that does not surprise me. You see, everybody looks at Samantha and what she has done here at the Hall. I mean, managing the estates, dealing with the tenants, supervising the breeding of the Ashley hunters, and things like that, which Mama is always prosing on about as no fit occupation for a female. Anyway, outsiders often see her as one of those dreadful managing females, always telling people what to do."

She paused and grinned at him. "I wouldn't mind betting you thought her pretty stiff-rumped yourself when you first met."

"Certainly not," Carrington protested mildly. "I found her most agreeable and entirely . . ." He searched for an appropriate adjective. "And entirely biddable," he finished rather lamely.

"That's a whisker if ever I heard one," crowed Felicity. "I can tell she has pulled the wool over your eyes and no mistake.'' She poured herself another cup of tea and sent a footman off to the kitchen for a jug of ale for Carrington.

''The truth is that Samantha has a streak of the romantical in her. Oh, I know you will disagree,'' she added quickly, seeing Carrington's quizzical expression. ''But I know my sister. And she is quite different from me.''

''Now *that* I have no difficulty in believing, my dear girl,'' Carrington acknowledged cheerfully.

''But not in the way you think, my lord,'' she countered. ''I am consistently mistaken for a schoolroom chit and a feather-headed widgeon, one of those simpering misses who are forever saying goosish things and care for nothing but new gowns and other fripperies. Why, just look at me, Philip! Didn't you think when you first saw me that I was a silly peagoose?''

Carrington had to admit this was true. Even as he examined her across the breakfast table, he could not imagine that this fairylike creature, who stood barely five feet three inches tall in her tiny slippers, with a halo of the palest golden hair clouding round her heart-shaped face in the most delicate of curls, could be anything but a beautiful, capricious, and spoiled child. If he had not already experienced her sharp, teasing wit, he would have been thoroughly taken in by the innocence of those immense pansy-blue eyes that now regarded him in blank wonder.

Yes, he thought, Lady Felicity Ashley was a rare Beauty indeed, with all the outward appearance of a feather-headed heartbreaker.

''As a matter of fact, I did,'' he admitted, knowing she would demand complete honesty from him. ''But not for long, my girl.''

A roguish twinkle replaced the blank stare, and Felicity grinned her knowing grin. ''I told you so. It happens every time. Gentlemen are such nodcocks, you know,'' she added in a serious tone. ''I have yet to meet one who can see the real me. Some have even written sonnets to my hair; can you believe such fustian nonsense?''

''Indeed I can, my dear. The world is full of fools.''

''I was beginning to think you might turn out to be one, too, Philip,'' she said with her customary frankness. ''Because you took so long to come to Samantha's rescue. Only a complete shuttlehead would have failed to snap up such a prize, and . . . By the way, what *did* take you so long?''

"I don't think we should be discussing your sister in this unseemly way, do you?" Carrington remarked coolly.

"Ah! You don't want to tell me," Felicity shot back. "I expect you found it hard to get away from your *chère amie*. Is that it?''

"Nothing of the kind, young lady," the marquess replied in shocked tones. "And you will oblige me by not talking like a tattle-monger, Felicity. Such things are not for you to know anything about.''

"Fiddle!" she said rudely. "You sound like Mama. And don't take that starched-up air with me, Philip. Samantha won't like it, either, let me tell you. She doesn't take kindly to a stiff-rumped approach.''

"Where is your sister, anyway?" the marquess enquired. He felt he needed a respite from this disconcerting chit who looked like an angel but seemed to have the curiosity of the devil himself.

"She is out in the stables with those famous horses of hers," Felicity answered carelessly. "You would think they were her children, the way she fusses over the great beasts. I'll take you out there, if you like," she added graciously, but with a telltale gleam in her eyes. "I suppose you want to kiss her again, Sir Knight? Is that it?" she murmured teasingly and whisked herself out of the door before the marquess could think of an appropriate set-down for the saucy minx.

Samantha had passed a restless night. The memory of that lingering kiss in the library had triggered a host of fantasies she didn't know she was capable of. She had only a vague recollection of sitting down to dinner and none at all of the conversation at table.

Afterwards, the marquess had disappeared into the library with Lady Midland, and Felicity had drawn her into the Blue Saloon and badgered her unmercifully to reveal what had transpired between her sister and Carrington before dinner. Had the White Knight come up to scratch? she wanted to know. Had he thrown himself at her feet and clasped Samantha's hand to his bosom?

Samantha had never considered herself a missish female, but she found herself quite unable to cope with Felicity's teasing. On the pretext of needing a shawl, she escaped up to her bed-chamber and sat for a full twenty minutes before the bevelled mirror on her dresser, trying to regain a modicum of her habitual composure.

Finally, Lady Midland had come up to gather her eldest daughter in her arms and congratulate her on her betrothal. They had shed a few tears together and then gone down to spend the rest of the evening playing silly parlour games under the direction of Felicity, who seemed to sense her sister's desire to avoid a second tête-à-tête with her White Knight.

This morning she had called for her cup of chocolate at an earlier hour than usual and then allowed Sally to help her into her new green velvet riding habit. She saw no reason to break her daily routine of supervising the exercising of the hunters just because she had become engaged.

So shortly after seven she made her way down to the stables in the semidarkness of the December morning, where old Matt Cooper, her father's head groom, had already set a team of stable-lads to currying and brushing the prize cattle for which Ashley Hall was justly famous.

Fifteen minutes later Samantha was sedately cantering round the enclosed arena on her pride and joy, Raspberry Treat, a dark roan stallion whose offspring had been known to bring over a thousand pounds at the yearly spring auctions held at the Hall for as long as Samantha could remember.

It was here that Felicity and the marquess found her over two hours later when they came in to inspect the stables. By that time Raspberry Treat had long finished his morning canter and was being rubbed down by one of Matt's most trusted lads.

Lady Samantha was putting a promising young gelding, Raspberry Torte, through his paces when she became aware of an audience. She turned her horse and cantered over to where the marquess and her sister stood beside the door.

"Good morning, my lord," she called out as she pulled her fidgety mount to a halt beside them. "I do think this horse would be up to your weight if you care to try him out," she offered, annoyed at the tingling sensation in her chest the presence of her betrothed seemed to provoke.

Carrington reached up to stroke the fine-looking roan between the ears, but his eyes were on Samantha, admiring the healthy colour of her cheeks.

"You are looking in prime twig this morning, my love," he murmured and was rewarded with a smile. "Felicity has promised me a canter on one of the famous Raspberries," he added, returning her smile. "I can see now why the Ashley hunters are so sought after. This is a magnificent specimen. I would certainly like to try out his paces."

The next hour was pleasantly spent in putting several of Raspberry Treat's offspring through a series of jumps rigged for that purpose in the exercise arena. Both young ladies showed themselves to be at home to a peg in the saddle, and Carrington found Raspberry Torte so much to his liking that he seriously considered purchasing the animal for his own stables at Silverdale Grange, his country seat near Guildford, in Surrey.

By noon the winter sun had warmed the air enough to melt most of the previous evening's snow, and Felicity insisted that they take the marquess on a tour of the estate.

"We can show him off to the locals," she announced as they trotted down the curving driveway to the pillared entrance. "By now the village will be all agog to see Samantha's new beau."

Carrington glanced at Samantha and saw a moue of annoyance cross her face.

"All you will gain with that vulgar talk, Felicity," she said sternly, "is that Lord Carrington will turn tail and flee back to London to escape any further contact with such a rag-mannered family as ours." She turned her amber gaze on him and added, "Isn't that true, my lord?"

"I might be persuaded to overlook Felicity's disregard for etiquette, my dear, if you will promise to call me Philip instead of my lord." He grinned. "Otherwise I can't guarantee what I will do."

"That seems a fair enough exchange, Philip," Samantha replied calmly, wondering why the sound of his name on her lips caused her so much sensuous pleasure.

"Well, now that's settled, can we take the short-cut through the Home Wood, Sam?" Felicity wanted to know. "We can show Philip the trout-pound and the raspberry patch which gave Great-grandfather Ashley the name of his first show mare, Raspberry Fancy." Without waiting for her sister's reply, Felicity yelled, "Race you, Philip!" at Carrington and galloped off across the Park.

With difficulty Carrington forced Raspberry Torte to forego the gallop and drew him alongside Lady Samantha's mare, who was also fidgeting to race.

"It must be rather exhausting to live with that girl," he remarked and was rewarded with a faint smile from his promised bride.

"Felicity can be a sad romp at times," Samantha agreed. "But she is really a dear, so full of good sense for a child her age. You would never think it to look at her."

Her face had softened as she spoke of her sister, and Carrington felt a quite unreasonable desire to take her in his arms and kiss away all her cares. Could it be that this White Knight nonsense Felicity had started was beginning to grow on him? he wondered. To dispel this uncharacteristic maudlin mood, he suggested they let their horses stretch their legs and catch up with the silly chit who had reached the Wood and was waiting for them.

But Lady Samantha hesitated. "There are several things we need to discuss, my lord . . . I mean, Philip," she corrected herself nervously. "Concerning our . . ." She looked at him, and he detected a note of reticence in her voice.

"Concerning our forthcoming marriage, my dear?" he prompted her.

"Yes. Perhaps after our ride. That is, if you agree?"

"Of course. I realize there will not be enough time for all the normal preparations and fanfare associated with a *ton* wedding, which females set such store by and which you have every right to expect, my dear. I am sorry for it, but I promise to make it up to you, my love," he added gently, reaching over to touch a stray curl which had escaped from beneath her fur beaver. "Shall we join that rattle of a sister-in-law you are saddling me with?"

He relaxed his hold on Raspberry Torte's reins, and the roan shot forward eagerly. Samantha followed suit, wondering just what she was getting herself into by accepting a man who had offered for her out of a sense of duty to his dead father, but whose touch could reduce her to a state of incoherence.

With Felicity in the lead, followed by Samantha, and the marquess bringing up the rear, the party trotted down the narrow bridle-path through the Wood. Much of the forest had been cleared of undergrowth, but in occasional clearings they passed huge clumps of blackberry bushes and scraggly gorse, which tore at the trailing skirts of the ladies' riding habits.

"I must have one of the lads come in and cut some of these briers back," Samantha said after a particularly tenacious blackberry cane had caught her habit so tightly that Carrington had to dismount to pluck her free from it.

"Thank you, Philip." She smiled at him. "We enjoy the blackberries so much in the summer that we forget how easily they can get out of hand and overrun the path."

She had turned away to continue her way, leaving Carrington to remount the restive Raspberry Torte, when she was startled to hear a sharp explosion behind her.

As she steadied her own mount, she glanced back and saw a terrified Raspberry Torte rear up and come plunging towards her. Samantha whirled her mare across the path, and as the runaway horse crashed into her, she grabbed the flying reins and brought the roan gelding to a shuddering, snorting halt. With both hands occupied in controlling two frightened horses, she watched helplessly as the Marquess of Carrington, the front of his riding jacket liberally splattered with blood, slid from his saddle and rolled over, his pale face half buried in the damp snow.

For a dreadful moment Samantha felt paralysed. Then she turned blindly to Felicity, who had come trotting back to see what had happened.

"It's Philip," Samantha managed to choke out. "He's been hurt! Oh, Felicity, he may even be dead." She suddenly became aware that hot tears were streaming down her face.

"Hold on there, old girl," her sister said in a strained voice. "Don't go all mawkish on me, Sam." She dismounted quickly and handed the reins to her sister. "Here, hold my horse for me, and I'll see what can be done."

Bending over the prone form of the marquess, Felicity gently rolled him over onto his back. He groaned. She unbuttoned his hunting jacket and paled at the amount of blood that covered his chest.

"He's alive!" she cried in relief.

Samantha, who had moved the nervous horses farther down the path, looked back at her sister anxiously. From where she sat, she could see that Carrington's shirt-front was now bright red. How could he still be alive after losing that much blood? The sight of it made her feel faint.

"Are you sure, Felicity?" she called.

"Oh, I'm sure all right," came the subdued reply. "But he won't be for long if we don't get him to a doctor quickly."

"Whatever shall we do?" Samantha asked in a quavering voice.

"Get back to the Hall as fast as that mare will take you, and send some of the servants with a litter. And tell Biddle to send for Dr. Graham immediately. I will try to stop the bleeding. But do hurry, Sam," she pleaded, her voice betraying her anxiety. *"Please hurry!"*

Afterwards Samantha remembered nothing of that mad ride back to the Hall. She must have made it in record time because less than twenty minutes after the marquess had been shot, she was back with several sturdy grooms, headed by Matt Cooper himself. Gently they laid the unconscious man on a rough litter and carried him through the Wood and across the Park to the Hall.

Mrs. Biddle had prepared a brick for the wounded gentleman's bed and set out an array of bowls with hot water and various other things she knew the doctor would require.

When the marquess had been undressed and put to bed, Felicity was called to staunch the renewed flow of blood from the bullet-hole in his shoulder. As Samantha helped her sister to clean the wound and bind it with strips of torn sheets, she watched Carrington's pale face anxiously. An occasional groan escaped him as they raised him to pass the bandage around the shoulder; and each time this happened, Samantha's heart gave a lurch.

When Dr. Graham arrived, he examined the wound and declared himself satisfied that the bullet had gone straight through the shoulder without touching the bone.

"The gentleman was lucky," he announced in his gruff voice. "A shade lower and the lung might have been affected. With Lady Felicity to look after him, he should be all right and tight again in a week or two."

He promised to return the following day but made it clear to Lady Samantha that her guest had several days of strict confinement to his bed ahead of him.

"We don't want to start that wound bleeding again," he told her. "The gentleman has lost far too much blood as it is. It's a good thing he is not one of these scrawny foppish young men you see around nowadays. He would have been dead by now."

This blunt evaluation of Carrington's narrow escape gave Samantha ample food for thought as she sat by the patient's bedside later that afternoon.

As she reviewed the events leading up to the accident, Samantha forced herself to consider the possibility that the shooting had not been an accident at all. Matt Cooper had immediately assumed that it had been one of the local poachers who occasionally trespassed on Ashley land to lay their traps for hares and partridges or shoot a fat pheasant or pigeon. Samantha was not so sure. How could someone who was not blind and deaf dare to shoot off his fowling piece so close to a party of riders? Unless, of course, the shooting had been deliberately aimed at the marquess.

The implications of this possibility could not bear thinking about. Who could possibly want the marquess dead?

Samantha tried to avoid the obvious answer to this question for several minutes. Finally, however, she had to admit that, unless Carrington had dealings in his past of a truly shady nature, the only person in the vicinity who would profit by his death would be her own cousin, Gerald Ashley.

If this were true, then Gerald must be in desperate straits indeed. What would he do when he learned his attempt on Carrington's life had failed? The thought made Samantha sick with apprehension.

8 * The Emerald Ring

At four o'clock, Lady Midland insisted that Samantha leave the sick-room and take her tea downstairs with Felicity in the small drawing-room. Such was her anxiety, however, that she barely took the time to gulp down one cup of scalding liquid before rushing upstairs again to see if there had been any change in the patient's condition.

"I doubt Carrington will wake up before the dinner-bell, my love," her ladyship remarked, rising from her seat by the bed. "Dr. Graham did give him a draught to make him sleep, you know."

"You won't mind if I have a dinner-tray sent up here, will you, Mama?" Samantha asked. "Felicity has promised to help me change his dressing, and it is sure to make him uncomfortable."

"If you insist, dear." Lady Midland sighed. "But I do think you might allow Morgan or Mrs. Biddle to sit with him while you have your dinner in peace." However, she knew her daughter better than to expect this advice to be heeded.

When the marquess did finally open his eyes, Samantha's dinner-tray had long since been removed and the thick curtains had been drawn across the windows to keep out the winter draughts.

Memory returned to him slowly, and he looked about the room with dazed eyes before his gaze came to rest on Samantha. She sat by the fireside, an open book on her lap, gazing abstractedly into the dancing flames. The sight of her brought a slight smile to his lips, and he was content to observe her for some time before a twinge in his shoulder caused him to stir.

Instantly she was at his side, her hair making a reddish-gold halo about her anxious face in the candlelight as she gazed down at him. When she saw his smile, she relaxed a little.

"How are you feeling, Philip?" she enquired with gratifying tenderness. "Can I tempt you with a little light gruel that Mrs. Biddle has prepared especially for you?"

He grinned crookedly. "I'll need something stronger than gruel if I'm to be on my feet by tomorrow, lass."

"There will be no getting up for you tomorrow, my lord," she said sternly. "The doctor has prescribed complete rest in bed for the next few days. So you can put that idea out of your head, sir."

"But I must get up, my dear."

"And why must you, may I ask?"

He looked at her intently for a moment, then asked quietly, "Has my cousin arrived yet?"

"Mr. Dalton? Why, no, I don't believe so. When did you expect him?"

"Sometime late this afternoon." He paused, casting her a significant look. "I trust he has not met with another odd *accident* along the way."

Samantha looked uncomfortable. "I doubt that two such accidents could happen in one afternoon," she said stiffly.

"Don't try to bamboozle me, my dear," he retorted. "You know as well as I do that was no accident."

"Matt thinks it may have been a poacher," she said defensively. "We do get them occasionally at this time of year."

"If that was a poacher, then I'm a prize turkey," Carrington replied with such force that his shoulder twitched painfully, and he had to lie still for a moment until the pain subsided.

"You are right, of course," she admitted grudgingly. "But please do not get into a pelter over that." She observed his pale face anxiously. "Dr. Graham was most insistent that you not overtax your strength. You had a narrow escape, Philip. In fact, not to wrap it up in clean linen, you nearly got notice to quit, as Felicity would say."

He smiled at her attempted levity. "Where is that brat, anyway? The last thing I remember is her tugging and pulling at me, and it hurt like the very devil."

"She is down in the drawing-room playing piquet with Mama," she replied. "Shall I send for her?"

"No, no," the marquess said quickly. "There is something

I want you to do for me before we are interrupted, my love.''

Samantha looked at her patient apprehensively.

He laughed weakly at her wary expression. ''Don't be a peagoose, Samantha. I'm much too done up to make improper advances to you, my dear, if that's what you're afraid of.'' More's the pity, he added silently, thinking that his betrothed looked particularly enticing in the firelight.

''You flatter yourself, my lord,'' she said briskly. ''No such unseemly thought entered my head. Now, what can I do for you?''

He waved weakly in the direction of his dresser. ''In the top drawer you'll find a leather toilet case. Bring it to me, will you?''

Samantha did as she was bid, placing the leather case on the bed near his hand. He tried ineffectually to release the brass catch.

''Open it for me, love. I'm as weak as a cat.''

Deftly she undid the clasp and pulled the case open. Carrington rummaged around in it, and when his hand reappeared, he was holding a small, square velvet box. The effort seemed to exhaust him.

''Here, my love,'' he murmured after a few moments. ''I had intended to give it to you last night, but I was outmaneouvred by that chit who would not leave us alone.

''Here, take it,'' he urged when she hesitated.

Gingerly Samantha took the velvet box from his nerveless fingers and opened it. She let out an unmistakable gasp of surprise and pleasure. There in the nest of green velvet lay a magnificent emerald ring. The enormous square-cut stone was surrounded by clusters of diamonds, and in the flickering candlelight, its green depths appeared to be in constant and mysterious motion.

If Philip had wished to surprise his betrothed out of her usual reserve, he had certainly succeeded. Samantha looked up at him, her eyes soft and glowing with pleasure.

''The Silverdale Emerald,'' he said briefly. ''Been in the family since before Queen Bess's time. Every bride of every heir to the title has worn it. Bit of a white elephant to wear about the house every day, but I'll get you something more appropriate when we get back to London.''

This speech seemed to tire him, and he lay back against the pillows and closed his eyes.

"It's the most beautiful thing I've ever seen," Samantha whispered, quite dazzled by the glittering emerald.

Now I am truly betrothed, she thought with a flicker of panic. She gazed at the man in the bed, and a wave of tenderness replaced the momentary fear which had assailed her. This is what Papa had wanted. And, if she was to be completely honest with herself, this was what she wanted, too.

She picked up the Silverdale Emerald and slipped it on her finger.

Her revery was suddenly shattered by raised voices in the hall outside, and then the door burst open and Felicity bounced in, followed more sedately by Mr. Anthony Dalton.

"Mr. Dalton," Samantha greeted him warmly. "I'm glad you're here. Your cousin has been anxious about you."

"Devilish glad to see you, Samantha," Dalton said as he bent over her proffered fingers.

"Ah!" he exclaimed as his eyes lit on the emerald ring. "I see that I must wish you happy and welcome you into the family, my dear. Congratulations. I'm glad to know that Carrington has some sense after all. How is the old fellow, anyway?"

"Samantha!" Felicity whooped before her sister could reply. "What a sly baggage you are. Why ever didn't you *tell* me!" she cried, holding her sister's hand and gazing delightedly at the emerald. "Now you can take the shine out of that stuffy Miss Stoddard and her paltry ruby, and no mistake! I can't wait to see her face when she sees this."

"Felicity!" Samantha said sharply. "Will you stop babbling in such a vulgar way. Whatever will Mr. Dalton think of you?"

"Oh, fiddle," came the inelegant reply. "As if I cared for such fustian rubbish. Besides, *somebody* thinks I'm top-of-the-trees, don't you, Philip?" She came over to the bed, raised Carrington's head, and plumped his pillow.

"There. That's more comfortable, isn't it?" She examined his drawn expression more carefully. "What's up? You look as queer as Dick's hatband." She glanced accusingly at her sister. "What have you been doing to him, Sam? I'd wager my best hunter you have put him into a pucker about something."

"I have *not!*" Samantha glared at her. "But he would not touch the gruel that Mrs. Biddle sent up," she added, hoping to divert her outspoken sister's attention to the patient.

"We'll see about that," Felicity said briskly, picking up the bowl of offensive liquid and advancing upon the marquess with a martial gleam in her eyes.

Carrington groaned and caught his cousin's amused eyes above Felicity's diminutive golden head. "Save me, Tony," he begged weakly.

"You keep out of this, Mr. Dalton," Felicity ordered over her shoulder. "I know what's good for an invalid. So oblige me by not abetting any foolishness." Resolutely, she brought a spoonful of gruel to Carrington's lips and held it there relentlessly until he opened his mouth and swallowed it.

"Good," Felicity said encouragingly. "That wasn't so bad now, was it?"

The marquess groaned again, but offered no further resistance.

"I never thought I'd live to see the day you'd be bested by a mere slip of a girl," Dalton remarked when the bowl was empty.

"Don't tease him," Felicity remonstrated. "He very nearly stuck his spoon in the wall, you know."

"Felicity!" her sister cried in embarrassment, but both men laughed.

"I despair of ever making a lady out of you, my girl," Samantha complained. "Such stable-talk may be amusing here at home, but if you use cant terms in the London drawing-rooms, you will find yourself ostracized by all the important hostesses, my love, and certainly denied a voucher for Almack's."

"Oh, how devastating," her unrepentant sibling retorted sarcastically. "And, of course, I will go into a decline and fade away into an old ape-leader if I am not allowed to parade myself at that insipid gathering of swivel-eyed Tabbies, and drink the weak tea I hear they serve there?"

"Bravo!" cried Mr. Dalton delightedly. "You are an original, Lady Felicity, and will undoubtedly be all the rage when you make your come-out next Season. I look forward to it."

"Please do not encourage her freakish starts, Mr. Dalton," Samantha rebuked him. "Come, Felicity, let us leave the gentlemen alone for a while before we change Lord Carrington's dressings."

Felicity reluctantly obeyed but paused in the doorway to throw a saucy glance at the marquess. "I shall tell Mrs. Biddle how much you enjoyed her excellent gruel," she said, laughing. "Perhaps she can be persuaded to send you up another bowl."

As soon as the door closed after the ladies, Carrington turned to his cousin, who was gazing at the door with a bemused look on his face. "You have to help me get back on my feet, Tony," he demanded.

"Seems to me you are in excellent hands already, coz. Can't say I'd mind having two dazzling beauties at my beck and call all day.

"I say, coz," he added with a note of awe in his voice. "That Felicity chit is a Diamond of the First Water."

"Also a rag-mannered brat and an incurable hoyden," grumbled Carrington morosely, still smarting under his defeat over the gruel.

"She's going to turn the Town on its ears one of these days," Dalton remarked. "And I want to be there to see it."

"You're welcome to the pesky chit," his cousin responded sourly. After a short pause, he gave voice to what was uppermost in his mind. "I'm glad you're here, coz. It wasn't an accident, you know."

Dalton looked startled. "Surely you don't mean someone took a deliberate potshot at you, old man?"

"That is exactly what I do mean. And you can see what that implies, can't you?"

"Can't say I do, old man," came the puzzled reply. "Not handing me a Canterbury tale, are you, coz?"

Carrington looked at his cousin disgustedly. "I can guarantee that my wits have not gone begging. There is something smokey going on here. Someone wants me out of the way, Tony."

"Doing it a bit too brown, aren't you, old man? I mean to say, why the deuce would anyone want to shoot you? Damn it,

Philip, you don't even know anyone in these parts—except the family, of course.''

"That's exactly my point," the marquess replied, closing his eyes as a wave of pain ran through his shoulder. After a short pause, he opened them again and looked up at his cousin. "Tony, there is only one person I know who would benefit from my being out of the way. And that's Gerald Ashley. He stands to get both Ashley Hall and the fortune if I don't marry Samantha before December the tenth. That's Wednesday, the day after tomorrow. Today is Monday. Do you see now why I have to get back on my feet?"

"Actually, I don't," Tony replied, wondering if his cousin had been hurt more seriously than he had supposed. "I hear the sawbones wants you to stay in bed for a week at least."

Carrington closed his eyes and moaned softly. He felt himself slipping down into a bottomless black pool. He struggled one last time to make his cousin, who seemed to be unnaturally slow-witted today, understand the urgency of his case.

"Got to tie the knot right away," he mumbled. "Can't waste any more time. Tony . . . Tony, got to get hitched first thing tomorrow." He forced his eyes open and looked up at Dalton, who seemed to be swaying about alarmingly. "Help me, Tony. Please . . ."

Tony Dalton watched in panic as Carrington's eyes closed and his head rolled to one side. He stepped to the bellpull and yanked it vigorously.

Almost before he had released the silken cord, Felicity burst into the room and hurried to the patient's side.

"Now what is the matter, Philip?" she demanded, flitting across to his bedside and placing a small white hand on his brow. "Oh. The fever is coming back. Ask Mrs. Biddle to send up some fresh rosewater, Samantha," she said to her sister, who had followed her into the room. "And, Tony, please hold his head up while I give him some of this potion Dr. Graham left. Then you can help me change the dressing, while Samantha applies cold presses to his brow."

Dalton was happy to follow these instructions and was impressed at Felicity's total lack of squeamishness in handling the patient. When the marquess was sleeping comfortably again, he offered to share the night vigil by his cousin's bedside with the two young ladies, both of whom seemed determined to spend the whole night in the sick-room.

Although his offer was declined, he did manage to have a few words in private with Lady Samantha before he retired for the night.

"Philip is very anxious for the marriage to take place as soon as possible," he informed her. "He is labouring under the strange delusion that your cousin, Gerald Ashley, wishes him dead."

"I think he may be right, Mr. Dalton," Samantha replied. "I dislike accusing any kinsman of mine of such nefarious dealings, but I fear that in this case, there may be some cause for alarm. I suspect that Gerald is well and truly dipped this time. He has lived on the edge of ruin most of his life, but recently he has been spending more than usual; based on his expectations of becoming master of Ashley Hall, I fear." She looked at him uneasily. "I find it hard to believe that . . ." She paused, unable to come right out and say what was on her mind.

"That Carrington's coming up to scratch has put Ashley's nose out of joint in more ways than one?" Dalton ventured to complete her sentence.

"Well, yes. You might say that," Samantha agreed reluctantly.

"Then Philip was right to insist on the marriage taking place immediately," he continued. "It stands to reason that while there is still a chance of the marriage promise remaining unfulfilled, there is still hope for Ashley to inherit all that blunt."

Samantha was intensely distressed at this plain speaking, but she strove to maintain a clear head. "What do you suggest we do? The wedding is planned for tomorrow evening just before dinner. Is that soon enough, do you suppose?"

"No, I don't," Dalton replied forcefully. "Don't you see, my dear, that every hour you remain single, Carrington's life may be in the gravest danger? We must contrive to have the wedding tonight, just as soon as he regains consciousness."

"Now?" Samantha was shocked into exclaiming. "Do you

know what time it is? And the vicar has probably retired for the night already. This is the country, my dear sir.''

''What's all this about the vicar?'' demanded Felicity, entering the room in time to hear her sister's remark.

''Mr. Dalton has conceived the hare-brained notion of having the wedding ceremony now, in the middle of the night. Poor Mr. Fulton will think we have taken leave of our senses if we send for him to perform his offices at this hour.''

Felicity stared at them for a moment, her pansy-blue eyes wide and sparkling. ''A midnight marriage!'' she exclaimed gleefully. ''What a splendid idea, Sam. And how disgustingly romantic. Does our White Knight know what is in store for him?''

''White Knight?'' Dalton repeated in a bemused voice.

''Yes, of course, silly.'' Felicity gave him a roguish smile that quite left him speechless. ''The marquess is our White Knight, you must know, who appeared on our doorstep in the middle of a snowstorm—not quite crawling on his hands and knees, but close enough—to rescue us from that toad Gerald.'' She smiled up at him engagingly, obviously waiting for an answer.

''I see,'' Dalton murmured, not quite sure that he did.

His answer seemed to satisfy her, for she turned to her sister. ''Leave everything to me, dearest. Mama and I will take care of all the details. You and Tony can stay here with Philip. It is better that he gets all the rest he can. And at the stroke of midnight we will wake him with this wonderful surprise.''

After her sister had bounded out of the room, Samantha looked down at the sleeping marquess and then glanced uneasily at Mr. Dalton.

''We are still in time to stop this madness,'' she ventured to suggest. ''I cannot believe that Lord Carrington will agree to be a party to such a havey-cavey affair. He may well conceive a distaste for the whole idea, and I can't say I'd blame him.''

''You have no faith in White Knights, Samantha?'' Dalton teased.

Samantha glanced down at the pale face on the pillow, made even paler by the shock of black curls that tumbled around it, and her expression softened.

''Yes,'' she whispered gently. ''Yes, indeed I do.''

The envious thought flitted across Mr. Dalton's mind that his cousin was a very lucky dog.

9 * Midnight Wedding

WHEN THE MARQUESS NEXT OPENED HIS EYES NEARLY TWO HOURS later, it was several minutes before he recognized where he was. He still lay propped up in the same bed, and this was certainly his bedchamber, but what a magical transformation it had undergone.

The soft firelight had been augmented by a veritable blaze of candlelight from the numerous silver candelabra placed on every available surface. The fire had been built up to a crackling mountain of logs, and in the centre of the room a round table covered with a white lace cloth was set for some kind of celebration. He saw plates of pastries, thin slices of Yorkshire ham, a raised pie, a dish of cold salmon, and numerous assortments of jellies and fruit compotes. On the dresser, several bottles of French champagne stood among at least a dozen long-stemmed glasses.

The sight of so much food reminded him that he had eaten nothing more substantial than a bowl of weak gruel since a light nuncheon yesterday. He was wondering if he could risk getting out of bed to sample a tempting slice of ham when the door opened and his betrothed walked in. The sight of her obliterated all thoughts of food from Carrington's mind.

For reasons she could not entirely explain, Samantha had taken considerable trouble with her appearance for this strange marriage into which she was entering. Since she had no proper wedding dress, she had chosen one of her recent London purchases, a diaphanous sea-green gauze draped becomingly over a deeper green satin underskirt in the same hue as the Silverdale Emerald, which adorned her left hand. Her bodice, cut fashionably low, was edged in ivory lace, which complemented the creamy tone of her throat and bare arms.

Around Samantha's slender neck Lady Midland had, only moments before, clasped an impressive necklace of diamonds arranged in five fan-shaped clusters, each cluster centered by a large, pear-shaped stone of perfect purity and brilliance.

When Samantha, who was not given to ostentation, suggested mildly that this magnificent piece was a trifle ornate for the simple occasion of a bedside exchange of vows, Lady Midland had adopted one of her rare immovable poses.

"This was given to me on the day of my own betrothal to Ashley by your grandmother, who received it from her own mother on a similar occasion. My own great-grandmother—so the story goes—received it from her father as part of her dowry. It seems he had won it at cards and considered it a good-luck gift for his beloved only daughter. I hope it brings you as much happiness as it brought me, my love," she had added rather emotionally. "The Lucky Tears, we used to call it, and it goes down through the female line instead of the male. Wear it and be happy, my love."

Samantha fervently hoped that the charm of the diamonds would work their magic for her in the years to come. Tonight would be her wedding night, and she devoutly hoped she would not live to regret this hurried and rather ramshackle affair.

When she saw Carrington was awake, she went over to his bedside. He looked so much more vulnerable here than he had in London, she thought. Not nearly as stiff-necked as she remembered him. She liked him much better this way, although that was probably a mistake. In a marriage of convenience such as theirs would be, it was always unwise to allow one's emotions too much free rein. Especially when the husband had the rakish reputation Gerald had warned her about. She must guard against the notorious Silverdale charm. Well, she thought philosophically, forewarned is forearmed, as the saying goes. And she must endeavour to remember that this marriage would save Ashley Hall and her father's prized hunters from being put on the auction block by her spendthrift cousin.

Carrington caught her fingers and brought them to his lips for a warm kiss. Damn the man for being so attractive, she thought, feeling her pulses race at the lazy smile and the frank approval in his eyes.

"You outshine the very stars tonight, my love," he whispered caressingly. "Can I count on you waking me every night at midnight with this vision of loveliness? I could become addicted to this kind of surprise, my dear.''

''We have quite another kind of surprise for you tonight, my lord,'' she replied cautiously, hesitant to inform him baldly that the vicar was downstairs waiting to leg-shackle the elusive marquess.

''I trust you will not be too cut up at the manner in which this affair is being handled,'' she continued. ''It was your cousin's idea, and there was no fobbing him off once he had made up his mind.''

''That sounds like Tony, all right. But what is this latest start of his that has you in such a pucker, my love?''

Samantha looked around the brilliantly lit room helplessly. She was saved from having to reply by the precipitous appearance of her sister, closely followed by Mr. Dalton. Both seemed to be in high gig.

''Well, Philip,'' Felicity burst out paying no attention to Samantha's warning glance, ''has Samantha told you we are going to get you well and truly riveted tonight? I swear I haven't had so much fun since Squire Johnson's prize Jersey bull got loose at Lady Cottingham's garden party two years ago. I never would have guessed that prissy Miss Stoddard could run so fast. Hiked her skirts right above her knees, she did, and—''

''Felicity!'' Samantha cut in sharply, ignoring Mr. Dalton's shout of laughter. ''Will you never learn to watch your tongue, child?'' She turned apologetically to Carrington, a flush of embarrassment adding colour to her glowing cheeks. ''I will not blame you a bit if you decide to cry off, my lord,'' she managed to say through her teeth. ''This hoydenish sister of mine always manages to put everyone to the blush.''

''Not me,'' Dalton expostulated between gasps of merriment.

''Nor me,'' the marquess added, squeezing her hand gently. ''In fact, I am quite prepared to get riveted, as Felicity so elegantly put it, without any further delay if I am allowed to sample some of that York ham over there.'' He waved at the tableful of food.

Felicity could not repress a giggle. ''How could you, Philip?

When poor Mrs. Biddle has prepared an entire tureen full of gruel for you to celebrate this momentous event.''

Samantha was shocked that her noble bridegroom did not seem to take umbrage at this intentionally provoking remark.

"Minx!" he said. "The very first thing I shall do when I get up out of this bed is to put you over my knee and give you a well-deserved thrashing.''

"That may be the second thing you do," Felicity retorted, a saucy gleam in her blue eyes. "But I doubt it will be the first."

"Go downstairs immediately, Felicity," Samantha snapped, her ears burning at the implications of her sister's scandalous words. "And ask Mama to bring Mr. Fulton upstairs."

Afterwards, Samantha had difficulty remembering the details of what Felicity had rightly dubbed a momentous event. What emerged most clearly out of the jumble of emotions was Carrington's weak yet firm voice promising to have and to hold her until death parted them.

She also remembered being pulled down to receive her first kiss as the Marchioness of Carrington, amid the applause of those present, led by an uninhibited Felicity. Carrington, resplendent in a gold-braided purple dressing gown, had wanted to get out of bed for the ceremony, but Felicity had bullied him into staying in a more comfortable reclining position, bolstered up by extra feather pillows.

Due to the lateness of the hour and despite Felicity's pleas to continue the party until the wee hours, Lady Midland had ordered the table dismantled and the candles extinguished by half-past one. The vicar, Mr. Fulton, had departed almost as soon as he had congratulated the new couple and toasted them with some excellent Ashley sherry.

Samantha was relieved when her mother, disregarding the protests of the two gentlemen, packed both her daughters off to bed and told her new son-in-law that Miss Morgan, the girls' governess who now served as her own companion, would sit up with the invalid as soon as Mr. Dalton retired for what remained of the night.

"That fairly beats the Dutch, coz!" Dalton exclaimed as soon as the door had closed behind Lady Midland. "I hope I don't have to spend my wedding night alone."

His cousin grinned weakly at this sally. "You had better not get yourself shot up by a demmed rival on your wedding day,'' he retorted. He closed his eyes for a moment, feeling a familiar drowsiness coming over him. "Tony," he mumbled as sleep began to relax his overexcited brain. "Tomorrow I want you to go down to the local alehouse and set the word about that Samantha and I are wed. Will you? Ashley must be apprised of that fact as soon as possible."

Carrington need not have worried about getting the word of his marriage out. As it happened, the sister of one of the scullery maids at Ashley Hall was walking out with the cousin of a stable-lad at the Black Boar Inn. As a result, the news of the midnight marriage was common knowledge in the taproom of that establishment when Mr. Dalton made his scheduled appearance there shortly before ten o'clock the next morning.

The unwelcome news had greeted the sixth Earl of Midland upon his descent to the private parlour earlier that same morning. Upon his curt request for breakfast to be served at once, he began to experience the immediate effects of his cousin's marriage on his financial standing.

"Begging your pardon, milord," Mr. Tubbs, the portly innkeeper replied stiffly, his round face red with embarrassment. "But Mrs. Tubbs asked me to tell ye, sir, that we canna keep afeeding ye unless you put down some of yer blunt, milord, and that's a fact."

Mounting indebtedness did not usually cause Gerald Ashley any loss of sleep; he had lived one step ahead of his creditors for far too long. However, when his stomach was affected, he tended to react violently.

"The devil take you for an impertinent rascal," he growled at his host, who stood regarding him passively in the open doorway of the parlour. "You'll get your money tomorrow, you scurvy rogue. And if I don't get more respect from the likes of you, I'll take my business elsewhere when I become master over at the Hall. Now don't stand there gaping like a big looby. Bring me my breakfast."

Mr. Tubbs regarded the irate earl pityingly. He was not above taking a grim satisfaction in putting this obnoxious and overbearing lord's nose out of joint. "From what I hear, milord, ye'd best not count those chicks before they're hatched."

Ashley turned from the fire, where he had been warming his hands. "What are you saying, you fool?" he thundered, thoroughly out of patience with these locals who did not seem to appreciate the favour he was doing them by gracing their establishment with his presence. He glared at Mr. Tubbs condescendingly.

The host permitted himself a thin smile. "I was saying, milord, that ye had best not count on the Ashley guineas to get ye out of this hobble. Have to use yer own gingerbread for that, I'm thinking."

"Stop playing games with me, you villain, and tell me what you mean before I take a whip to you."

The innkeeper seemed unmoved by this threat and merely smiled at the surprise that awaited this poor excuse for a gentleman. "You may have stepped into the old lord's shoes, sir. And more's the pity he had no sons of his own to carry on the line. But you'll not be master up at the Hall now, milord."

Gerald turned pale as the unpleasant possibility occurred to him that perhaps that Ashley chit had indeed brought Carrington up to scratch. Not only had the earl been forced to pay the outrageous sum of five guineas to that old scoundrel Tom Mcgee to put a bullet through his rival, but he had learned last evening from the veteran poacher himself that the money had been wasted since Carrington had escaped with only a flesh wound.

"What are you saying, you swivel-eyed scoundrel?" he demanded hoarsely, unable to believe that his plans were threatening to go awry.

"The word is out that Miss Samantha is now the Marchioness of Carrington," Tubbs said smugly. "Got herself buckled to the marquess last night at midnight, according to thems that know."

A string of curses met this unexpected piece of bad news, and Gerald Ashley pushed past the stolid Mr. Tubbs and strode toward the door. He would go up to the Hall himself and put an end to these rumours.

If he had been less distraught, Gerald might have glanced into the taproom, where Mr. Dalton was enjoying a mug of Mr. Tubbs's home brew. But he did not do so, and ten minutes later was driving his new curricle and team of prime matched bays at breakneck speed towards Ashley Hall.

The earl's thoughts were murderous. He sorely regretted having trusted that dolt Tom Mcgee with the attack on Carrington. It was not distaste for murder that had prompted Ashley to hire the poacher to do his dirty work for him. Gerald knew himself to be an indifferent shot and had believed Mcgee when the rascal had assured him that he could pick off a fat pigeon at twenty-five yards. The fool must have been bosky, he thought savagely. And now, if what Tubbs had said was true, he would shortly find himself in the devil of a hobble. The five guineas he had given to Mcgee had reduced his funds to almost nil. The regrettable truth was, he admitted sourly, he hadn't a feather to fly with, and once the word got out about his cousin's marriage, his creditors would descend upon him like a pack of dogs.

Venting his frustration on the magnificent team of bays he had, until recently, been so proud of, but which he would now undoubtedly be forced to return, Gerald racked his brain for a solution to his present dilemma.

Getting married at midnight had not prevented Samantha from rising at her usual early hour the next morning and going down to the stable. When she came in from exercising her hunters an hour later, she looked in on Carrington and discovered Felicity sitting at his bedside supervising his breakfast of weak tea and toast.

"I swear this hellion will be the death of me," the patient complained weakly as Samantha entered the room, dressed in a smart navy-blue riding habit with fashionable gold epaulettes. "I am being slowly starved to death, my love. I appeal to you to do your duty, Samantha, and see that your husband gets a plate of ham, roast kidneys, and scrambled eggs sent up immediately."

Samantha briskly bid her new husband good morning but carefully refrained from enquiring if he had spent a restful night.

His amused gaze regarded her appreciatively. "You are looking enchanting this morning, my sweet. But I warn you,

you'll be a widow before the week is up if this heartless minx persists in feeding me nothing but thin gruel and weak tea.''

Felicity laughed merrily. ''What a pesky patient you have turned out to be, Philip. You can have a small portion of boiled capon for lunch and perhaps a little asparagus, but don't talk to me of roast mutton or pigeon pies, because the answer is no.''

''I'll never get my strength back at this rate,'' he grumbled, taking a reluctant bite of toast. ''I shall complain to the good doctor as soon as he arrives.''

Samantha envied her sister the easy camaraderie she had already established with the marquess. She herself felt a tremour of nervousness in his presence and escaped as soon as she could to change out of her riding clothes. When she returned, thirty minutes later, she was in time to hear Dr. Graham assure Carrington that if his fever was completely gone by noon, he might sit downstairs for an hour or two without any harm.

The marquess had to be content with this, and when Felicity left the room to accompany the doctor downstairs, he regarded Samantha with an amused twinkle in his dark eyes.

''Sit with me awhile, my dear. I have had no chance to talk to you since we became man and wife. In fact, to be quite frank with you, I don't feel leg-shackled at all.''

Samantha busied herself arranging her primrose silk gown on the chair so that she might avoid meeting his gaze. ''That is not to be wondered at, my lord,'' she began calmly. ''The circumstances of this marriage were rather odd, to say the least. I don't feel any different myself,'' she ventured to add, glancing up at him through her thick lashes. ''But no doubt we will grow accustomed to it in time.''

''The devil we will,'' Carrington responded forcefully. ''That's not precisely what I had in mind, my sweet. And the name is Philip.'' His gaze had grown so intense that Samantha lowered her eyes in confusion at the unfamiliar warmth that invaded her body. This was not going as she had planned. By rights she should not be feeling these disturbing emotions which now rioted in her breast at the glance of a man she scarcely knew. She was behaving like a ninnyhammer, she thought crossly, and that would never do.

She raised her eyes and regarded him with a calmness belied

by the throbbing of her pulse. It would be wise for her to set things in proper perspective before Carrington began to think she was panting to get into his bed, she decided. After all, he was a rake and a libertine, wasn't he? She had it on good authority. Surely her own Aunt Eliza had said so when she was in London?

"I had meant to discuss this with you yesterday, Philip," she began.

"Yes, I remember your saying something to that effect just before I was shot," he said, one dark eyebrow raised enquiringly.

"I understand from the letter you brought from Mr. MacIntyre in London that when you last visited him, you signed all the agreements he had drawn up to protect my position here at the Hall and my control of Papa's fortune."

"That is correct," he replied shortly.

"I would, of course, welcome your advice on my father's investments in India, since they so closely concern your own. However, anything concerning the running of the estate and the Ashley stables will remain entirely in my hands, as it has been for the past five years."

"That is also correct," Carrington remarked in a bored voice. "All this is in MacIntyre's letter, which I presume you read and approved before you took your vows last night." He smiled his slow smile at her, and Samantha felt her heart lurch uncomfortably.

"Yes, I did. Mr. MacIntyre confirms that you have behaved with extraordinary generosity in not challenging any of the conditions he and I drew up in the marriage settlement," she continued, trying to sound calm and unaffected by the sight of the mat of dark hairs spilling from his loosely fastened dressing-gown. "I have not had a chance to thank you, Philip. You have saved Ashley Hall for me and rescued my mother and Felicity from having to remove to Northumberland. I can never hope to repay you for what you have done for us all."

"I fancy we will soon think of something to even the scales, my sweet," he drawled, his smile broadening.

A blush rose in her cheeks as she suspected what he was thinking, but she did not look away. "There *is* one other thing . . ." She hesitated, not quite sure how to phrase her request. She had little practice in flirtation and no notion whatsoever of how a man as obviously virile as Lord Carrington might react to being asked to give up his marriage rights.

"And what might that be, love?" His voice was gentle, and his eyes glowed with a special light that caused Samantha to question the wisdom of the request she was about to make.

This attack of mawkishness quickly passed, however, and she sat up straighter in her chair and took a deep breath.

"My father had a great affection for you, Philip," she began. "As you know, he regarded you as a son. You were as close to him—perhaps even closer—than I was." She paused briefly. "But you and I are still such strangers to each other."

There was a pause during which Samantha saw with alarm that the smile had disappeared from his eyes. "Just what are you suggesting, my dear?" he said in a flat tone.

Samantha swallowed and tried to speak lightly. "I was merely pointing out that we have not had the advantage of a normal courting period during which two people who are to wed can develop a deeper understanding of each other."

"I think I understand you pretty well, my pet."

"I wouldn't be too sure, my lord," Samantha contradicted him. "And I can assure you that my ignorance of you is abysmal. Why, I don't even know what you like to eat for breakfast," she added with a small smile.

Carrington laughed. "If that's all that is bothering you, my dear, we can remedy it immediately."

"That's not exactly all," she forced herself to say.

He looked at her for a moment in silence, then she heard him sigh. "That's what I was afraid of. You see, I know you better than you think, Samantha. You wish me to forego the pleasures of the marriage bed, is that it?"

Samantha blushed painfully at this bluntness and looked down at the white knuckles of her clenched hands. There was a coolness in his voice that wrenched at her heart. "I find it distressing to be thrust so suddenly into the intimacies of marriage," she heard herself murmur. "Especially an arranged marriage such as this to a virtual stranger." Her voice sounded odd to her, almost like a strangled cry coming from someone else.

"I'm sorry to hear you say so, my dear," he replied softly, touched by her obvious agitation. "I cannot say I suffer from similar misgivings, myself."

She heard the wry humour in his voice and dared to raise her eyes. "That does not surprise me, sir. You are a man, after all."

"I'm glad you've noticed," came the rueful response. "There is hope for you yet, my love.

"This is the one condition your esteemed parent did not think to prescribe for me," Carrington remarked after a prolonged silence. "Just how long do you expect me to sit around kicking my heels while you—what was it you said— develop a deeper understanding of me? A week? A fortnight? A whole month?"

Samantha raised her amber gaze and looked at him pleadingly. "I feel that six months would be adequate time to—"

"Six months?" he roared and struggled to sit up in bed. The movement jerked his wound and made him grimace with pain.

Samantha anxiously leaped to her feet and rushed to arrange his pillows and settle him back into a semireclining position.

"You are all about in the head, my dear," he groaned, trying to arrange his throbbing shoulder in the most comfortable position. "You cannot possibly expect me to agree to such a hare-brained idea. Besides," he argued more calmly, "I have business to attend to in London. I cannot stay here above a week or ten days. And how will you learn to understand me if I am in London and you are here?"

Sensing that his opposition to her scheme was weakening, Samantha pressed her advantage.

"Before you came, we had made plans to spend Christmas with my Aunt Eliza in London. And if you are well enough to travel by then, you and Mr. Dalton could escort us to Town. That is if you agree," she added with a conciliatory smile.

"As my wife, I expect you to stay at Carrington Court when you are in London, my pet. And there will be no concessions on that point."

Samantha was startled. She had not yet stopped to consider the duties she would have to assume as the Marchioness of Carrington. But he was right, she realized. Sooner or later she would have to take her place as his wife. It would seem very odd if she stayed at Fathington House with her mother and Felicity.

She saw that he was amused at her hesitation and had probably guessed her thoughts.

"Very well," she agreed reluctantly. "You are right. It shall be as you wish, Philip. That is, if you agree to the six months I have requested," she could not resist adding with a tentative smile.

"You drive a hard bargain, love. Here"—he seized her by the arm and pulled her down on the bed—"let us seal it with a proper kiss, wife."

Samantha found herself crushed ruthlessly against his chest and her lips claimed in a searing kiss that left her breathless. She could feel the heat of him through the front of her silk gown as his right arm, like a band of steel, clasped her firmly to him.

After what seemed like an eternity of floating in a deliciously warm and paralyzing haze, she felt his arm relax and his lips move down her neck in a slow, tantalizing motion.

"If you don't want me to ravish you here and now, my sweet," he murmured against the smooth swell of her breast, "you had best escape while you still can."

Samantha reluctantly pulled free of the warm nest of her husband's arms and ran out of the room.

10 * The Tarnished Knight

It was nearly noon when Biddle sought Lady Samantha out in the small drawing-room, where she was going over the accounts of the Home Farm with Henry Miles, the Ashleys' long-time estate agent, to inform her that the Earl of Midland had called on urgent business.

"I have put his lordship in the Blue Saloon, milady. Most insistent he was on speaking with you. Most insistent indeed." Biddle's lips pursed into a thin line of censure.

Knowing her butler as she did, Samantha interpreted this carefully worded understatement to mean that her cousin had forced himself into the Hall.

"Shall I inform his lordship that you cannot receive him, milady?"

"No, thank you, Biddle. Please tell the earl I shall be with him shortly."

Samantha did not relish this encounter with her cousin, but neither could she very well avoid it. As head of the family, he did deserve to be informed officially of her new state. She owed him that much. But if she were honest with herself, she would have to admit that she was thankful to be rid of his fawning attentions. She had never mistaken his persistent declarations as evidence of any tender feelings for her but rather as proof of his insatiable desire to fill her father's shoes and become the true master of the Ashleys of Ashley Hall.

When she thought about it, she felt sorry for her cousin. The only son of an invalid mother and an improvident father, Gerald had had little opportunity to enjoy his childhood. Even during the summers he had spent with his uncle's family at the Hall, he had—in unguarded moments—revealed to his two younger cousins a deep-seated bitterness at being only the nephew of the Earl of Midland and not his son. As a child,

Samantha had sensed this frustration in her cousin, and it made all protestations of goodwill from him suspect in her eyes.

So it was with mixed feelings that she entered the Blue Saloon a short time later to find the object of her misgivings standing before the fire, an impatient scowl on his thin face.

"So there you are, Samantha," he barked in obvious ill humour, ignoring her mild greeting. "What is this gossip I hear about a clandestine marriage, my girl? Surely you have not sunk so low as to compromise your good name? And my reputation, I might add, since it behooves me, as head of this family, to dispose of your hand as I see fit."

"Papa has already disposed of my hand, thank you, Gerald. So you need not trouble yourself on my behalf."

"Fiddle, my girl! Your father has been dead this twelve-month," he retorted impatiently. "And I, for one, see no reason for you to regard that ridiculous will as anything but the delirious ravings of a failing mind. Marry whom you will, lass, if you won't have me. And with my blessing. In fact, I'm even prepared to settle a fat sum on you to tempt any buck who may not want to be leg-shackled to a dowerless chit."

He glared at her from under hooded lids, as if to gauge her reaction to this unexpected show of benevolence. But Samantha merely stared at him in suppressed fury and indignation.

"Of course, I would much prefer that you accept my offer, Samantha," he continued in a softer voice. "We Ashleys should stick together, don't you think?"

"No, actually I do not," Samantha responded sharply. "And it is pointless for you to break squares with me over something which is already settled. You must know, Cousin," she added resolutely, determined to get over this hedge as lightly as possible, "that the rumours you have heard are true. I was married last night to the Marquess of Carrington, as my father wished."

The effect of these words on the earl was instantaneous and confirmed Samantha's suspicions that her cousin lacked any real regard for her. The fury of his reaction, however, made her blench.

"I absolutely forbid it," he barked harshly, striding up and down the room nervously. "As head of this family, I can and shall have the marriage annulled immediately, you ungrateful, willful chit." His usually pale face became infused with a dull purple flush of anger, and his eyebrows twitched uncontrollably as he glowered down at her, his expression so full of fury that Samantha involuntarily quailed.

"Yes, you may well tremble, my girl," he snarled. "If I had my way, I'd take a horsewhip to you, which is what you deserve for disregarding my advice. Didn't I tell you that Carrington is a gambler and libertine of the worst kind? Doubtless he is badly dipped at cards and thought to repair his fortunes at your expense." He smiled thinly at Samantha's startled expression. "Don't say I didn't warn you, you silly chit. I know for a fact he dropped ten thousand pounds two weeks ago at White's. And that new ladybird of his must be costing him a pretty penny," he added with a lewd snigger.

Noting Samantha's quick intake of breath, Ashley smiled wolfishly. "You don't imagine for a minute that he's down here on *your* account, now do you, lass?" He gave a short bark of mirthless laughter. "You're a skitterbrain innocent if you believe *that*. Living down here in the country, as you have these past five years, has addled your brain, my girl. You are not up to snuff on the way a Town Buck spends his blunt nor on how much it takes to live in the style Carrington is accustomed to."

"And am I to believe that you are, Cousin?" Samantha asked through gritted teeth.

Gerald looked at her sharply. "None of your impertinence, my girl," he snarled. "You should be thankful that I am here to save you from utter disgrace and ruin." He paused to stare down at her with repressed malice flickering in his pale eyes. "Why do you suppose it took Carrington so long to get down here, my love?" he murmured, an unctuous smile curving his thin lips. "Because Lady Sylvia Towers was still in Town, that's why." He grinned maliciously. "Carrington couldn't bear to tear himself away from his new *inamorata*, you silly chit. And I'll wager you thought he was doing the pretty for you, didn't you?"

Samantha felt a growing revulsion for this whole interview. One part of her mind adamantly rejected everything that Gerald was saying. Her very own White Knight could not be the kind of man Gerald was describing to her in such revolting detail.

But a tiny voice within her wavered. After all, hadn't she asked herself why the marquess had waited until the last minute to put in his appearance? And she could not deny that she had seen him several times in the company of that shining Beauty, the incomparable Lady Sylvia. He had seemed to be utterly enthralled by the undeniable magic of that lady's presence, as had all the other gentlemen who clustered around her.

"Well, I shall take care of that rakehell for you, Cousin, and send him about his business," she heard Gerald saying with relish. "If necessary, I shall call in the magistrate."

"Don't be ridiculous, Gerald!" Samantha was startled into exclaiming. "Only think of the scandal, and besides," she added, pulling herself together with an effort, "you seem to forget yourself, Cousin. Remember that I am mistress of Ashley Hall. You will not insult any guest of mine, and much less my husband, if you do not wish to make a complete cake of yourself. I suggest that you accept, as gracefully as you can, the fact that the conditions of my father's will have been met. If you cannot do so," she said calmly, "I must ask you to leave immediately."

The earl had gone very white at these words, and although Samantha was pretty sure he was bluffing, his face became so twisted with ire that she thought for a moment he was going to strike her.

"You vindictive little hussy," he snarled. "You always hated me, didn't you? Ever since those dreadful summers I used to spend here at the Hall. You couldn't bear it that your precious father recognized me as his heir. You were jealous, weren't you? And now you cannot pass up the chance to get your revenge."

"That is simply not true, Cousin," Samantha protested, shocked and saddened at the unfair accusation.

"Oh, yes, it is," Gerald fumed, his years of repressed frustrations and envy coming to the surface. "You actually had the gall to tell me that you pitied me, you spoiled, selfish little doxy."

Shocked as she was by the vulgarity and passion of her cousin's words, Samantha could not help pointing out the inconsistency in his argument. "How could I be seeking revenge on you, Gerald, if I am supposed to pity you?" she enquired.

"I don't want your pity!" Gerald fairly screamed at her. "All I want is what is rightfully mine. And you are depriving me of that birthright. It is I who should be master of Ashley Hall, not you. And certainly not that Town Tulip you have seen fit to marry against my express wishes, and who will fritter away the Ashley fortune on one fancy piece after another."

"You are quite wrong there, Gerald," Samantha managed to say in the midst of this irrational tirade. "The Silverdales are as plump in the pocket as ever father was, so I have absolutely no reason to believe these vicious lies."

"Lies, are they?" Gerald nearly choked. "You will soon find out that Carrington is not as well breeched as he would have you believe, you silly twit. And if you are expecting him to play the dutiful husband, you are wide of the mark, my dear." He smiled grimly. "After all"—his eyes raked her slim figure insultingly—"you can't hold a candle to the Towers woman, and Beau Carrington is used to the best in his women and his horses."

Outraged at this vulgar display of pique, Samantha moved over to the hearth and tugged the bellpull violently. "You will leave this house immediately," she hissed between clenched teeth. "For my poor Aunt Mary's sake, I will try to forget the venomous things you have said to me today. But believe me, Gerald, if you so much as whisper any of your lies about the marquess outside this room, I shall refuse to pay a single one of the numerous bills I imagine you have run up in Twyford."

She was gratified to see that this threat, at least, had hit home. The earl's fury seemed to have evaporated and was replaced by the same sulky pout she remembered him using as a boy when one of his devious schemes backfired.

"I trust you are satisfied, Cousin," he remarked smoothly, as if no angry words had passed between them. "I leave you a ruined man. One whose heart has been trampled into the mud and whose honest concern for a cherished cousin scorned. A man can take only so much ridicule, Samantha. And this time you may have pushed me too far."

Samantha was left speechless at this duplicity.

Then suddenly he smiled that secret, sly, vindictive smile

she remembered so well from their childhood. Samantha felt a familiar chill invade the pit of her stomach. She had learned to dread such a smile, for it always preceded one of her cousin's particularly hurtful revelations. She felt as though she were twelve years old again as she watched the sly smile slowly widen into a cruel grin.

"And I have yet to tell you the worst, my sweet little innocent," he hissed between tightly clenched teeth.

She knew from experience that he was savouring every moment of whatever cruelty he was preparing to inflict upon her.

His thin lips curled up at one corner as she had known they would. Here it comes, she thought. But what dreadful thing could Gerald have to say to her at her age that would hurt her as much as he had been able to when she was only twelve?

"One day you will be sorry you thought yourself too good for me, my girl," he finally said harshly. "At least I would never have foisted off my by-blows on you."

Samantha stood transfixed, holding her breath as the implication of these ugly words began to sink in. She wanted to scream out a denial, but no words came. Her cousin only smiled his wolfish smile, thoroughly enjoying her discomfort.

At this precise moment, Biddle opened the Blue Saloon door and Gerald swung on his heel and stalked out, leaving Samantha with her mind in a turmoil of doubt. If her cousin's intention had been to disturb her peace of mind and plunge her into a whirlwind of misgivings, he had succeeded beyond his wildest dreams.

How much of what Gerald had told her was true, and how much the product of his jealous rage? Samantha had asked herself the same question a dozen times in the past hour but could find no satisfying answer. Was her new husband indeed burdened with gambling debts? Ten thousand pounds seemed to her a considerable sum to lose, but then again, had Carrington really lost it?

Suddenly her mind flashed back to that afternoon in London when the marquess had taken her driving in the Park. She could not remember precisely how the casual mention of bribery had arisen, but she did recall explaining the special settlement of ten thousand pounds a year to sweeten the unusual conditions of her father's will. She remembered, too, her fear of insulting her companion by mentioning such a bequest. But Carrington had not been insulted, and at the time she had dismissed his noncommittal reaction to the information as mere politeness. Now she wondered if there might not be another reason for his apparent disinterest. Had he, in fact, been in need of that money but naturally unwilling to admit it to her?

Angrily Samantha closed the account books she had been trying to work on ever since Gerald had left her and rose from her father's desk. Much as she distrusted her cousin's motives for blackening Carrington's reputation, she was uneasily aware that many gentlemen of his station did indeed gamble away huge fortunes at cards and spend untold sums of money on frivolous wagers and even more frivolous females. She had heard that some of them even had children with favourite mistresses. It was common knowledge that the Prince Regent himself was a prime example of such lax concern for propriety.

She had been quite prepared to lend a blind eye to the frivolous females the marquess might feel the need to maintain discreetly in London, or at least, that is what she had told herself. In a marriage of convenience, a wife was expected to be complaisant of her husband's baser pursuits. Where there was no love, she had told herself reasonably, there could be no loyalty, could there? But what if he asked her to acknowledge his bastards, as Gerald had suggested he might? She pushed this unwelcome thought to the remotest part of her mind.

Samantha sighed. All this foolishness about White Knights that Felicity had teased her about was pure nonsense and nothing more. She hadn't believed it for an instant. Or had she? No, certainly not. Only in romantical fantasies did gentlemen behave with passionate abandon, motivated by true love. The marquess was not doing this for love, that was pretty obvious. How could he? He scarcely knew her. In that, at least, Gerald was absolutely correct. But if her cousin was correct in anything more, then her White Knight would be irrevocably tarnished, wouldn't he?

For some reason this conclusion made Samantha feel downright lachrymose, a condition she usually scorned as being too missish by half for a female of her solid good sense. But the condition persisted until Felicity burst into the room with her usual exuberance at two o'clock to announce that their reluctant patient was asking for Samantha and demanding to be allowed to come downstairs to take tea with the family like a normal human being.

Samantha welcomed this distraction from her gloomy thoughts and trod upstairs with Felicity, envying her little sister her cheerful acceptance of the marquess as already part of the family.

They found Mr. Dalton sitting with the patient, engaged in a friendly game of piquet.

Samantha felt Carrington's quizzical gaze on her face as she stood at his bedside listening to a heated discussion between Felicity and Dalton on the best way to transport the invalid downstairs to the drawing-room. Felicity favoured calling in two stalwart footmen with a litter piled high with cushions to carry the reclining marquess triumphantly down the stairs like some obese Roman emperor.

"I am nowhere near obese," Carrington complained. "In fact, I grow hourly more skeletal on this diet of gruel and toast. If you want me to be a Roman emperor, Felicity," he joked, "you will have to bring me some hearty English roast beef in place of this debilitating slop."

Felicity giggled. "Poor Mrs. Biddle will be mortally offended if she hears you. She is literally depleting the henhouse in order to provide you with fresh chicken broth, because I told her you enjoyed it so."

"Minx! Didn't anyone ever warn you that telling such Banbury stories will make hairy warts grow on your nose?"

Involuntarily Felicity's hand flew to her nose, and then she caught the amused glance of the marquess and giggled again.

"I intend to walk down," Carrington announced suddenly. "There is, after all, nothing wrong with my legs. If you ladies will retire for a few minutes, I will rig myself out in my toga."

When he appeared in the drawing-room twenty minutes later, resplendent in scarlet dressing-gown, and leaning easily on his cousin's arm, Carrington seemed to have regained something of his former self. He bowed gracefully over Lady Midland's hand and allowed Samantha and Felicity to settle him in a wide plush armchair near the fire. If he noticed that his new bride was rather more quiet than usual, he did not comment on it but spent his time listening good-humouredly to the merry discussion between Felicity and Mr. Dalton regarding their imminent journey up to London.

Although Carrington had stoutly maintained that he would prolong his stay downstairs to dine with the family, the afternoon's activity had exhausted him, and he allowed himself to be overruled by Dr. Graham when that worthy looked in on his patient later that day.

"I trust I may have the pleasure of your company while I dine on Mrs. Biddle's gruel, my dear," he said in a teasing voice to Samantha after the doctor had left.

When her daughter seemed to hesitate over her reply, Lady Midland answered for her. "Of course you may, my lord," she gushed effusively. "I shall ask Cook to send up a tray for Samantha, too, so that you may enjoy a quiet dinner together." Her ladyship seemed much taken with this romantic notion. She was obviously charmed with her new son-in-law, but her faintly apprehensive glance at her eldest daughter's serious face was not lost on the marquess.

He wondered what bee had gotten into his lady's bonnet that caused her to observe him so thoughtfully when she believed he was not watching her.

Later, when they were alone together in his room, he put the question to her, but Samantha was deliberately evasive. She had no wish to confess the misgivings that Gerald Ashley had raised in her mind about Carrington's debts or high-flyers, and much less about his possible illegitimate offspring. So she smiled reassuringly at him and replied offhandedly.

"My cousin called on me this morning, and he was particularly unpleasant when he found out that his hopes of being master here were dashed." Her face clouded at the memory of those particularly ugly accusations Gerald had made.

"Why didn't you tell me, my dear?" he exclaimed. "I would have sent Tony down to plant him a facer. My cousin is very handy with his fives and would have thoroughly enjoyed a turn-up with the likes of Ashley."

She shook her head and smiled, but made no reply, concentrating instead on the mutilation of her roast mutton. Her earlier desire for a bout of tears in the privacy of her bedchamber had disappeared, but it had been replaced by a strange heaviness in the region of her heart. She would have to shake off this ridiculous missishness, she told herself sternly. She was neither the first nor the last female in England to find herself in a loveless marriage, so there was no use repining. From somewhere deep within her, she must find the strength to become the complaisant wife the marquess obviously expected her to be. And the sooner she began to subdue her romantic heart and accept that role, the more comfortable everyone would be. At least, she fervently hoped so.

She raised her eyes and smiled tentatively at her husband. The expression in his dark eyes was unreadable.

"I can see that Ashley has said something to distress you, Samantha," he said softly. "What was it, my dear?"

"Oh, nothing that I haven't heard before," she replied quickly. "Gerald is notoriously small-minded and vindictive, which makes conversation with him rather tiresome." She smiled again, and this time it reached her eyes.

"What kind of things?" he insisted.

"Nothing of any real significance, actually." Gerald's bitter voice floated through her mind again, every ugly insinuation burning its mark on her brain. She wondered if she would ever be able to get rid of those tainted thoughts he had so deliberately planted there.

"Humour me, Samantha. If I don't know what lies he has burdened you with, I cannot protect you, can I?"

"He threatened to have the marriage annulled," she confessed reluctantly, selecting the least offensive of Gerald's accusations.

Was it her imagination, or did Carrington look relieved?

"He cannot do so," he said with a grim laugh. "You are of age, and the clause in your father's will is quite explicit. This estate is not entailed, neither are the Indian investments, so don't fret your pretty head over that. Your precious cousin was bluffing."

"I know it," she replied lightly. "And so I told him. But I could only put a stop to his vile ranting by threatening not to pay his shot at the inn, which I am sure poor Mr. Tubbs will expect me to do."

"You are under no obligation to do so, my dear," Carrington pointed out, his brows lowering in annoyance. "Let Midland learn that he cannot apply to you to get him out of debt every time he finds himself under the hatches. Do the fellow good, no doubt."

"Yes," Samantha agreed. "But Mr. Tubbs should not have to suffer for Gerald's profligate ways."

"You are right, of course, my dear. But if Midland continues to be a drain on your purse, I want to know about it."

"He called you a rakehell and threatened to send you about your business," Samantha said, a glimmer of amusement in her eyes at the absurdity of the picture her cousin's words conjured up.

Carrington gave a crack of laughter. "The devil he did! And are you saying that I have you to thank for warding off this ignominious fate?" He laughed.

His eyes caressed her face with a warmth that set Samantha's pulse beating wildly. How could a man look at her like this and be all the things Gerald said he was? she asked herself. She found herself remembering their embrace this morning. How much she had revelled in the feel of his warm lips on her neck, on her breast. His kisses had been a revelation to her, stirring senses she did not know she possessed, making her very blood sing in a way she had never in her wildest dreams imagined possible.

His laughter died; his eyes deepened and took on a hungry look that caused Samantha to catch her breath.

"Come here, love," he murmured hoarsely, holding out his good arm invitingly. "Give your husband a good-night kiss."

Samantha fought to suppress a wild urge to throw herself into the warm nest of his arms she had discovered so much to her liking this morning. Why was he doing this to her? Tempting her to behave like some lightskirt he had a mind to tumble in a night of illicit passion at one of the posting houses he frequented. Obviously being a complaisant wife was not going to be easy. The cool, chaste kiss she had steeled herself to bestow on him before retiring to her own cold bed was out of the question. His eyes promised a much, much warmer embrace.

But she dared not let him touch her in her present state of

agitation. To run into his waiting arms as she longed to do would be to act in a manner totally unworthy of a lady of good breeding, she told herself sternly. Such romantic starts were all very well for little servant girls who knew no better, or for the headstrong heroines of novels from the lending library, who still believed in White Knights and love matches.

No, indeed, she thought. She would not allow herself to be tumbled in his bed like one of his mistresses. If she had committed herself to be the complaisant wife of a tarnished knight, his lordship must learn that in return for her complaisance, he would be expected to treat her with all due respect, since love was not part of their bargain.

Samantha stood up and moved stiffly to the door. Glancing back at him, she noticed that her lord's eyes had lost their hot glow of anticipation. He looked like a child deprived of some special treat, she thought irrationally. For one mad moment she actually contemplated imitating one of those headstrong heroines who were always getting themselves thoroughly kissed by tall, dark, mysterious strangers in the most compromising situations.

For a heartbeat in time she seriously considered throwing discretion to the wind. Then the complaisant wife in her took over, and she opened the door.

"I shall ask Biddle to bring you up a small glass of brandy, my lord," she said in a voice she hardly recognized as her own.

Then she escaped into the safety of the dark hall and closed the door behind her.

11 * The Anniversary

AFTER A RESTLESS NIGHT, FULL OF FLEETING DREAMS OF BLACK-masked horsemen racing recklessly through snowstorms, Samantha rose betimes that cold anniversary of her father's death. She struggled into the warmest of her winter riding habits, a chocolate-brown velvet lined with heavy silk, and threw a fur-lined cloak over her shoulder.

When she entered the dimly lit stables, she found Matt Cooper and his lads already leading out some of the brood mares and their colts for their morning exercise in the arena. The Ashley stables on a winter morning, with that warm comforting smell of horseflesh and fresh straw, had been Samantha's favourite hiding place as a child. As a young woman with a lot on her mind, she still felt the calming effect of the soft sounds of horses nibbling on hay, currying brushes sliding vigorously over sleek hides, and well-shod hooves trotting round and round the central arena.

"Top of the morning to you, milady," Matt greeted her in the same jovial manner he had used with her ever since Lord Midland had first carried his baby daughter down to the stables to meet the famous Raspberry Delight, future grandsire of the Ashleys' present stud, Raspberry Treat.

Her first instinctive reaction to the horse had been a loud crow of delight which had won for her Matt's eternal respect and devotion. Later, when Matt himself had held her up on the smoothly muscled back of the famous stallion, she had gurgled with joy and plunged her fingers deeply in the dark mane.

Raspberry Delight, better known in those days as Samantha's Delight, had been dead for six years now, but the Ashley stables were full of his offspring, each one dear to Samantha's heart. On impulse, she got Ned, one of the lads, to saddle Raspberry Torte for her, the horse Carrington was riding on that fatal outing in the Home Wood. The horse was fresh and frisky, and Samantha spent a vigorous half hour with him in the jumping ring, all thoughts of her husband's debts and mistresses banished from her mind.

Two hours later she had ridden five horses and discussed their strengths and weaknesses in detail with Matt. She felt pleasantly tired and hungry but much calmer in spirit as she walked back to the house to change for breakfast.

When she descended shortly after nine o'clock, having changed her riding habit for a warm blue merino gown, she found Mr. Dalton being entertained by a vivacious Felicity in the breakfast parlour. The gentleman rose to greet her, but she waved him back to his seat.

"Pray do not stand on points with me, Tony. You are quite one of the family now, you know," she said pleasantly. "I did not expect you down so early. I thought that Town Beaux did not rise till noon, and then spent an hour tying their cravats, but perhaps I have been misinformed," she added with a smile.

"I'm afraid you have a very poor opinion of me, Samantha. Neither the Silverdales nor the Daltons have reputations as Town Beaux as far as I am aware."

"What's a Town Beau?" Felicity wanted to know.

"A rackety sort of fellow who is up to every rig in town and cares more for the size of his cravat and the shine of his boots than in paying his debts," Dalton answered smoothly. "You wouldn't want to meet one, Felicity. Believe me, they are very dull dogs."

"Then I can quite see you are not one, Tony." Felicity regarded him candidly as she bit into a thick piece of toast. "Neither is your cousin. Of course, he's a bit stiff-rumped when you first meet him, but I suppose being a marquess does that to a man. Makes him full of his own consequence, I mean," she added with a twinkle in her blue eyes that Dalton found entirely enchanting. "I'm glad you're not one."

"Felicity," her sister felt obliged to remark. "Such rag-tag manners are not pleasing in a young lady, as Mama has told you dozens of times.

"And how is your cousin this morning, Tony?" She glanced at her guest, and when she met his quizzical stare, she realized that the question was rather an odd one coming from a newly

wed bride about her husband. She returned his gaze calmly,
however, ignoring the faint blush which rose to her cheeks.

"The shoulder is healing nicely, thank you, but his nibs
seemed to be a bit blue-deviled when I looked in on him this
morning. He misses Crofts, his valet, I imagine. Found him
trying to tie his own cravat, which is a caper-witted thing to do
with only one good arm. Made the mistake of telling him so
and got my head bitten off for my pains."

"Then he is up and dressed?" Samantha exclaimed. "Do
you think it wise for him to be out of his bed so early?"

"I cannot think of anything that might keep him there
against his will, can you?" This seemingly innocent reply
again brought a tinge of colour to Samantha's cheeks. What
was the matter with her? she thought. She was behaving like a
maudlin girl in the throes of her first infatuation.

"I gather he intends to accompany us to the service for your
father in Twyford today," Tony explained, wondering what the
deuce was going on between the delectable Samantha and his
cousin to make her colour up so. "Your mother was kind
enough to invite me last night at dinner, and when my cousin
heard of it, he insisted on going, too. And when Carrington
makes up his mind to something, there's little anyone can do to
stop him." He laughed ruefully.

"That sounds just like Samantha," Felicity remarked, pouring herself another cup of tea. "They should deal famously
together," she added with a teasing glance at her sister.

Samantha ignored her. After informing Mr. Dalton that she
had ordered the carriage for eleven o'clock to take the family
into Twyford for the service the Reverend Fulton had prepared
in memory of the late earl, she excused herself and retreated to
her father's study.

It was there that Carrington discovered her an hour later, so
absorbed in her own thoughts that she jumped visibly when he
strolled over and stood before her desk looking down into her
startled amber eyes.

"I didn't mean to alarm you, my dear." He smiled, and her
heart leapt into her throat at the sight of the tender amusement
on his lean, handsome face.

"I fear that last night I alarmed you in quite another way,
Samantha. And I want to assure you it was not my intention to

do so.'' He was looking at her intently now, and Samantha rose nervously to her feet.

"There is nothing to apologize for, my lord," she murmured huskily, wishing that the lump that had suddenly appeared in her throat would go away.

"Oh, but there is, my love. And every time you call me my lord instead of Philip, you are confirming my suspicions that I have offended you in some way."

Samantha was appalled. "You are quite mistaken, my . . . Philip," she replied in obvious agitation. "On the contrary, you have done me a great favour for which I shall always, always be in your debt." She paused to regain her composure. "Only think, sir. If you had not come when you did, we would all be on our way to London at this very minute, banished from our home forever."

"Yes, I know, my dear. And you have all thanked me more than enough for it. So, let's hear no more of that, or it will begin to get tiresome." He smiled at her to take the sting out of the words. "I want you to know, Samantha, that coming here was both a duty and a pleasure. A duty that I owed to my father and to yours and which could not be ignored, even had I wished to do so, which I did not. I want you to believe that, Samantha; it is important to me that you do." He looked at her keenly, as if willing her to take his word for it.

"Oh, I do believe it, Philip. I do," she whispered.

"And as for the pleasure," he continued, a slow smile spreading across his face, "the pleasure, of course, is all mine." His gazed dropped to her lips and his smile deepened, bringing a quick flush to Samantha's cheeks. "And yours, too, my love, just as soon as you get over this foolish fear you have of me."

He took her by the hand and led her over to the hearth.

"I don't know what you mean," she stammered, chiding herself for being unable to control the tremor in her voice. "I do not fear you, Philip. Whyever should I?" She looked up at him wide-eyed and attempted a small smile.

"Can you honestly say you were not afraid of me last night, Samantha?" He caught both her hands in his and raised them to his lips, his eyes laughing at her. "Why, then, you little peagoose, did you refuse me a good-night kiss? I never realized

I was such a monster.'' He chuckled. "I confess you left me quite downcast after such a cruel cut.''

Samantha could not avoid a sudden gurgle of laughter. "Dr. Graham specifically ordered complete quiet and rest for you,'' she pointed out in a calmer tone. "I was merely following his orders.''

"If you think I am going to swallow that rapper, young lady, then you have a surprise in store for you. You were distressed last night, Samantha, and that distressed me, too, to think that I was the cause of it. Was the thought of kissing me so distasteful to you, my dear?''

"Oh, not especially so,'' Samantha replied without thinking. "It's just that I am not used to flirting, you see, and I was upset with what Gerald had told me, and—''

"Not especially so?'' Carrington burst out with a crack of laughter. *"Touché,* my dear. That's the most devastating set-down anyone has given me in a long while.'' Bemused, he gazed at the long lashes curling against her blushing cheek and the sweet curve of her full mouth and wondered just how long he would be able to resist the wild longing he felt welling up inside him and the need to crush her in his arms and teach her what being married was all about.

He must have groaned aloud, for she raised alarmed eyes to his face. He grinned sheepishly. "Just my bruised ego complaining, love. But I should tell you, Samantha, that there is nothing improper in a wife flirting a little with her husband, if it's done in private, and with good taste. And kissing is very much *de rigueur* among married couples. Again, in private, of course.''

His grin slowly faded as his eyes devoured her face, and Samantha stared in fascination as he metamorphosed before her eyes. The smiling, mildly flirtatious gentleman became a dark stranger with that hungry look in his eyes she instantly recognized from the latest romantic novels as a sure sign of impending ravishment.

Nervously she tried to withdraw her fingers from his grasp. Her movements seemed to break his concentration, and he shook his head as if awakening from a daze. His face broke into a guilty smile.

"There,'' he said contritely. "I've done it again. Forgive

me, Samantha. Although I must say in my own defence that it is perfectly natural for any man not in his dotage to wish to kiss you, my sweet. You are far too beautiful for your own good. And for mine," he added after a tiny pause.

"It seems to me that you are making a great piece of work about nothing, and that does alarm me," Samantha exclaimed, determined to put an end to this embarrassing exchange. "You will have us all believing you are running a high fever again if you don't have a care.

"How is your arm this morning?" she enquired, changing the subject so abruptly that Carrington had to laugh.

"Still sore," he admitted. "But on the mend, I am convinced. Thanks in no small part to the offices of the redoubtable Mrs. Biddle and her magic gruel. There, that's much better, my dear," he said when Samantha found herself smiling at his nonsense. "Let's at least be friends if we cannot be lovers. Or should I say, *until* we can be lovers. I think I like that better, don't you?"

When Samantha turned away in confusion, he became suddenly serious. "Don't be afraid of me, Samantha. I have promised to give you six months' grace, a foolish promise if ever I made one, but it is made and you have my word on it. I am not a man to break his word, or to take an unwilling woman to my bed."

He paused, then with a finger under her chin, he lifted her face and smiled crookedly. "Even if she is my wife," he added, brushing her lips briefly with his.

Samantha felt a weight lifted, at least momentarily, from her heart.

"If you can wait six months for me, my sweet," he murmured, his dark eyes inscrutable, "then I shall have to wait that long for you, now, won't I?"

The anniversary service in the little church at Twyford, presided over by the Reverend James Fulton, went off better than Samantha had expected. Held at noon on December the tenth, it was very well attended. The late Lord Midland had been well loved by his tenants and dependents, most of whom were there. The local gentry was also well represented, and Samantha was surprised and touched to find the Dowager

Countess of Rockford, an irascible matron of well over eighty summers, seated prominently in her regular pew, her lantern jaw firmly clenched in her heavy-jowled face.

The Marquess of Carrington, interestingly pale and with his left arm in a sling, sat beside Samantha in the Ashley pew and was the object of many curious glances from the congregation. During the lengthy eulogy, delivered by Mr. Fulton in a moving voice, Samantha was suddenly overcome with emotion and had to brush a wayward tear from her cheek. She was unaccountably comforted when Carrington quietly laid his strong fingers over hers and held them lightly until the good reverend's speech came to a close.

This tender gesture did not go unnoticed, and rumours immediately began to circulate that the old lord's eldest daughter had made a love match for herself and a wealthy one at that. This rumour even reached the chronically deaf ears of Lady Rockford, whose stentorian felicitations Samantha was forced to endure at the church door with every appearance of complacence.

When at last they were able to escape from the crush of well wishers, the marquess and his lady joined a tearful Lady Midland and a subdued Felicity on the short journey to Ashley Hall, where a light nuncheon had been set out for them in the small dining-room.

The food seemed to revive their spirits, and it was not long before Felicity, fortified by a generous helping of cold chicken, asparagus, and several of Cook's gooseberry tarts, began to regale the company with stories of Lady Rockford's notorious and long-standing quarrels with various neighbours and relatives.

"Speaking of relatives," she said suddenly, breaking off in the middle of a story. "Where was Gerald? Did you see him, Samantha? I wouldn't be surprised to hear that our coxcomb of a cousin had gone scrambling off to London without a by-your-leave."

"Under the circumstances, you could hardly expect him to come up and congratulate Carrington and your sister on their marriage, now could you, my dear?" Dalton replied. His eyes lingered caressingly on Felicity's lively face and the fleeting expression of wistfulness which crossed his own countenance was not lost on Samantha.

She shot a startled glance at Carrington and found him regarding her with faint amusement. She raised her brows enquiringly, but he only shrugged his shoulders imperceptibly and turned to listen to Lady Midland, who was engrossed in trying to establish a remote connexion between the Silverdales and her second cousin on her mother's side.

The idea of his carefree cousin losing his heart to a chit barely out of the schoolroom caused the marquess no little amusement. An adamant believer in the sowing of wild oats for as long as his indulgent parents would countenance such behaviour, Tony Dalton had been courted unsuccessfully by every hopeful mother in London for his sunny good looks, charming manners, and substantial fortune ever since he began to go about with his elder cousin on his twenty-first birthday. While not precisely the best catch of any particular Season, Dalton was definitely a very good matrimonial candidate. His mother was a Silverdale, and his father, younger brother to the Earl of Alton, owned a very tidy estate near the family seat in Hampshire.

Carrington remembered the stories he had heard from his father about Aunt Amelia's marriage to the younger Dalton. She had been pressured by her family to accept an offer from the elder brother. But she had chosen young Arthur, in spite of the undeniable fact that the heir to an earldom was considered a far superior match for a Silverdale. As far as the marquess knew, she had never regretted her choice, and in time had presented her lord with six healthy boys. When he came into the title, George Dalton had married a lady of great beauty but frail constitution, who had been unable to give him any children at all and had died in the attempt after only five years of marriage. Since the earl had never remarried, Anthony Dalton was the heir to his uncle's title and estates.

Carrington's eyes strayed to Felicity, who appeared to be teasing his cousin, for Tony smiled and bent to whisper something into the lady's ear which set her off into whoops of laughter. Yes, this could well be another love match in the making. Unlike his own, he thought ruefully, glancing at his wife, who was listening earnestly to the vicar's peroration on his latest contribution to the *Times*.

He could not really blame her for being reluctant to throw herself into his bed and become his wife in more than name only. She was right; they were still strangers. And six months' respite was not an unreasonable request, under the circumstances. He had been a fool to kiss the wench, but she had been so delectable, and so vulnerable. He was a much greater fool to think he could come down here and marry a female with so many obvious attractions as Lady Samantha and then ride back to London to resume his round of bachelor activities as if nothing had happened. He was more than a fool; he had been a complete sap-skull to imagine that this action he had taken to fulfill a promise made over twenty years ago would leave him unaffected.

"You have been wool-gathering, my boy," Lady Midland chided him good-naturedly. Then her friendly face took on an air of genuine concern. "Or is your shoulder giving you pain, my dear boy? Forgive me. Here I am chattering away while you have been standing there in pain."

Before he could agree that yes, perhaps he was a trifle exhausted by the morning's activities, she called out to her daughter. "Samantha, my love, our dear Philip is quite fagged to death by all this bustle. I insist that you help him up to his room at once so that he can get some rest. We must all have windmills in our heads to make the dear boy stand around like this. I wouldn't wonder if he has not contracted another fever. I think I shall send for Dr. Graham, just to be on the safe side."

Samantha had turned to look at him as soon as her mother started speaking, but blushed rosily when she saw the quizzical look in Carrington's dark eyes.

"Please do not bring the good doctor out on my account, madam," he remonstrated to Lady Midland. "Nothing ails me that a little bedrest will not remedy. I seem to have overdone things, but Lady Samantha will soon put that to rights, won't you, my dear?" he said with deceptive blandness.

There was a veiled challenge in his words and in his steady gaze which seemed to dare Samantha to renege on her wifely duties. Confused by the double-entendre she hoped only she had read in Carrington's words, Samantha stood stock still for a few seconds, ignoring her husband's outstretched hand.

"Oh, *I* will," exclaimed Felicity impulsively, unaware of the warning look that flashed between Carrington and his cousin. "Tony can help me, won't you, Tony?" She turned her pansy-blue eyes on him appealingly, and Dalton felt a sudden shortness of breath.

"I'm sure Samantha can manage very nicely, my dear," he remarked smoothly. "And besides, I thought you wanted to learn how to drive a curricle and four, my pet, and today's as good a day as any. That is," he added mendaciously, "if my cousin will trust us with those high-steppers of his."

Lady Midland, sublimely unaware of the little scene which was being played out among the young people, settled the matter. "If your cousin will be so kind," she murmured, glancing enquiringly at her son-in-law, "that would be a splendid idea, Mr. Dalton."

"Oh, would you, Philip?" Felicity squealed in delight. "Please say you will. I promise not to spring 'em," she teased.

"I should hope not, you minx," Carrington replied shortly. "And I shall hold you entirely responsible for my cattle, Tony," he cautioned his smug-looking cousin. "They must be very fresh, so take my Tiger Ned with you."

"Oh, we shall be very careful," Felicity promised breathlessly. "I shall insist upon it. And thank you so very much, Philip. You are a brother-in-law past price!" Before anyone realized what she was about, Felicity had rushed up to the marquess, pulled his head down, and planted a swift kiss on his astonished face. By the time he had recovered, she was gone, dragging a willing Dalton after her.

"I shall ask Biddle to help you up the stairs, Philip," Samantha said quietly, when the sound of her sister's eager chatter had died away.

"That will not be necessary, my dear. As I have said before, there is nothing the matter with my legs. I shall walk upstairs myself." He smiled at her, and she felt her heart give a wild lurch. "You can, however, if you would be so kind, lend me your arm."

With her mother fondly looking on at what must have appeared to her as a tender scene between the newlyweds,

Samantha could hardly refuse to escort Carrington up the stairs.

"Whew!" he said as soon as they were out of earshot. "I had to sacrifice my cattle, which went against the grain, my dear, but it was worth it to escape from your sister's ministrations for a while and enjoy a few moments with you."

"You are talking nonsense again," Samantha replied dampeningly. "And you have much to thank Felicity for. Dr. Graham told us that by stopping the bleeding so quickly, she hastened your recovery."

"I can indeed believe it, my dear, and shall be eternally grateful to your little sister. But I fancy she will enjoy driving out with my cousin more than attending to me. Don't you think so?"

"She has always enjoyed being outdoors, and horses are her passion as well as mine," she replied calmly, choosing to ignore the implications of his words.

When they reached his room, she stopped and tried to withdraw her arm, but he would have none of it.

He opened the door and glanced down at her. "Afraid to enter the lion's den?" He smiled, and Samantha again heard a challenge in his voice.

"Of course not," she snapped, angry that he had succeeded in provoking her. "You said you were tired and wished to rest. I fail to see how I can help you."

"Do you?" He smiled softly, letting his dark eyes wander over her face and figure until she wished the ground would open and swallow her up. Or that he would crush her against his chest and cover her face with the hot kisses she had read about so often, she thought recklessly.

"Then I fear you have a lot to learn, my sweet," she heard him say through a blur of emotion.

Samantha shivered slightly as the implication of his words sank into her befuddled mind. She felt torn between two conflicting impulses. One told her to remove herself instantly from this danger zone. The other hinted at unknown delights which she might have for the asking.

Carrington broke the spell by walking into the room and saying casually over his shoulder. "I could use some help in getting out of this tight coat, my dear. That is, if you do not object to being my valet for a moment. Believe me, I would not dare to ask if Crofts were here to assist me. But since he isn't and this deuced arm is still so sore . . ." He looked at her helplessly.

Samantha knew she could not deny him such a small favour. Gently she tugged the well-cut coat off his shoulders and held it while he shook his right arm free of the clinging material. Then she gingerly eased the left sleeve off, trying to avoid any jerking movement that might cause him pain. When is was off, she shook it and went to hang it in his dressing-room next door.

When she returned, she found him fumbling awkwardly with his cravat.

"Here, let me do it," she said briskly and untied the white lace folds with quick fingers, keeping her eyes firmly on her task.

"Thank you," he said briefly. "Now, if you could just help me undo these buttons." His fingers plucked ineffectually at the front of his white shirt.

Samantha glanced up at him suspiciously but could detect nothing in his expression to alarm her.

Tentatively, she reached up and unfastened the top button with the tips of her fingers. Then she moved down to the second. By the time she had unbuttoned the third, she saw with a start that a thatch of black hair had pushed its way out of the opening and was now curling over the edges of the material. The sight of it made her feel unreasonably weak at the knees. Her fingers trembled slightly, and she forced herself to concentrate on avoiding any contact with the dark mass.

It occurred to her rather belatedly that she would soon be in a very awkward position. What should she do when she reached the last visible button? Should she ignore the others which must surely be tucked into the waist of his tightly fitting breeches? Or should she venture to tug the shirt out of the waistband? Heaven forbid, she thought, feeling a hot flush spreading over her cheeks. She was quite sure that ladies should not be thinking the thoughts that were occurring to her at that moment.

Carrington had not said a word nor moved a muscle all this time, and Samantha began to feel she had acquitted herself rather coolly and kept her head in a disturbingly intimate situation. This complacency was short-lived, however, for as soon as she had unfastened the last visible button, Carrington's strong fingers closed over hers and pressed her open palm against his bare chest.

The touch of those black hairs unnerved her and sent tremors of longing through her entire body. She raised her eyes to his face and saw that he was smiling, but that his gaze was hot and fierce, and vaguely threatening.

"Thank you, my sweet," he said slowly, with a hoarseness she had never heard him use before. "You make a fine valet. With a little more practise, you will become perfect." He moved her palm over his chest slowly until it tingled. "What do you want in payment," he murmured, raising her hand to his mouth and kissing her palm lingeringly. "Anything you want, my love. Anything at all."

His smoldering eyes dared her to give in to the intoxicating sensations his kiss was promising. And for a moment that seemed like an eternity, Samantha stood on the brink of total capitulation. Then she shuddered and drew her hand away quickly.

"I want no reward for doing my duty, my lord," she said faintly, feeling as though she had just stepped back—with a strange sense of regret—from the edge of a fascinating precipice.

With her hand on the doorknob and the safety of the hall already in sight, she breathed a sigh of relief and glanced back at him, an almost flirtatious gleam in her eyes.

"And if I were you, my lord, I would not stand around with my shirt hanging open. You will certainly catch a cold."

Without waiting for an answer, she swept out and closed the door softly behind her.

12 * Nicholas

THE FOLLOWING MORNING, SAMANTHA LEARNED FROM BIDDLE, WHOSE daughter worked for Mr. Tubbs at the Black Boar Inn, that Lord Midland had departed the village on the very afternoon of his uncle's anniversary service. He had left in the company of one Sir Joshua Fieldham, a gambling crony of dubious reputation, who had been visiting in the neighbourhood. The two gentlemen had gone off in the earl's new curricle without putting down so much as a groat on the considerable reckoning his lordship had racked up at the inn.

The information saddened though did not surprise Samantha, who was well versed in her cousin's cavalier dealings with tradesmen. She immediately instructed Biddle to determine just how badly Midland was dipped in the village and to bring her a list of his local creditors.

"You should let the Bow Street Runners come after him," Felicity grumbled to her sister that evening as Samantha was dressing for dinner. "A short stay in Debtors' Prison would do him a world of good."

"Perhaps you are right, dear. But just think of the scandal. How could we ever face our neighbours knowing that a member of our family is in such a disgraceful situation? Besides," she said as she stepped into the new orange silk gown as she had chosen to wear that evening. "It is not entirely Gerald's fault that he is such a spendthrift, you know."

"No, I don't know," Felicity answered shortly. "And if our dear cousin did not fancy himself a Tulip of fashion, he would not be obliged to lay out his blunt on so many new clothes. Do you remember that green and gold striped waistcoat he wore to church once? I swear I thought Lady Rockford was going to burst her stays when she saw it." She grinned mischievously at her sister's shocked expression.

"Felicity, that is no language for a lady, and you know it."

Samantha sighed. "So why do you deliberately provoke me by using it? I shudder to think what Carrington will take us for if you don't mend your ways."

"Oh, I don't care a fig what Philip thinks," Felicity answered flippantly. "He's too busy making sheep's eyes at you to take any notice of me anyway." She was satisfied to see the colour rise into her sister's cheeks at this calculated remark. It was just as she thought. Samantha was not quite as cool as she pretended to be about the marquess.

"Felicity! I forbid you to talk about his lordship in that disrespectful manner." Samantha was uncomfortably aware of her young sister's amused gaze. "Watch your tongue, young lady."

"Why, whatever is the matter, Sam?" came the innocent response. "Don't you *want* him to look at you like that? I thought that's what the romantic heroines in your novels are always pining for. Some poor fool to make a cake of himself over them."

"What do you know about the heroines in my novels? I thought you never read them."

"Well, of course I don't actually *read* them. But I do glance at them occasionally. How else would I know what maggoty ideas are getting into your head, Sam? I declare, you are a slow-top sometimes." She smiled angelically, and Samantha, who knew that Felicity had nothing angelic about her, held her breath.

"Here you are, in the middle of a romantic situation straight out of the latest novel, one that most females would kill to have happen to them, and what do you do?" Felicity gave a snort of disgust. "I wager you haven't even kissed him, much less . . ." She paused, suddenly conscious of the impropriety of what she was about to say.

Samantha gasped in horror at her little sister's embarrassing lack of modesty. "And just what do you know of such things, miss?" she enquired frostily, drawing herself up to her full height and glaring down her nose at Felicity. "Mama shall hear of this latest start of yours, you may be sure."

Realizing that she had really upset her beloved Sam this time, Felicity rushed over and flung her arms around her sister. "Forgive me, Sam. I didn't mean to set up your hackles, truly

I didn't.'' She looked so sincerely contrite that Samantha hugged her tightly. ''I only want to see you happy with your White Knight.'' Felicity murmured. ''He really is bang up to the nines, you know. I just can't understand why you are not in alt over the whole affair.''

A sudden thought occurred to her, and she glanced up at her sister, an expression of comic dismay on her beautiful face. ''Don't you love him at all, Sam? Is that it?''

Samantha disengaged herself and smoothed out the skirt of her silk gown with unsteady fingers. ''I *like* him well enough,'' she began hesitantly, reluctant to describe her confused feelings for Carrington in any stronger terms. ''But this is an arranged marriage, don't forget. And we are practically strangers, dear.''

''Oh, fiddle! What has that got to do with anything? Why cannot you form a strong attachment for a total stranger? It happens all the time in novels,'' Felicity added blithely. ''And Philip is hardly that, is he?''

''Real life is not fiction, my love.''

''Tony says it is often much better than fiction,'' Felicity put in. ''And you know something, Sam. For a gentleman, Tony has an extraordinary amount of good sense.''

Samantha glanced at her sister curiously. ''That is praise indeed, coming from you,'' she remarked dryly, clasping a string of pearls around her slender neck and examining the effects in the pier glass above her dresser. ''What has Mr. Dalton done to deserve such accolades?''

''He is amusing, and witty, and does not flirt with me or tease me with silly remarks about my hair and eyes as most of the gentlemen around here do.'' She wrinkled her nose in disgust. ''He is comfortable, if you know what I mean, Sam. And I feel that I can talk to him about anything, and he won't be shocked or say I am being improper.''

Her sister looked at her in alarm. ''I hope you are never improper, my love. You don't want Mr. Dalton to think you are rag-mannered, even though we both know you are.'' She laughed.

''Oh, Tony doesn't mind a bit. He says he likes it when I speak my mind. He can't bear mealymouthed creatures who put on languishing airs and burst into tears at the least

provocation. He says that all his brothers will like me excessively. He has five, you know. Harry and Ben are still at home,
but George and William are up at Oxford, and James is in the
army. What fun it must be to have five brothers,'' she said
wistfully. ''I can't wait to meet them. Tony says—''

''It seems to me that Tony does a good deal of talking.''
Samantha laughed. ''You seem to be exceedingly well informed about our new relatives on the Dalton side. But what of
the Silverdales? Who can we look forward to meeting there?''

''You already know that Philip is an only child and both his
parents are dead,'' Felicity explained. ''That is why he spends
so much time with his cousins. Tony is like a brother to him,
you know. And then there is Nicholas, of course. Tony says
that Philip always spends Christmas with him, and this year he
will bring him up to London. I think that very considerate of
him, don't you? Considering who he is, I mean.''

Samantha felt a stab of panic in the pit of her stomach. Here
it is, she thought. This must be the love-child Gerald had
thrown in her face the other day. But surely Carrington would
not recognize the child so openly? Or would he? Could it be
that her husband intended to include the boy in their Christmas
plans without consulting her? Was he to stay at Carrington
Court? Would Carrington really expect her to lend her countenance to such an arrangement? A chill hand seemed to clutch
at her heart.

''And who is this Nicholas?'' She forced herself to speak
with a calm she did not feel.

Felicity, who had been rummaging distractedly through her
sister's jewelry box, turned to her in surprise.

''Philip has not told you about Nicholas?''

''As I have already explained to you,'' Samantha replied
stiffly, ''we are practically strangers. There is much we do not
know about each other.''

''He doesn't seem like a stranger to me, and I am not
married to him,'' Felicity pointed out. ''If you were to spend as
much time with your husband as you do with your horses, you
might know more about him,'' she added rather more tartly
than she had intended. ''And Nicholas is Philip's godchild.
Both his parents are dead, poor little fellow. Tony says that
Philip is raising him as if he were his own son.''

Oh, I can well believe it, Samantha thought angrily, pushing the Silverdale Emerald onto her finger and twisting it viciously. Godson indeed! A likely story. She stared at the glittering green stone through a mist of unshed tears. And this . . . this godson was to spend the Christmas holidays in Carrington Court, her new home. And doubtless she would be expected to go on as if it were nothing out of the ordinary to have one's husband's illegitimate brat staying under the same roof. Well, she would have to see about that, wouldn't she?

"Come along, child!" she exclaimed peevishly to a perplexed Felicity. "We should not keep the gentlemen from their dinner."

Samantha was more than a little relieved that her mornings were fully occupied with exercising her hunters and discussing estate business with Mr. Miles, her agent. She was thus able to avoid all but the briefest encounters with Carrington. Her afternoons, however, were a different matter, and she could not neglect the entertainment of her two guests.

Contrary to Samantha's assumptions about London gentlemen, both Carrington and his cousin were avid outdoorsmen. Luckily, the weather remained fine for several days, and Samantha took advantage of the crisp, sunny afternoons to drive her guests around the Ashley estates and surrounding neighbourhood.

If she had thought to avoid a tête-à-tête with Carrington, however, Samantha had reckoned without her little sister. Felicity was a consummate and enthusiastic rider and had little trouble persuading Dalton to take to the saddle with her and leave the carriage to the convalescent Carrington and his new bride. Much as she would have preferred to be on horseback herself, Samantha could hardly refuse Carrington's request that she show him the paces of an Ashley team.

"If my shoulder were not still so sore," he told her somewhat mendaciously, "I would drive you in my own rig. But I know you to be a very fine whip, my dear, so I place myself confidently in your hands."

There was nothing else for it but to order up her own team and hope that they would be mettlesome enough to keep her fully occupied.

On one such afternoon they paid a social call—at Felicity's insistence—on Mr. and Mrs. Stoddard and their daughter Miss Leticia Stoddard. This unfortunate young lady, so recently betrothed to a young titled gentleman during her first London Season, was the object of Felicity's particular wrath for having paraded her large ruby engagement ring and broadly hinted that, at twenty-three, Lady Samantha was already on the shelf. It was only after considerable argument that Felicity was prevailed upon not to punish her for this piece of impertinence by comparing the offending ruby ring with the Silverdale Emerald on her sister's finger.

"You are a spoilsport, Sam," Felicity complained as the party passed out of the gates on the return home. "That Leticia deserved a sharp set-down if anyone did. She had the gall to suggest that rubies are all the rage this year."

"That is no reason for you to be rude to the girl," Samantha replied calmly. "It is no crime to prefer rubies, after all."

"Well, I prefer your emerald over that paltry ruby any day, Philip," she declared stubbornly. "And furthermore, that pimply-faced, beardless wonder she is betrothed to cannot hold a candle to you," she added, her eyes glinting with ingenious admiration as she addressed her brother-in-law. "And did you see the size of his shirt points? He could hardly turn his head and had to peer at me sideways like a startled horse. What a rasher-o'wind he is, to be sure. I feel quite sorry for Leticia getting herself leg-shackled to such a sorry-looking pudding-head."

Carrington watched her with a lazy smile on his lips. "Thank you for your flattering opinion of me, Felicity. I shall endeavour to live up to it."

Felicity flashed him a dazzling smile and cantered off with Dalton in close pursuit.

"Your sister has the makings of a Diamond of the First Water," he remarked as the curricle shot out of the narrow gate in fine style and the matched roan team—all Raspberries of one kind or another—settled down to a mile-eating pace that only the best cattle can sustain. "Add a little Town bronze, and she will play havoc with the young bucks when she makes her come-out. I can see an eventful Season ahead of us, my dear. Carrington Court may never be the same again."

"Carrington Court?" Samantha glanced at him quizzically.

"Yes. I have persuaded your mother to let us present the chit next April. There is no reason to burden your aunt with that responsibility, is there? I am assuming, of course, that you would like to have Felicity make her debut under your sponsorship."

"Yes, I would like that excessively," Samantha confessed, and Carrington was rewarded with a warm smile. "That is very generous of you, Philip. I had no idea you planned to be in Town for the Season."

"Well, I certainly will be if you are going to be there. I assume you will want to attend your sister's come-out parties. After that, I would like to take you to Silverdale Grange, my family seat. The staff will be wanting to meet you. It's close to Dalton's home in Alton, and you will enjoy meeting his family, especially my Aunt Amelia. She is a beautiful, head-strong, independent woman; she reminds me a little of you, Samantha."

Samantha kept her eyes on the road. Somehow all this travelling around and staying with Carrington at his estate had not entered into her plans at all. She had expected to remain quietly at Ashley Hall with her mother and Felicity. But suddenly she had been made to realize that this plan was not going to be so simple after all. Felicity had grown up, and the look in Dalton's eyes warned her that her little sister would not be single much longer.

And what about herself? In accepting Carrington, she had tacitly accepted all the honours and responsibilities that went with her new title. Could she really expect to continue as the reclusive Lady Samantha Ashley of Ashley Hall? She was now mistress of not one but two new establishments, Carrington Court in London and the family seat, Silverdale Grange. Would it be fair to neglect her role as Philip's wife merely because she had made him agree to allow her an extraordinary amount of freedom for a woman in her position? Papa would hardly have approved; she doubted he had that in mind when he made his will. He would, she very much feared, have been thinking of his grandchildren. For the first time, Samantha allowed herself to consider what it might be like to bear Carrington a son. The idea did not seem repugnant at all.

And what about Nicholas? Who was he really and how was she to live with the knowledge that Carrington had, as Gerald had warned her, foisted his love-child upon her?

These and other heavy thoughts occupied her so completely that she failed to perceive the silence which grew between them, or the speculative gaze that Carrington cast upon her during their drive home.

At the end of the week, the marquess was pronounced fit to travel by Dr. Graham on his usual afternoon visit to his noble patient.

"But not on horseback, my lord," he warned Carrington. "We don't want to run the risk of aggravating the wound, which is still very tender."

"He will travel in the coach with the ladies, the lucky dog," his cousin remarked after the doctor had left and Lady Midland had ordered a tea-tray sent up to the Blue Saloon. "While I shall have to drive all alone, in solitary splendour, in your curricle, coz. I almost wish it had been me that poacher hit with his stray bullet," he said with a laugh. "The pain would have been well worth it to have three lovely ladies waiting on me."

Carrington noticed that, although his cousin spoke of three ladies, his eyes were resting fondly on only one, who immediately responded to his comment with unexpected severity.

"That's a nonsensical thing to say, if ever I heard one," Felicity declared sternly. "And unworthy of you, Tony. I thought you had more sense than to wish to suffer in order to gain our attention. You must be hard up indeed to contemplate such caper-witted strategies. Shame on you, sir."

"Don't be so hard on Mr. Dalton, child," her mother remonstrated gently. "It was very prettily said."

"Well, I think it was silly," Felicity insisted, refusing to look at the culprit and concentrating all her attention on the plate of pastries in front of her. "As for myself, I would give my eye-teeth to ride in the curricle instead of that stuffy old coach," she added ingenuously.

Dalton caught his cousin's bemused glance and grinned wryly.

"Lady Felicity is absolutely right," he said contritely.

"Only a sap-skull would wish to be shot. I hope you can bring yourself to overlook this momentary lapse of wit, Felicity."

Felicity examined him speculatively for a moment while she finished off a gooseberry tart. Then an angelic smile spread over her face and a mischievous twinkle made her eyes sparkle.

"Only if you will take me up in the curricle with you, Tony."

Although Mr. Dalton would have been only glad to comply with this request, he had to agree with Lady Midland that an open carriage was no place for a delicately reared young lady during the winter.

"Well, let me tell you, Mama," that same young lady argued hotly, "I am not delicate at all. Quite the contrary, as it happens. I'm as strong as a horse. Ask Samantha if you don't believe me. Oh, how I do hate to be mollycoddled."

Samantha agreed, with as straight a face as she could muster, that her sister was indeed as strong as a horse, but that propriety demanded that she ride in the carriage with her mother.

Felicity threw her sister a look of utter disgust. "I don't see why that should signify. Tony is family now, isn't he? He's like a brother, aren't you Tony," she demanded, turning appealing eyes upon Mr. Dalton.

Carrington took pity on his cousin and came to his rescue. "Yes, Felicity, Dalton may seem like a brother, but the truth is, he is not. What Lady Midland wishes to avoid, I am sure, is any unnecessary gossip which such an escapade may cause. I'm convinced you can appreciate the need for a young lady to act with discretion at all times."

Felicity stared at him with horror, momentarily struck dumb that such fustian farradiddle could come from someone she so admired. "But I would be the soul of discretion," she wailed. "I wouldn't even ask to handle the ribbons. Unless Tony insisted, of course." She looked at them as a new thought struck her. "You are all talking as if you expected Mr. Dalton to run off to Gretna Green with me," she said with an irrepressible giggle. "That's an insult to his intelligence, of course. And if he did suggest anything so hen-witted, I would shoot him myself."

There seemed to be nothing left to say after this unladylike sally, and the subject was dropped until the following morning when the party assembled in the front hall, where a mountain of trunks, bandboxes, and valises had been steadily accumulating since the previous afternoon.

"I'm afraid that travelling with three females is not what you are used to, Philip." Samantha smiled ruefully at her lord as he descended the stairs to find her directing the disposal of the luggage in the second carriage, which was to accompany them to London.

"My father always managed to leave before us so that he might avoid all the clutter and bustle," she said.

"Pity I didn't think of that myself," Carrington replied. "I can't say I blame him, though. This looks like a regular deployment of army baggage for a whole regiment. Am I right in assuming that this collection will be augmented by sundry purchases from London modistes?"

He looked at her quizzically, and Samantha felt a glow of contentment at the warm friendliness she perceived in the depth of his dark eyes. Since learning of the existence of Nicholas from Felicity, she had adopted a cool reserve with the marquess, which he had not tried to violate. She had dreaded being cooped up with him for several hours in the Ashley travelling coach, but for the past few days he had shown no inclination at all to flirt with her, so her apprehension had diminished considerably.

Observing him as he stood beside the carriage, his many-caped driving coat flung carelessly around his broad shoulders and his tall felt beaver perched jauntily on his dark head, Samantha caught herself wishing that they had met under different circumstances and that a little boy named Nicholas had never been born.

13 * London Reception

THE JOURNEY TO LONDON WAS ACCOMPLISHED WITHOUT MISHAP AND IN a fair degree of comfort thanks to the Ashleys' luxurious travelling chaise, which was well sprung and well appointed with burgundy velvet upholstery and tightly insulated against the cold.

At Carrington's request, and much to Felicity's chagrin, Mr. Dalton had gone ahead in his cousin's curricle-and-four to alert the household of their imminent arrival. So it was that in the late afternoon of the second day, when their carriage finally pulled into the ornate porte-cochère in front of the Carrington town house on Cavendish Square, the entire staff was gathered in the marble-tiled entry hall to receive their new mistress.

Momentarily daunted by the prospect of facing so many new faces, Samantha thought back wistfully on the less formal and infinitely more affectionate greeting that had awaited them at Fathington House. She envied her mother and sister, who, at this very moment, were certainly seated around the tea-tray in her Aunt Eliza's cozy drawing-room engaged in comfortable family gossip. She had exchanged the briefest hug with her aunt herself, and tarried only long enough to allow Lord and Lady Fathington to wish her and her new husband happy, before Carrington bundled her back into the carriage for the short trip to Carrington Court.

Now the vaguely dreaded moment had finally come. She was about to enter her new home in the company of her new husband. They were now an officially married couple in the eyes of society. At Ashley Hall, she had been able to keep this fact in abeyance and carry on as she had always done. The wedding itself had been almost like a dream, agreed upon and performed too quickly for it to have much reality in her mind. But here, reality was catching up with her. Once she stepped across this threshold, her life would never be the same again.

However much she had wanted to keep things unchanged, she knew that they had changed, irrevocably so. No amount of documents carefully drawn up by Mr. MacIntyre to protect her freedom could alter the fact that this tall stranger helping her out the carriage was now in control of her destiny.

A shudder ran through her.

Carrington glanced at her and smiled. "It's not going to be as bad as you think," he said softly, as if he had read her thoughts. He pressed her fingers before handing her down to his butler, who had himself placed the steps for his new mistress to descend from the coach.

Samantha gave him her hand. "It's Turner, isn't it?" she inquired with her customary graciousness.

"Yes, milady," replied the butler. "It's very kind of you to remember, ma'am."

How could she forget? Samantha thought fleetingly, remembering that first embarrassing incursion into her lord's house to seek out the man who had promised his son to her in marriage. That day seemed to be only yesterday, and yet here she was entering the same house with that promised husband.

"Give his lordship a hand, Turner," she said. "He will not admit it, but he is not yet fully recovered from his injury."

She was right, Carrington had to admit. He was unaccountably weary from those long hours of sitting in the coach and accepted Turner's proffered arm gratefully. He knew from her small shiver and by the way she clung to his arm as they mounted the steps that Samantha was dreading the ordeal ahead of her. It pleased him to note, however, that she made no attempt to hurry the introductions, but proceeded leisurely down the line, accepting the bobbed curtsies and bows with a smile and a murmured comment.

"We will go straight upstairs, Turner," he said, divesting himself of his greatcoat and felt beaver. "Her ladyship will want to rest, but if you send up a tea-tray to the Silver-Room, I am sure it would be most welcome."

"Yes, milord. I shall bring it up myself immediately, just as soon as Mrs. Collins takes her ladyship to her room."

The housekeeper bustled forward eagerly, but the marquess waved her away. "I will attend to that myself, thank you, Mrs.

Collins. Have her ladyship's valise taken up, Turner. The rest of the luggage should be arriving shortly.

"Where is my cousin?" he enquired suddenly.

"Mr. Dalton is upstairs in the nursery with Master Nicholas," the butler replied. "Shall I inform him of your arrival?"

"Yes," Carrington said briefly, glancing at Samantha, who had turned towards the staircase as he spoke. "Is the boy fully recovered from his head cold?"

"Oh, yes, milord. Master Nicholas is in fine gig and asking for you since early this afternoon. Shall I send him to you, sir?"

"Later, Turner. After we've had our tea."

They climbed the stairs in silence. Carrington wished now that he had been more frank with his bride regarding the presence of Nicholas in his household. It had not seemed important at the time, but now he wondered if perhaps he should have brought up the subject sooner. Felicity had known about Nicholas; she had told him, with characteristic enthusiasm, how much she looked forward to meeting him. And he had assumed that she had told her sister. But perhaps he should have done so himself.

He glanced at Samantha's profile beside him and got the distinct impression that she had withdrawn from him. Well, he would explain everything to her after she met the boy. No, he thought, not everything. He couldn't tell Samantha of all people the whole truth about Nicholas. To protect the boy from scandal, he would have to continue in his role of godparent to a motherless child. That much at least was true, he consoled himself. Nicholas's mother was indeed dead.

For her part, Samantha had received a severe shock upon hearing that Carrington's godchild—or at least one he claimed as his godchild—was actually here in the house with her. She would have to be strong. She must pretend she didn't care, she told herself firmly. She would act as though it didn't matter to her how many illegitimate sons Carrington might have scattered throughout the kingdom. It would undoubtedly break her heart, but she would do it.

Samantha schooled her face to reflect a calmness she was far from feeling. But when her husband threw open the door of the master suite withdrawing-room, better known as the Silver-Room, she could not suppress a gasp of delight.

The room was obviously designed for the intimate comfort of the master of the house and his lady. There was a profusion of deep armchairs and inviting sofas smothered with plump, gaily-coloured cushions, convenient knick-knack and candelabra tables, and even a silver-enamelled piano in one corner. The Aubusson carpet covering the entire floor had given the room its name, for it was an intricate design of pewter-coloured leaves and birds on a silver background. The crackling fire under the slate-grey marble mantelpiece gave the whole an air of cozy informality which warmed Samantha's heart.

This would undoubtedly be her favourite room, Samantha decided instantly and said as much to the marquess, who stood awaiting her reaction.

"It's beautiful," she breathed, truly enchanted by the silvery lightness of the furnishings. "And so inviting. I love it!" she cried impulsively, turning a smiling face to the man at her side, her previous annoyance with him quite forgotten.

"I'm glad you like it, my dear. It was my mother's favourite, too. She spent most of her time here when she came to London. I thought I would leave it exactly as she had it. You can order what changes you think fit after you are settled in."

"Oh, I wouldn't change a thing, Philip," Samantha declared. "It is perfect as it is."

"Your bedchamber is over here," he said, walking over to a door to the left and opening it. "I have had this refurbished for you, but if it is not to your liking, you must change it."

Samantha passed apprehensively into the luxurious room and glanced around, her eyes skipping nervously over the enormous four-poster bed in the center of the floor. It had a sea-green eiderdown spread upon it and was surrounded by clouds of pale green, gauzy curtains, tied back by satin cords with silver tassels on them. The erotic visions which flitted unbidden through her mind at the sight of so much splendour made Samantha's cheeks glow with embarrassment.

"My mother preferred blue, but I thought this green might be more appropriate to the colour of your eyes," Carrington explained, watching his wife's reaction to the huge bed with lazy amusement. Six months seemed to loom like an eternity before him, but perhaps, he thought, as he watched Samantha's graceful form move over to the tall window overlooking the small garden area now devoid of flowers, perhaps Lady Carrington would find that big bed rather too lonely for her taste in the weeks to come.

A discreet knock from the other room announced the arrival of the tea-tray, and they returned to the sitting-room to find Turner busy arranging a silver tea-set on a low table before the fire.

"Cook has sent up a plate of pastries in case her ladyship should wish to eat something," he murmured. "Our cook is rather well known for her apricot tarts, milady," he explained to Samantha, who had taken her place in front of the tea-table.

"Now, don't split hairs, Turner." Carrington laughed. "We all know that Cook's tarts are the envy of every hostess in London."

"Thank you, Turner," Samantha said. "And please thank Cook for being so thoughtful. I am indeed hungry after all that jolting about."

Turner looked gratified at this response, and after making sure that everything was to her ladyship's liking, he hastened down to the pantry to assure the housekeeper that it was just as he had predicted, the new mistress was indeed a pearl past price.

Carrington leaned negligently against the grey marble mantel, one gleaming Hessian resting on the brass rail, admiring the picture of quiet domesticity presented by his lady busy at the tea-table. Her eyes were lowered as she poured the cups of tea, and Carrington marvelled at the thickness of her dark lashes against her cheek.

On the whole he was pleased at the way things had turned out. His hand had been forced, it was true, but it was time he settled down and produced an heir to his line. For the first time in his thirty-two years, he considered the possibility of setting up his own nursery. The need had never before struck him as being urgent. There had always been Tony and his five brothers standing between himself and the extinction of the title. But as he stood gazing down at his wife's delicate face and alluring form, he was conscious of a strong desire for a son of his own, a Silverdale to carry on the name as well as the title. The thought caused his blood to stir in anticipation.

At that moment Samantha raised her amber eyes and looked directly at him. Her hand, proffering a delicate Wedgwood cup, wobbled alarmingly as she met his gaze. Recognizing that lean, hungry look as a sign of danger, she made a valiant attempt to smile. "Wool-gathering, my lord?" she asked incautiously. "I'll give you a penny for them."

Carrington laughed. He stepped forward and took the cup from her trembling fingers. "I was merely thinking how very charming you look, my dear, sitting here at the tea-table. You have brought new life to this room, which my mother loved so much. We never used it, my father and I, after her death two years ago. And I've missed it." He looked at her warmly. "Now we can enjoy it together."

"You must have loved your mother very much," she remarked, ignoring the implications of shared intimacies in his remark.

He turned back to the fire and kicked at a half-burnt log with his boot. "Yes, I did. And my father adored her. We were a happy family, although I know my mother had wanted a bigger brood, and especially a daughter. But it never happened, so she had to make do with me," he added, a smile softening his well-shaped mouth.

"I hope we have more luck, because I find I rather fancy the idea of a nursery full of little Silverdales." He grinned at her. She had coloured up at his remark, and he wondered idly if that rosy hue which now suffused her cheeks had spread down over her beautifully rounded breasts. He promised himself the pleasure of discovering the answer in the near future.

"I shall endeavour to oblige you, my lord," she murmured. His words had moved her, and she suddenly realized how painful it must be for a man like Carrington not to be able to recognize his first-born son as his rightful heir. Well, she reasoned, he should have thought of that before he . . . before he—she could not quite bring herself to think of that intimate event which must have preceded the appearance of the child. An unexpected wave of sympathy for the mother of that child washed over her.

"To tell you the truth, I had never given it much thought

before," her husband was saying. "In fact, I had thought to go to my grave a bachelor." He smiled at her startled expression. "Yes, Tony and I have been successfully dodging match-making mamas for many years now. Spending so much time in India has helped, of course. And now, thanks to you, my dear, I don't have to dodge any more."

"Were there no eligible young ladies in Bombay, then?" Samantha asked curiously. The thought crossed her mind that perhaps Carrington had met Nicholas's mother in India.

"Very few, as it happens. The climate is not kind to England's fair beauties. And what females of quality there are can have their pick of the gentlemen."

Samantha said nothing. She could well imagine that with his rank and fortune, Lord Carrington had been among those picked. And even had he lacked these two important qualities, his dark good looks must surely have won him the attention of even the most fastidious ladies. For some inexplicable reason she found herself envying those ladies in Bombay.

"And what about the charming Mr. Dalton?" she enquired. "Am I correct in assuming that he was one of those picked?"

"Dalton has far more charm with the ladies than I can boast of," he replied candidly. "But I have never seen him so taken with a member of the fairer sex as he is with your sister, my dear. I can only hope he does not make a cake of himself," he added.

"Would it be so terrible if he were to fall in love with Felicity?" she asked, more than a little displeased at his flippancy.

He smiled in amusement at her ruffled countenance. "Love is for green-headed moonlings and Johnny Raws," he replied mildly. "A vastly exaggerated and romantical myth, from all I hear."

"Do you mean to tell me you have never felt the slightest tendre for one of my sex?" she exclaimed in mock surprise. "And how cynical of you to disparage your cousin for being in danger of falling prey to Cupid's arrow."

"I count myself lucky to have escaped unscathed from just such a fate," Carrington drawled, intrigued by the sparkle of indignation in his lady's eyes. "Do not tell me, my love, that you harbour such secret romantical notions in that pretty head of yours?''

She was saved from having to find a suitable reply to this piece of drollery by a discreet knock on the door and the appearance of Turner, who informed the marquess that Mr. Dalton and Master Nicholas were downstairs asking for him.

''Ask them to step up here, Turner, and bring some more pastries for that young scamp. That is''—he turned an enquiring glance on Samantha—''if you do not mind the invasion, my dear?''

''Of course not,'' Samantha heard herself respond through suddenly frozen lips.

The following morning, when Samantha looked back on that scene in the Silver-Room, she had difficulty remembering much of what had transpired. The door had burst open, and Dalton had appeared on the threshold holding a small boy by the hand. That she recalled clearly enough.

Then her eyes had focussed on the child, and her heart seemed to leap into her throat. He was a beautiful, well-shaped little boy of about six, but what twisted the knife in her heart was his colouring. His hair was a mass of tumbled dark curls which bounced appealing when he ran across the room to fling himself joyously into Carrington's open arms.

His cry of welcome tore at Samantha's nerves. And when her husband had swung the child up into the air until he squealed with delight, and then hugged him affectionately against his broad chest, Samantha could plainly see that their colouring was almost a perfect match.

Seeing the two dark heads together made Samantha feel almost ill. But the worst was yet to come. When Carrington brought the child over to meet her, it took all her willpower to remain calm and respond coherently as Nicholas gazed up at her with eyes that were as dark and enigmatic as Carrington's.

''And this is my godson, Nicholas,'' she heard him say, as if from a great distance. ''Nicholas, make your bow to my lady, like a real gentleman. You are never too young to learn good manners, boy.''

''Can't I kiss her, Uncle Philip?'' the child asked, his serious little face suddenly transformed by a pixie smile.

Both Carrington and his cousin laughed at this. "You'll have to ask her first!" Dalton exclaimed. "It's always bad form to kiss a lady without asking her permission, Nicky. You don't want to be taken for a gapeseed, now do you?"

Both gentlemen had regarded her with amusement, and she remembered her anger at being placed in that impossible situation. She had felt trapped and for an awkward moment seriously contemplated flying into a pelter and rushing out of the room. Luckily she had not disgraced herself with such a vulgar tantrum. Instead she had looked into the boy's eyes and seen such confident expectancy there that she had impulsively leaned forward to embrace him and allow him to place a wet kiss on her cheek.

He had remained close to her, standing within the circle of her arms, and the warmth of his little body leaning so confidently against her had dispelled her anger.

"You smell nice," he had told her with innocent candour. And she had been forced to laugh and succumb to the sudden urge to smooth his rumpled black curls back from his forehead.

"Uncle Philip says you are to live here with us. Is that true?" He gazed up at her intently, as if her answer really mattered to him.

"Why, yes, that is certainly true, Nicholas." She found that saying his name had not been as difficult as she had expected.

"For always and always?" he had insisted.

She gazed at him in perplexity, wondering at the note of longing in his voice. Had she imagined it, or did this little lad stand in need of a woman's affection?

"That all depends." She smiled. "Do you wish me to?"

The pixie smile had flooded his face again, and he had flung his arms about her neck, crushing her gown and knocking several pins form her hair. "Oh, yes!" he had crowed excitedly. "Yes, if you please. We can have such fun. Uncle Tony has promised to take me out in his curricle tomorrow if it is fine. You may come with us if you like," he added. "Uncle Tony drives to an inch, you know. He may not be a member of the Four-Horse-Club, like Uncle Philip, but he is a first-rate fiddler. He is going to teach me how to feather my corners with his sixteen-mile-an-hour-tits when I get bigger. I'm sure he would show you, too, if you asked him."

"Lady Carrington is already a first-rate whip, young man." Carrington remarked with a laugh. "As you will soon find out. Now get off the lady's lap, you ragamuffin. You must learn to kiss a lady without pulling her hairpins out, or you will set up her bristles, my lad."

After that the evening went by in a drowsy glow, whether because of her own exhaustion or the comforting warmth of the room, she could not tell. Perhaps the intense feeling of relief that her meeting with Nicholas had not, after the first few moments, been painful at all had something to do with her sense of well-being.

When his Nanny, Mrs. Hudson, had been sent for to take him off to bed, the child had again hugged her quite as unself-consciously as he had done with Carrington and Dalton.

She had been surprised when Carrington invited his cousin to stay and share the light supper he had ordered Turner to have sent up for them. Dalton had looked at her quizzically, but when she had added her invitation to her husband's, he had accepted. He had made the meal so enjoyable with his charming chatter, that Samantha had forgotten to be self-conscious with Carrington. Only when Dalton opened a bottle of champagne and proposed a toast to the newlyweds, did she feel a blush rise to her cheeks.

Now, as she sat propped up against feather pillows in her immense bed, drinking hot chocolate brought up personally by her own abigail, Samantha remembered her promise to visit Nicholas in the schoolroom.

"Sally," she said, putting the cup down on the ornate lacquer table by her bedside and throwing off the covers. "You can prepare my bath now. I have slept quite long enough. And lay out my new green merino, will you. I plan to pay a call on my aunt this morning."

"You'll be wanting a breakfast tray sent up, my lady?" Sally helped her mistress into a warm dressing gown and then rang for the hot bath water to be brought up.

An hour later, after a warm bath and a light breakfast, Samantha left the relative safety of her bedchamber and made her way up the stairs to the third floor.

14 * Lady Sylvia Towers

THE NURSERY WAS A LARGE, AIRY ROOM OVERLOOKING THE BACK gardens, and when Samantha made her entrance, Nicholas was alone at the window gazing out anxiously.

As soon as he saw Samantha, his face cleared. "It's going to be a fine day for a drive in the park, isn't it?" he cried, running across the room to embrace her with obvious enthusiasm. "I hope Uncle Tony will not forget his promise to take me."

"I'm sure he won't, Nicholas. But if Mrs. Hudson can spare you for a little while this morning, I would like to invite you to accompany me to visit my Aunt Eliza. Would you like that?"

"Oh, yes!" the boy cried, his eyes sparkling with excitement. "I'll ask Mrs. Hudson if I may go." He planted another wet kiss on Samantha's cheek and dashed out of the room, calling to his nurse at the top of his voice. Samantha gazed after him, a bemused look on her face.

Twenty minutes later, muffled up to the eyebrows against the chill December air, Samantha bundled a jubilant Nicholas into the Carrington town carriage for the short trip to Brook Street.

No sooner had the carriage pulled out of the porte-cochère, however, than Samantha began to have second thoughts about this impulsive visit to Fathington House. What maggot had got into her head? she wondered. Wasn't she about to deceive her own family by bringing Carrington's love-child into her aunt's house? Of course, she would not introduce Nicholas as such, but that was what he was, surely? Gerald had warned her, and he had been right. She hated to admit it, but surely she could not doubt it? Mrs. Hudson had indicated that Nicholas had no friends in London and that Lord Carrington never had the boy downstairs when he received visitors other than Mr. Dalton. Wasn't that evidence enough that he was ashamed of the child? Perhaps he would be angry with her for taking the child out in public, even if only to her aunt's home. Belatedly, Samantha realized she should have consulted Philip before presuming to entertain his son.

As she listened to the child's happy prattle and felt the warmth of his small hand clasping her own, a great wave of sadness washed over her at the unfairness of life. Why should this innocent child be ostracized by society because his parents had not been married? A tremor of guilt shook her as she recalled that only yesterday she herself had been determined to ignore his existence.

"Are you cold, Aunty Sam?" Nicholas paused in his story about the pony he hoped to receive from his Uncle Philip for Christmas to regard her with his dark velvety gaze. The child's eyes were so like Philip's that Samantha felt again the stab of jealousy for that lady in Bombay who had obviously shared an intimate part of her husband's life.

"No, darling, not at all." She smiled. "Tell me, do you really think you will get your pony?"

"Oh, yes," came the instant response. "Uncle Philip promised me one, and he always keeps his promises. And Uncle Tony promised to show me how to ride it." He regarded her seriously for a moment. "Do you keep yours?"

"My what?" She stared at him uncomprehendingly.

"Your promises, of course," he prompted. "Don't you remember? You promised you would live with us for always and always."

"So I did." She smiled. "And I hope to keep all my promises to you, Nicholas. But you must understand that I have an estate of my own in Hampshire to manage, Ashley Hall, with lots of horses on it, so I may not be with you and your Uncle Philip as much as you wish."

He seemed to ponder this information for a minute or two before replying. "Can't we go with you? I would like to see your horses. Tell me about them, please."

Avoiding the first question, Samantha launched into a detailed account of the Ashley hunters and found that, for a six-year-old, Nicholas was surprisingly knowledgeable about horses. He was soon confessing that one of his most cherished dreams was to learn to be a bruising rider to hounds and wear a red coat, taking his fences in bang-up style.

By the time the carriage pulled up in front of Fathington House, Samantha found herself promising to take Nicholas to Ashley Hall and initiate him into the rites of hunting.

"But only if you are good, Nicholas," she warned him. "And, of course, if your uncle agrees and you can convince my mother, Lady Midland, that you are a well-mannered young man."

They were still arguing about these conditions, which Nicholas considered entirely superfluous, when they were ushered into Lady Fathington's morning-room by a beaming Jaspers.

Any qualms Samantha may have entertained about her family's reception of Nicholas were soon laid to rest. But the warmth of their acceptance caused a flicker of guilt to twist in her heart.

"Nicholas!" Felicity cried, jumping up from her seat beside Lady Fathington as soon as Samantha entered the room and rushing to hug her sister and the small boy whose hand she still held. "I have heard all about you from Tony, and if you are first oars with him, I know we'll get along famously. He's one of my very favourite friends."

"Oh, he's one of mine, too," Nicholas replied, undaunted by this tumultuous welcome. "He's going to take Aunty Sam and me driving in the park this afternoon. You can come, too, if you want."

"Of course I do," Felicity answered gaily. "But let me introduce you to these ladies first, then you and I can enjoy some of these lemon tarts which are Mrs. Jaspers's specialty." She detached a willing Nicholas from Samantha and took him over to her mother and aunt, who sat watching this scene with a mixture of amusement and curiosity.

Samantha regarded them anxiously. Would they notice the striking resemblance between the child and her husband? Felicity hadn't seemed to find anything amiss, and neither had Lady Fathington. But her mother was gazing at the small boy with a startled look on her face as the child made his bows and then insisted on kissing both ladies on the cheek.

Lady Midland raised her eyes and met her daughter's anxious gaze over the child's dark head. Samantha could not read anything but a faintly quizzical expression in her mother's glance, but that was enough to make her uneasy.

"And just who is this child, my love?" her Aunt Eliza asked as soon as Felicity and Nicholas, entirely in harmony with each other, had moved away to inspect the plate of pastries on a nearby table.

"He is Philip's godson," Samantha replied as calmly as possible. "His parents both died in India, Philip tells me, and Philip was appointed Nicholas's legal guardian."

Her mother, who had not said anything, now regarded her daughter pensively. "The child reminds me of someone," she murmured. "But I can't for the life of me recall who. Is the boy to live with you, my dear?" she enquired.

Samantha felt a stab of apprehension at her mother's words. Would she recognize the boy's resemblance to Philip? she wondered. And if that happened, what would she say to her daughter for harbouring one of her husband's by-blows under her roof? One of them? The appaling thought that there might be others suddenly struck her again.

"Philip has brought him up to Town for the Christmas holidays," she answered mechanically. "Otherwise, he has been staying at Silverdale Grange with Mrs. Hudson, his nurse."

"He is a sweet-tempered little lad," Lady Fathington remarked pensively. "I only wish . . . But then, it does no good to repine on what might have been. I was obviously meant to dote on my two nieces instead of on daughters of my own."

Samantha knew that her aunt, happy as she undoubtedly was in her marriage to Lord Fathington still regretted not having any children of her own. She did not often refer to her disappointment, however, and Samantha realized that the sight of little Nicholas had turned her aunt's thoughts into that melancholy channel again.

"And on your great-nieces, my dear Aunt!" Samantha exclaimed impulsively, taking Lady Fathington's small hand in hers and squeezing it affectionately.

"What!" her aunt cried, effectively distracted from her own fruitless musings. "Never tell me that you are breeding already, my love? How delightful! I claim the honour of being godmother to your first daughter, my dear. Nothing could make me happier, I assure you.''

Samantha felt the blood rush into her cheeks as both her mother and aunt stared at her expectantly.

''No,'' she mumbled hastily, her eyes flicking instinctively to the small boy who was deep in earnest conversation with her sister. ''I have barely been wed two weeks, you know.'' And am still as innocent as Felicity, she added to herself, wondering for the first time if the moratorium of six months she had imposed on her new husband had not been a trifle excessive.

''Never mind, love.'' It was her aunt's turn to pat her hand tenderly. ''All in good time, dear. All in good time. But I will insist on being a godmother, don't think I won't.''

''What's all this about godmothers?'' drawled a voice from the door, and Samantha raised her eyes to find Tony Dalton regarding her quizzically. ''Am I missing something, Cousin? Or is the event still a secret?''

It was a tight squeeze, for a gentleman's curricle was not designed for family accommodation, but Tony Dalton insisted that if one of the ladies were to hold Nicholas on her lap, there would be enough room for Felicity to accompany them on a drive in Hyde Park.

Before she realized what she was doing, Samantha had claimed this privilege, and the party set out from Fathington House in high spirits.

The feel of Nicholas's little body so close to her own was strangely comforting, and his dark hair, which tickled her nose each time he squirmed around in her lap to look up at her, smelled sweet and clean. The thought of having a little boy of her own began to look more appealing than ever, and she wondered just how she could convey this notion to Carrington without appearing immodest and forward beyond what was pleasing. For the life of her, she could not think of a ladylike way of inviting a man into her bed, especially when she had banished him from it for six months.

''He will crush your dress, Samantha,'' Tony had warned as he handed her up into the vehicle and swung the wriggling bundle up to her. ''And you, young man,'' he addressed

Nicholas sternly. "Sit still, or I shall never take you up with me again."

This threat was sufficiently severe to keep Nicholas quiet for nearly three whole minutes, but as soon as Dalton guided his vehicle through the gates of Hyde Park, his bubbling curiosity got the better of him.

"Why is that fat man creaking so?" he whispered loudly as they came abreast of a portly gentleman astride a thoroughly dejected-looking hack.

Dalton and Felicity tried in vain to repress their giggles, but Samantha felt it behooved her to point out that only rag-mannered gapeseeds made such impolite comments about the appearance of complete strangers.

"But he *is* creaking," Nicholas insisted. "Can't you hear it, Uncle Tony? He sounds like one of the hay-wagons they use at Silverdale Grange."

"That is because he is wearing whalebone stays," Samantha murmured, trying to avoid the aggrieved stare of the portly gentleman, who was now regarding them with bulbous eyes set in a puffy, mottled face.

"And please don't stare, Nicholas," she admonished. "You will only embarrass the poor man or make him so angry he will insist on an apology."

"Uncle Tony will call him out if he does anything so bacon-brained," Nicholas said confidently. "You will, won't you, sir?"

"Of course he will," Felicity answered before Tony could think of a reasonable excuse for not living up to the boy's expectations of him.

"In fact," Felicity continued with unabashed enthusiasm, "he will send his seconds to arrange a meeting as soon as we get home. Philip can be one of your seconds, can't he, Tony?" She looked at Dalton expectantly. "And please say we can all go and watch you put a bullet through his fat hide. You'd like that, wouldn't you, Nicholas?"

Nicholas gazed up at Dalton, adoration writ plainly on his cherubic countenance. "Above anything," he said reverently. "Even more than going to a mill or riding to hounds."

"I hope you appreciate the honour that is being bestowed on you, Tony," Samantha remarked, amusement making her amber eyes sparkle. "You had best contract for a reputable surgeon, too, just in case the fat gentleman shoots back."

By this time Dalton's team had outstripped the portly rider, and the discussion moved on to less violent topics. Samantha gave a sigh of relief and exchanged an amused glance with Dalton as Felicity began a detailed description of the wonderful coloured ices to be found at Gunther's Pastry Shop during the Season.

Nicholas was listening with round-eyed fascination to the list of flavours available at that fashionable tea-shop, when his attention was suddenly diverted by the sight of a familiar figure on horseback.

"Oh! There's Uncle Philip." He chortled delightedly, pointing a somewhat grubby finger at the man seated on a restless black horse beside an elegant barouche which was blocking the traffic ahead of them.

Their carriage had come to a stop and Samantha had ample opportunity to observe her husband, indescribably handsome in a brown riding coat moulded to his broad shoulders and fawn-coloured unmentionables outlining, what seemed to her critical eye, every muscle in his powerful thighs. He sat his horse with effortless grace and held the restless animal in check easily as he conversed with the occupants of the barouche.

As she watched, mesmerized by the aura of masculinity which seemed to emanate from his tall frame, Carrington threw back his head and laughed. The sound of his voice reached her across the various carriages and riders that separated them, and she felt a pang of envy at the ladies in the barouche who had provoked his amusement. She wondered idly who they could be.

At that moment her husband's horse sidled nervously, and the ladies came into view. Samantha caught her breath as she recognized the beautifully groomed woman whose exquisite face was turned up so enchantingly to Carrington. She was Lady Sylvia Towers, the woman Gerald had identified as her husband's latest mistress.

Samantha's face froze as she observed the tableau being acted out before her. The glittering smile that woman was bestowing on Carrington was definitely too intimate for a casual acquaintance, she told herself. It suggested an intimacy she could not bear to think of, an intimacy she herself had never enjoyed with her husband. Gerald must be right again, she thought desolately. He had been right about Nicholas, hadn't he? And now here was her husband, brazenly making eyes at his latest *chère amie* in the middle of the Park, for everyone to see. Had they no shame at all?

She felt Tony watching her and forced her lips into a brilliant smile. "Are we to sit here all afternoon catching cold while Carrington dallies with the ladies?" she enquired sweetly. The spitefulness of this remark shocked her, but she could not seem to control her mounting fury.

"Are you cold, Aunty Sam?" Nicholas asked innocently. "You're shivering."

"No, dearest," she managed to say through lips that were indeed trembling. "Are you all right?"

"Oh, it's nice and warm here on your lap, Aunty Sam. I just wish Uncle Philip would come over and ride with us. What can be keeping him?"

"He hasn't seen us yet, dear," Samantha replied shortly. She felt her eyes drawn in her husband's direction again and found him looking straight at her across the intervening distance, a strange expression on his face. He raised an arm in their direction but turned once again to respond to something the lady was saying. He had removed his tall beaver, and Samantha felt a sudden weakness at the sight of his dark head bowed over Lady Towers's hand as he took his leave.

The congestion had thinned, but as Dalton guided his team past the barouche, now surrounded by several other gentlemen of the *ton,* Carrington appeared beside the curricle. Nicholas squealed with delight and held out his arms, clearly indicating his wish to ride with his uncle.

The transfer was made with a considerable amount of excited chatter from Nicholas, a laughing warning from Carrington to sit still or he would spook Big Black, and a total lack of comment from Samantha. Her previous tender feelings towards the potential father of her children had been replaced by a burning desire to scratch his eyes out. To prevent this desire from being perceived by the object of her fury, she kept her gaze averted and pretended not to hear his amused exchange with Nicholas.

But the outing had been ruined for her. Although Dalton drove twice around the Park and stopped several times to exchange civilities with acquaintances, Samantha did not once cease wishing she were back home. The insipid gossip of the fashionable matrons bored her to tears, and the empty gallantry of the various gentlemen who came up to pay their respects to the new Lady Carrington seemed to reflect idle curiosity rather than true friendliness. And all the while her anger settled into the pit of her stomach in a cold, hard knot of despair.

By the time they stopped at Fathington House to set Felicity down, Samantha had determined that cold civility would be her only defence against the confirmed rake and libertine she had married.

As Dalton handed her down from the curricle, Samantha was strongly tempted to plead a headache and escape to her room. The thought of trying to be civil to her husband after his philandering behaviour in the Park made her nerves jangle. But she could not bring herself to be uncivil to Tony, who was, after all, her cousin and guest. So when Turner opened the door for them, she requested a tea-tray in the drawing-room.

"Unless, of course, you prefer something stronger, Tony?" she remarked as soon as they were settled before the crackling fire. "I know that some gentlemen cannot abide tea. As for me, I find there is nothing so comforting after an outing in winter as a steaming hot cup of tea. At Ashley Hall," she continued, stretching her cold hands out to the fire, "Felicity and I always used to build a huge snowman after the first real snowfall of the season. But the best part was afterwards, when we came in chilled to the bone to sit by the nursery fire and eat Cook's fresh crumpets smothered with butter and drink mugs of hot cinnamon tea."

She stared pensively into the flames, wondering if she would ever be that happy again.

Suddenly recalling her present duties as hostess, she smiled. "Forgive me, Tony. I did not mean to indulge in nostalgic reminiscences. But those were such happy times, when my father was alive. I hadn't a worry in the world beyond deciding which horse to ride on any particular morning."

"And now you are weighted down with worries, no doubt," Tony responded with a grin.

"I certainly feel that way," she confessed. "In the last month my whole world has been turned upside down. I feel so cut off from everything that was familiar and . . . and safe." Her voice faltered and she hesitated, embarrassed at her sudden loss of control, but unable to stop. "I miss Felicity terribly, and we've only been separated for one night. Already I feel she belongs to a part of my life that is gone forever."

"The present can be happy, too, Samantha," Tony said gently, evidently much moved by the anguish in her voice. "As we grow older, of course, we find pleasure in different things. But some things never change. Like building snowmen, for instance." He smiled. "When we go down to Silverdale Grange for the New Year, you will see what I mean. My cousin and I used to build snowmen, too. I am sure Felicity will insist upon it. And the cook down there will certainly know how to make cinnamon tea, my dear."

"Will Felicity be there, then?" she asked in surprise.

Dalton looked at her with a faint smile. "I don't doubt it. In fact, I shall insist upon it." His smile widened to a grin. "You can insist upon it, too, Samantha. Carrington will do anything to make you happy; you must know that. You have only to ask."

Samantha was saved from having to reply by the arrival of the tea-tray. While she waited for Turner to supervise the placing of the heavy silver service and the delicate Wedgwood cups on the low table in front of her chair, she was able to regain her composure.

"Thank you for letting me talk to you like this, Tony," she said as soon as they were alone again. "I'm not usually such a ninnyhammer. I didn't mean to burden you with my troubles, but it is a relief to talk to someone as kind as you are."

Dalton stared at her, a frown darkening his brow. "Are you telling me that Carrington does not know you are unhappy, Samantha?" he asked brusquely.

She shook her head, her gaze on the cup she was filling with steaming liquid. "It's not that I'm unhappy exactly, but—"

"But nothing!" he ejaculated. "Talk to him, Samantha. For heaven's sake, talk to him."

"Who is this man you are advising my wife to talk to, Cousin?"

Samantha slopped some of her tea in the saucer as her head jerked up to find Carrington standing in the doorway, his dark eyes fixed on her.

After a palpable pause, she pulled herself together. "Where is Nicholas?" she asked in a subdued voice. "I thought you would allow him to have tea with us, since we are alone today."

"He is upstairs in the nursery, where he belongs."

Although he spoke with polite civility, Samantha perceived a steely edge to her husband's voice. She glanced anxiously up at Tony and saw by his wry smile that he had heard it, too.

"You have not answered my question, Cousin." Carrington trod across the wide expanse of Axminster carpet and accepted the cup that Samantha had poured for him. "I am waiting."

"Dash it all, coz. Don't get on your high ropes with me!" Dalton laughed good-naturedly. "If you must know, we were talking about you." He regarded his cousin blandly. "I was merely suggesting that Samantha consult you on which guests you wish to invite down to Silverdale Grange for the New Year. Nothing momentous or earth-shattering, I should add."

An uneasy silence fell on the room.

After a few moments, Dalton set his cup down and smiled encouragingly at his hostess. "I must leave you, my dear. I am engaged to dine with the Fathingtons this evening, so will not see you again until tomorrow at breakfast, a pleasure I will certainly look forward to."

The door closed softly behind him, and Samantha heard his steps grow faint as he disappeared down the hall. She was hurt by his desertion but could not really blame him. The expression on Carrington's face had not been exactly inviting. She glanced up at her husband and found his gaze had softened.

"Another cup of tea, my lord?" She smiled tentatively.

"No, thank you," he said softly, replacing his empty cup on the table. He came to stand before the hearth and looked down at her. "Now, what is it you want to talk to me about, Samantha? And I don't mean that Banbury story my cousin concocted about guest lists." His voice was softer now, and there was the suggestion of humour in it.

Samantha lowered her eyes and wondered where all her previous anger at this man had gone. Where was that cool civility she had promised herself would be her defence against the pull of attraction she felt every time he came near her, every time he spoke to her in that caressing way of his? What was it about this man that seemed to sap her resistance, turn her insides into knots of anxiety, and fill her blood with strange longings?

"Samantha," he prompted her gently. "Are you going to talk to me or not, my love?"

It was the endearment that gave her back her anger. Who did this man think he was to address her as his love? If he had a love, she was not it; of that she was perfectly certain. And it was about time she ceased acting the shrinking violet and let him know that she would tolerate no hypocrisy in their marriage. If he had to have a mistress, so be it, she thought bitterly. She could not very well insist that he be celibate, could she? Much good it would do her if she tried, she thought, remembering the latent virility she had experienced in that one burning kiss they had shared.

She quickly suppressed the desire to dwell more fully on that unforgettable event. This was not the time for romantic daydreaming. A faint blush touched her cheeks, but she raised her eyes to meet her husband's penetrating gaze.

"As a matter of fact, my lord," she said coolly, "we actually were discussing the guest list. I did not know, for example, that you had invited my family to join us for the New Year."

"Only Felicity, my dear. Your mother opted to stay a while longer in Town with your aunt. She will join us in early January."

"Oh. I am so glad you have arranged everything," she remarked with a touch of asperity.

Her rebuff seemed to amuse him. "It does not meet with your approval, then?"

Her approval? What did her approval matter? she thought bitterly. She had been correct in her initial assessment of this man she had married. He was accustomed to ordering things to suit himself. He had a new mistress in London—a beautiful one, she had to admit—and had now arranged to keep his new wife in the country, undoubtedly taking care of his bastard son. How very convenient for him!

"I thought you would be pleased to have Felicity with us, my dear."

"Oh. I am very well pleased, my lord," she relented enough to admit.

"My lord? What happened to Philip?"

"I meant to say Philip."

"Just so. Now that's settled, tell me what else you discussed with my charming cousin."

"We talked of snowmen," she replied lightly. "Snowmen, winters in the country, Ashley Hall, nursery fires, fresh crumpets, hot cinnamon tea. Things like that."

"Sounds quite unexceptional," he murmured. "What else?"

"We also talked about you."

He raised an eyebrow. "Me? What about me?"

"Tony said you would do anything to make me happy," she said in a low voice, meeting his gaze fully.

There was a definite pause during which Samantha held her breath. Had she imagined it, or had his eyes veiled suddenly at her words?

"He is quite right," Carrington said at last, but Samantha was sure she detected a note of wariness in his voice. "Only tell me what I must do to make you happy, and it shall be done." His smile, too, seemed less spontaneous.

"You could tell me all about Nicholas," she replied at once. "I want to know everything about the boy. Who his mother was. His father." Here she paused for a long moment, regarding her husband intently. "How they met. How they died. How you came to be the child's godfather. Everything. Will you do that?" she challenged him.

Her voice trembled slightly towards the end of his speech. The change in his expression was obvious now. His face had closed down, eyes shuttered, lips compressed into a thin line. She felt as though she had touched some old wound which triggered painful memories in the man who stood before her, looking straight at her but not seeing her at all.

With a sigh, Carrington walked over to the window and stood for some time looking sightlessly out at the early winter twilight. Then he turned to face her, and her heart leapt up into her throat at the bleakness in his eyes.

"Very well, my dear," he said slowly. "I shall tell you all about Nicholas."

15 * Almost All the Truth

CARRINGTON LOOKED INTO HIS WIFE'S AMBER EYES FIXED ON HIM SO unwaveringly and thought he detected a glimmer of apprehension in them. Did she perchance regret the demand she had just placed upon him? No, that was not likely. Like most women, he supposed, she was just curious and would not rest until she had all the details of what she must imagine to be some kind of romantic affair between strangers in a far-off land.

He examined her upturn face dispassionately. His wife was a truly beautiful woman. Her complexion was almost translucent, and when she blushed, which she did with enchanting regularity, she reminded him of the personification of dawn he had read as a youth in the great epics of Homer. *Aurora's rosy fingers reaching across the sky.* Yes, that was it. As a callow young man at Oxford, he had not appreciated the classic beauty of the description, but now, looking at Samantha, he suddenly realized the depth of feeling that lay beneath the surface of the poet's words.

With difficulty, he pulled his thoughts away from his wife's attractions and considered how he could respond to her recent demand.

Tell me all about Nicholas, she had said. Obviously she had no idea what she was asking of him, but that didn't make it any easier for him to tell her about the boy. And, foolishly, he had agreed to do so. Of course, sooner or later, she had to know, but he would have preferred to wait until they were more comfortable together. Perhaps even until she had a son of her own. The thought of having a son with Samantha opened up all sorts of delicious possibilities which threatened to distract him again.

His wife's eyes were still fixed him expectantly. He sighed. How, he asked himself, could he tell her the truth about Nicholas without breaking a promise he had made when the child was born six years ago, a promise to someone he considered sacred? What kind of man would break a promise to someone now dead and buried in India?

Samantha's low voice interrupted his revery. "You have not even told me the child's full name, you know. Who was his father. Philip?"

If you only knew that, he thought, I would not be forced to lie to you now. He made the decision on impulse. It would be the lesser of two evils. Half the truth is better than none, didn't the saying go? Well, he would tell his wife almost all the truth and keep back only that one link which would undoubtedly cause her the most pain. The rest of it had to be told, and the sooner the better.

"Nicholas is illegitimate," he said bluntly.

For some reason he could not understand, this starting piece of information failed to shock her. He had expected a fit of strong hysterics, perhaps even swooning, and a need for the vinaigrette. Aside from a slight paling of her cheeks, Samantha had shown no signs of these usual feminine reactions to unpleasant news. He felt an unexpected satisfaction that his wife had so much spirit.

"I knew both his parents, but they were never married," he explained brusquely. "The boy's name is Sloughcum. Naturally, he took his mother's name. She was Victoria Sloughcum, visiting her uncle, Colonel Ned Sloughcum, military attaché to the viceroy." He paused, bittersweet memories crowding his mind.

"And his father?" Her voice was cool and strangely remote.

Carrington brought his attention back to his wife's face. She seemed to have turned even paler, and there was a tenseness to her mouth as if she were preparing herself for the worst possible news. The alarming thought flitted through his mind that perhaps she had guessed the truth. He dismissed this idea impatiently. The whole truth was something he was determined to avoid at all costs. He had a promise to keep.

"His father was rather well known both in India and in England," he explained, choosing his words carefully. "Marriage was out of the question; her family had betrothed her to another when she was a child."

"Betrothals can be broken."

"He had other obligations."

"What possible obligation can be more important than the protection of an innocent child?" his wife enquired, and he noticed two angry spots on her cheeks.

"Nicholas is protected, my dear," he replied firmly. "His future is secure with me."

"But he has been deprived of his father's name." She was glaring at him now, and he marvelled that she had put her finger on the exact core of this whole affair which had distressed him the most. Nicholas could never carry his father's name.

Samantha had risen from the blue brocade settee, and they stood staring at each other for several moments before she spoke again.

"You have yet to tell me who his father is," she said more calmly.

"That's right. I haven't, have I?" And he wouldn't, he thought. How could he? Not for the first time, he wished that he did not have the burden of this guilty secret to carry around with him.

"Well?"

"Well, what?"

Her eyes flashed dangerously. "Don't play games with me, my lord. What is the father's name?"

"I can't tell you," he replied, honestly enough. He was not about to break his promise.

"You said he was well known here in England. Are you afraid I might recognize the name?"

"Just so."

"Why would that matter?"

"It would cause you unnecessary distress, I imagine," he replied, striving to keep his voice casual.

"So, you are not going to tell me?"

"No, my love."

"You wish me to believe the very worst of you? Is that it? Very well, my lord," she said in a strangled voice. "If that is the way you want it." She turned on her heel and almost ran out of the room.

He stood watching her go, a startled look on his face.

The two remaining days before Christmas passed in a whirlwind of activity for Samantha. When she was not engaged in going over the last-minute details for the holiday festivities with Mrs. Collins, the housekeeper, she was paying extended morning visits to her Aunt Eliza, or helping Felicity choose gifts to be sent down to Ashley Hall for their long-time retainers.

Underneath all the excitement, however, she was conscious of a dull ache in her heart, which no amount of activity seemed to ease. Since many of her excursions included Nicholas, who was rapidly winning a place for himself in her family, Samantha was constantly reminded of that fatal interview with Carrington and his implicit confession of paternity. She had tried in vain to remind herself that he had not actually said he was Nicholas's father. But why else had he refused to name the boy's father? Surely no other name but his own could cause her the distress he seemed anxious to save her from.

Well, she would not fall into a fit of the dismals, she told herself firmly. Nothing was to be gained by moping around like a lovelorn schoolroom chit. She wished—as she had many times during the past year—that her father were still alive. He would have known what to do, she thought with a sigh. It had been a mistake to try to talk to Carrington. He had fobbed her off with some Banbury tale of a man well known in England who had other obligations.

What a whisker, she thought. Did he think she was such a noddle-head as to believe that bag of moonshine? He would soon realize she had more gumption that to be taken in by such an unlikely story. It suddenly occurred to her, however, that he would probably not notice anything at all, since she had been studiously avoiding him for the past two days.

She had breakfasted on a tray in her bedchamber, lunched at her Aunt Eliza's, and dined once with Lady Midland at a relative's informal dinner, and again at a more formal affair with both Lady Fathington and her mother. If these ladies had thought it odd that she should be escorted by Mr. Dalton on both occasions and not by her husband, they had not remarked it.

Now, as she watched Felicity comparing two bolts of Chinese silk from which she planned to purchase a dress-length for their mother, she felt a stab of envy for the uncomplicated relationship her sister had developed with Tony Dalton. She was not sure of her sister's feelings for her husband's charming cousin, but Dalton's eyes held an increasingly tender expression when they rested on Felicity. She wondered how long it would be before he requested permission to speak to her. Theirs would be a love-match; she was sure of it. How would it be, she asked herself, to have a husband who looked at one with love as well as passion?

"Samantha." Her sister's voice brought her back to reality. "I think the green satin would be best, don't you? Mama always did look well in green." She sighed. "I'm glad that's decided. Now we can go to Hatchard's to get that novel you wanted for Aunt Eliza." She smiled teasingly at her sister. "I hope you don't intend to get one for me, too, Sam. You know I don't set much store on fictional Prince Charmings."

"You don't have to, dearest, when you have a real-life one dancing attendance on you." Samantha was charmed to see her little sister succumb to that most feminine of responses: She blushed.

Instead of the laughing denial she had expected, Samantha was surprised when Felicity responded shyly.

"Do you really think so, Sam? I confess I have often thought he seemed partial to me. And I like him monstrously, you know. He is so comfortable to talk to, and not always trying to flirt with me like that odious toad Willy Stoddard."

She glanced up at her tall sister from beneath long curling lashes. "Is it fun to be married, Sam? I've been meaning to ask you. Is it pleasant to do whatever it is that married people do? Does Philip stay with you the whole night? And what exactly *does* he do?" she added breathlessly, quite aware that her sister was staring at her in shocked amazement.

"Felicity!" Samantha cried in agitation. She lowered her voice when she noticed two elderly ladies regarding them curiously. "How can you be so brazenly immodest?" she hissed, her cheeks on fire. "These are no thoughts for a young girl to fill her mind with. Such questions are totally reprehensible and hoydenish beyond belief."

Felicity's questions had not only shaken her composure; they had made her realize more clearly than ever that her marriage to Carrington was not the romantic union she had read about so often in Mrs. Radcliffe's novels. Furthermore, she could not answer any of them. How was she to know if Philip would spend the whole night with her? Or if what he would do to her—if she had not forestalled him, of course—would be pleasant or not? The truth was, she had only the most general idea of what it was he would have done had she not imposed that idiotic six-month ban on his doing anything at all.

Her mind was a jumble of confused thoughts as she marched Felicity forcibly out of the shop, ignoring the curious stares of the same two elderly ladies.

"I'm truly sorry to have upset you so, Sam," Felicity murmured, so contritely that Samantha almost relented.

Her face still flushed with embarrassment, she looked up and down the street for their carriage.

"We told John Coachman to wait for us outside Hatchard's, Sam. Don't you remember?" Felicity ventured to point out in a subdued voice. As they turned to walk towards the bookshop, Samantha was mortified to see Felicity, apparently fully recovered from her scolding, wave gaily at two gentlemen approaching them at a leisurely pace.

"Oh, look, Sam!" she exclaimed happily. "There's Tony. Do let's invite him to accompany us to Hatchard's. And that's Philip with him," she added without apparent embarrassment at her recent interest in her brother-in-law's nocturnal habits. "How fortunate. Now we can all go to Hatchard's together."

Samantha was in no mood to consider this chance encounter fortunate at all. Her embarrassment only increased as Felicity skipped unself-consciously up to her Prince Charming and took his proffered arm, leaving Samantha no choice but to accept the arm her husband held out to her.

As they followed the younger couple in silence, Samantha could not help but envy—once again—the easy confidence her sister seemed to enjoy with Tony Dalton. Even as she watched, he bent his head over Felicity's golden curls to whisper something which made her laugh gaily. If only Philip and I could rub along half so comfortably, she thought, I would feel better about this marriage.

"A pretty picture, aren't they?" Carrington remarked, a trace of amusement in his voice. "A regular pair of turtle-doves, and it still lacks three months till spring."

"At least they are happy." Samantha replied without thinking.

Carrington stopped abruptly and turned to look at her.

"Has our marriage brought you so much unhappiness, my love?"

Surprised at the tenderness in his voice, Samantha raised her eyes to his face and studied it for several moments without speaking.

''I don't recall that happiness was written into our marriage contract, Philip,'' she replied finally. This was not what she had wanted to say, but how she could explain all her doubts and suspicions to a man who probably believed himself innocent of any wrongdoing?

''Perhaps not in the contract, Samantha, but certainly in our marriage vows. I distinctly remember promising to love and cherish you forever.''

Samantha dropped her gaze, unwilling to let him read in her eyes how much she wished that vow had been sincere.

''I fear we are making a spectacle of ourselves,'' she said, suddenly realizing they had been standing in the street staring at each other for several minutes. ''And marriage vows were not written for arranged alliances such as ours, anyway,'' she remarked as they resumed their walk towards Hatchard's.

''Who *were* they written for, my dear?''

''For lovers, I suppose,'' she said, after a slight pause.

She heard a chuckle. ''Need I remind you, peagoose, that we could be lovers, too, if it were not for a certain promise you extracted from me when I was too weak to know what I was saying.''

Samantha blushed rosily and kept her eyes lowered.

''Now that you know me a little better, love, wouldn't you agree that six months is rather excessive?'' he murmured, covering her gloved hand with his and squeezing it gently. ''I dare you to tell the truth, Samantha,'' he added when she did not reply at once.

The truth? And what was the truth? she wondered. There seemed to be a deplorable lack of it between them, and not only on his part, either, she had to admit. Looking down at his strong, brown fingers covering hers, she felt a wild, unladylike desire to throw discretion to the winds and admit that yes, six months was far too long to wait to find out if he would indeed spend the entire night in her bed, or if he would leave as soon as his passion was sated. Her blush deepened at the immodesty of such thoughts.

''Well?'' he prompted, squeezing her fingers again.

''Perhaps.'' The word escaped her before she could stop it, but it was uttered so softly that she prayed he had not heard.

Carrington stopped dead in his tracks. ''Perhaps?'' he repeated. ''Am I to understand, my love, that you are contemplating commuting my sentence? Can it be that you are also getting tired of this nonsensical delay in—''

''Philip!'' she cried out in dismay at what he had been about to say in front of several interested parties who were standing about in front of London's most popular bookshop. ''You are putting me to the blush, sir.''

Disengaging her hand from his arm, Samantha almost ran up the steps and into the warmth of the shop, thankful that she had escaped having to answer Carrington's last question.

Her relief did not last long, however, for no sooner had she located Felicity and Tony in cheerful conversation with another couple and started towards them, than she wished she had remained outside.

At that moment Carrington came up behind her and, taking her arm again, said in an amused voice, ''You should not run off like that, my dear, and leave a fellow with half a question stuck between his teeth. Bad form. Aha!'' he added, following her rigid gaze. ''Come, Samantha, I want to introduce you to a good friend of mine. You will like her, I know.''

That is highly unlikely, Samantha thought, as she allowed herself to be guided across the room to join the animated group. After all, what is one supposed to say to the mistress of one's husband?

Lady Sylvia Towers was even more beautiful at close range than she had been at a distance. In spite of her prejudice, Samantha had to admire the perfect symmetry of her features and the flawless translucency of her complexion. As she returned the firm handshake, Samantha noted that the lady's eyes were large, expressive, and intensely blue. She was somewhat startled to see that they also glowed with unexpectedly warm friendliness.

''I was telling Philip only the other day that I was very eager to make your acquaintance, Lady Carrington.'' Her voice was soft and musical and made Samantha want to scream. Philip indeed! Who did this hussy think she was, flaunting her illicit intimacy in her face like this? She forced herself to smile and make an appropriate answer; what it was, she never knew.

''I confess I was excessively put out with him for keeping you a secret from us,'' Lady Towers explained. ''I think that is a shabby way to treat old friends, don't you?'' The silvery laugh that accompanied this jangled on Samantha's nerves.

"Indeed," Samantha replied with a slight smile. So they were old friends, were they? Was she expected to swallow that rapper? she wondered furiously. Or did they think she was some countrified ninnyhammer who would be bamboozled by this sickening charade?

"I would like to make you known to Sir Hugh Davenport," Lady Towers said, laying a white hand on that gentleman's sleeve and drawing him closer. "Hugh, this is Lady Carrington, whom Philip has been keeping to himself for so long."

"I can't say I blame him," Sir Hugh said, bowing gracefully from his considerable height over Samantha's unresisting fingers. "Enchanted, I'm sure, my dear. I applaud his lordship's impeccably good taste."

Samantha found herself being observed by a handsome, rather heavy-set gentleman in his late thirties, dressed in pale gray unmentionables and an elegantly cut puce-coloured riding coat, over a discreetly flowered waistcoat. His neatly tied cravat proclaimed him to be a careful rather than a flamboyant dresser, and Samantha found his smile to be admiring without any hint of flirtatiousness.

She smiled at him, feeling her lips gradually unfreeze from the forced smile she had adopted since joining the group.

"Philip, you're a dashed lucky dog, did you know that?" Sir Hugh added with a jovial laugh. "I'm surprised to see you in Town at this time of year, ma'am," he said, favouring Samantha with another of his wide smiles. "London's mighty thin of company in December. I'm only here myself because I've been commandeered to escort Sylvia and her aunt down to Kent after Christmas. Her uncle's estate lies next to mine, just south of Charing, so it is not out of my way at all."

"And if it were, you old fox, you would do it anyway," Carrington chided him. "Don't try to gammon us, Hugh; it won't fadge."

Samantha was surprised to see a boyish grin flash across Hugh's face, and when she intercepted a warmly affectionate glance from Lady Towers at that same gentleman, she was nonplussed. Could there be an *affair du coeur* going on between these two? And if so, where did that leave Philip? He did not seem at all put out that Sir Hugh was obviously wearing his heart on his sleeve for the beautiful Lady Towers.

So intrigued was she with the possibility that she may have misjudged the Incomparable Sylvia, that when the latter drew her away from the gentlemen to browse through the table of recently published books, she went willingly.

"I think it is very naughty of Philip to have kept you to himself like this, my dear!" Lady Towers exclaimed as they stood together by a table displaying the latest novels. "We are friends of very long standing, you know. Before my poor Bertram was killed in that hunting accident over a year ago, Philip used to spend part of his summers with us in Kent. He and Bertram were at Oxford together, and they developed a wonderful friendship."

"He has not mentioned that part of his life to me at all," Samantha said, conscious once more of how little she really knew her husband.

"That doesn't surprise me," Lady Towers replied. "My Bertram was a recluse in many ways, and Philip is, too, as you probably know by now. They got along famously, however, and Philip was really devastated when it happened." She paused, as if the memory were still painful.

"Please don't dwell on it, my lady," Samantha found herself urging, her tender heart touched by the sad story. "It must be devastating indeed to lose a loved one so early in life."

Lady Towers smiled mistily. "Yes, it was hard. We were so much in love, you see." She glanced at Samantha apologetically. "I really don't know why I'm telling you all this except that . . . well, you know how it is, one is supposed to keep a stiff upper lip, but it is so hard to do when one falls into a fit of the dismals, as I seem to have done this afternoon."

"I understand exactly what you mean, Lady Towers," she responded sympathetically. "I suffer from the same malady myself upon occasion."

The widow must have found that amusing, for she laughed gently and patted Samantha's hand. "You are much too young for such melancholy thoughts, my dear. And besides, you have Philip to dote on you, as he obviously does. I cannot recall ever seeing him so lighthearted. You have been good for him, Samantha. May I call you Samantha?"

"Why, of course," Samantha murmured, thoroughly in-

trigued by this new development and captivated by Lady
Towers's charm.

"I must confess that Philip was a godsend to me when
Bertram died. I could not have managed without him. Or
without Hugh, of course," she added with an affectionate
smile. "And Hugh's younger brother, Ned. They all came to
my rescue and set Bertram's affairs in order for me. I never did
have much of a head for business, but Philip was so patient
with me, you have no idea how much in his debt I am."

At that moment Felicity came up to ask if Samantha had
chosen the novel for their aunt's gift. Lady Towers immediately wanted to know if Samantha read romantic novels
herself; and before they knew it, the ladies found themselves
involved in a lively discussion on the various merits of the
latest popular romances.

Later, as Carrington helped her into the carriage for the drive
home, Samantha's mind was in such a turmoil that she paid
scant attention to Felicity's happy chatter. Gerald's accusation
regarding her husband's *chère amie* was still ringing in her
ears, but it no longer seemed so plausible. Could her cousin
have been mistaken or perhaps—heaven forbid—indulging in
a spiteful whim?

The lovely Lady Sylvia Towers was not at all what Samantha had expected. Her long-standing friendship with Philip
seemed legitimate. And at no time had she acted as mistresses
were supposed to act, at least, if one were to judge by the
numerous barques of frailty who appeared in Mrs. Radcliffe's
novels.

And she could not forget Sir Hugh Davenport and his
obvious affection for the attractive widow. Philip had not
seemed the least put out to learn that the handsome Sir Hugh
was to escort Lady Towers down to Kent.

Samantha's head began to ache with so many puzzling
questions. Much as she had been prepared to dislike her
supposed rival, she had been unable to do so. In fact, quite the
opposite was true. She actually liked Sylvia. Only time would
tell, she thought wearily, if her instincts had betrayed her.

16 * The Bribe

AT LEAST ONE THREAD IN THE CONVOLUTED SKEIN OF HALF-TRUTHS connecting Carrington with Gerald's accusations became clearer to Samantha as a result of her encounter with Lady Sylvia Towers at Hatchard's that afternoon. If nothing else, she had learned that if she wanted to know the truth, she would have to go out and search for it. Therefore, as soon as she had divested herself of her warm pelisse and gloves upon her return to Carrington Court, she sat down at the elegant escritoire in the library and dashed off a note to Mr. MacIntyre, her London man of business.

Papa had been right, as usual, she thought, as she tucked a rebellious red-gold curl back into place before signing her name to the missive with a flourish. One must take one's fences straight on, with no prevarication; it was the only way. Mr. MacIntyre would undoubtedly be able to contribute an important piece to the puzzle of Cousin Gerald's accusations.

When Turner arrived with the tea-tray, Samantha gave him the note and asked that a footman be dispatched immediately to the offices of MacIntyre and Hamilton in the City and await a reply.

Samantha felt rather pleased with herself for having had the wonderful notion of applying to her man of business to answer one of the questions which had been troubling her about Carrington. Gerald had told her Carrington was saddled with heavy gambling debts. Short of asking her husband outright, which she shrank from doing, Samantha had no way of confirming this accusation. Then she had remembered the ten thousand pounds her father had offered in his will, apparently to make the arranged marriage more palatable to the gentleman he had selected to be her husband.

"London gentlemen are often in need of ready cash, my lady," the solicitor had told her, permitting himself a thin smile. And she had agreed, but the thought that a Carrington might be one of those strapped gentlemen had never crossed

her mind. She had assumed he had refused the thinly veiled
bribe. Now she was not so sure. Mr. MacIntyre's response to
her note would relieve her mind of any doubt.

She had little time to mull over the state of her husband's
finances, however, for tomorrow would be Christmas Day, and
Mrs. Collins was in a twitter of excitement at the prospect of
entertaining the new Lady Carrington's family at Carrington
Court.

"It's been such an age since we have entertained here, my
lady," the housekeeper confessed anxiously. "Not since the
old lord died over a year ago. And even then, what guests we
had were usually gentlemen more interested in drinking and
gambling than in social niceties."

Accustomed as she was to running the large household at
Ashley Hall, Samantha had personally made all the arrangements and was fully confident that she had taken care of every
detail. "From what I have seen of Cook's culinary arts in the
past few days," she told Mrs. Collins, "we have nothing to
worry about. And now, if you will be so kind as to make sure
the mistletoe and holly boughs are in place by tomorrow
morning, I must run upstairs to dress. My aunt is expecting us
at seven o'clock, and it is already after six."

While Sally was putting the last touches to her shining hair,
piled modishly on top of her head with several red-gold curls
falling artfully to her shoulders, there was a knock at the door
leading to the Silver-Room. Samantha's heart leapt up into her
throat. She had not seen Carrington since earlier that afternoon
at Hatchard's. Their conversation there had been interrupted,
and she knew him well enough by now to be sure he would not
let his last question go long unanswered.

"Ready, my love?" he enquired, strolling casually into her
bedchamber as if he were at home there. He was dressed for the
evening in the palest blue satin knee-breeches and a coat of a
darker blue which could only have come from Weston in Conduit
Street. His snowy cravat was tied in the intricate *Trône d'Amour*,
and among its folds a large sapphire winked in the candlelight.

Samantha thought he looked magnificent. When he came
and stood behind her as she sat at her dressing table, she felt a
surge of pride that this man was hers. She lowered her lashes
so he would not guess her feelings, and felt his hands caressing
her bare shoulders.

"Yes," she murmured, gazing down at her open jewel-box. "I have only to select a necklace, and I shall be ready."

"Perhaps this will be just the thing, my dear." He laughed, pressing a flat jeweller's case into her hands and a warm kiss on her neck.

Samantha held her breath as she opened the case and stared down at the most beautiful sapphire and diamond necklace she had ever seen. "Oh, Philip," she breathed, suddenly conscious of a large lump in her throat. "Oh, Philip," she repeated, at a loss for words to express her delight at this unexpected gift.

He seemed to find her astonishment amusing, for he chuckled. Then, picking up the necklace, he placed it carefully around her throat and fastened it, the touch of his warm fingers sending tremors of sensation through her whole body.

Samantha had closed her eyes to enjoy the sensuousness of the moment to its fullest. When she opened them, it was not to admire the blaze of blue at her throat, but to search out his dark gaze above her and lose herself in it until his lazy smile disappeared and she recognized the flare of incipient passion in his eyes.

Quickly she dropped her gaze to the sapphires. "They are incredibly beautiful, Philip," she whispered, touching them gently with the tips of her fingers. "Thank you. Oh, thank you so very much. My diamond earbobs will make a perfect match with them."

"Here, my love," he said, catching her by the hand and drawing her to her feet. "Stand up and let's have a look at you." He paused for a moment to examine her with such a suggestive gleam in his hooded eyes that she blushed.

"I think we should be going, Philip. We don't want to keep my family waiting, do we?" she said hastily.

"The deuce take your confounded family, my sweet," came the soft reply. "I wish I had you all to myself tonight. We have some unfinished business to discuss, if you will recall."

Samantha blushed a deeper rose and refused to look at him. "We promised, my lord. It would look very odd if we did not appear. This is Christmas Eve, you know. We are to open our presents, and drink hot rum punch, and sing carols." She peeped up at him through her lashes. "We cannot disappoint Aunt Eliza. This is the first Christmas I will spend with her in over five years."

"Very well." He sighed. "But before we go, my pet, I have something else for you." He withdrew something from his coat pocket and, taking her left hand in his, slipped a stunning sapphire and diamond ring onto her finger. "Remember, I promised you a more fitting engagement ring to replace the highly impractical Silverdale Emerald."

Samantha could only stare speechlessly at the blue stone which fit so perfectly next to her engraved wedding-band. "I don't know how to thank you, Philip." She raised her eyes, misty with tears, to his face. "I just don't know what to say."

"No need to say a thing, my love," he replied hoarsely and pulled her into his arms. "But I will show you what you can do to thank me." He took her face in his strong fingers and lifted it gently to receive his kiss.

Samantha felt herself sway unresistingly towards him; one of his arms went round her waist and drew her tightly against his hard body. Her breasts were crushed to his chest, and she was sure he could hear the hammering of her heart. She could certainly feel his. Tentatively she reached up to pull his head into a more comfortable position and heard him groan as she moved against him. She felt his mouth grow more insistent and shivered with shock as his tongue gently pried her lips apart and explored the soft parts of her mouth.

"Samantha," he whispered against her neck as he traced kisses down it to her partially exposed breasts, leaving a trail of fire across her skin. "Let's send round our excuses, my love. Mmmm . . ." His lips moved up the other side of her neck. "You are delicious, my love. Let's say we are taken mortally ill and cannot go tonight. And I promise to show you the thanks I want from you, dearest."

Momentarily drugged by this assault on her senses and the seductive warmth of her husband's hands on her body, Samantha could not reply. Then gradually all the doubts and suspicions about this man, planted in her mind by her cousin, came flooding back to her, and she pulled away.

"Nonsense, Philip," she said shakily. "You are mad to suggest anything so rag-mannered." She looked down at her blue satin gown, to avoid looking at him. "And here I have just spent a king's ransom on this dress, my lord, and you have crushed it sadly."

Quickly she gathered up her fur-lined cloak and muff from the bed and, without casting a single glance in his direction, swept out of the room before he could utter a word of protest.

The evening went by in a whirl of happiness for Samantha. It felt wonderful to be surrounded by her family again without the fear hanging over her, as it had for the past year, of being evicted from Ashley Hall. How very different from the last Christmas they had spent together, with her dear father, unknown to them, so recently dead, and that odious Gerald making his ingratiating offers of a match between them. She shivered at the unpleasant memory.

"Chilly, my dear?" It had gratified Samantha that her husband had hardly stirred from her side the entire evening. He had sat by her at dinner, turned the pages for her as she played the traditional Christmas carols, and now stood near her chair, a tankard of punch in his hand, regarding her with tender concern.

"No. I was thinking of last year when we got that letter from your father with the news of Papa's death. It arrived in the middle of January, you know, when he had been dead for over a month. We had expected him for Christmas, and when he did not come and sent us no word, I had the premonition that something was very wrong." She was silent for a moment, her mind reverting to the Christmases of her childhood, spent with her dear Papa at Ashley Hall, with her mother and Felicity making the family circle tight and comfortably secure.

She sighed. "I miss him terribly."

"So do I, Samantha. But do not distress yourself repining on what cannot be mended, sweet. And don't worry your lovely head over that shabster cousin of yours; he can no longer harm you. You have me to protect you now, my love."

Oh, how she wished that were true. Tonight Samantha was tempted to put Gerald from her mind and bask in the warmth of the love and affection of her family. Her family, she thought with a sigh of contentment. A family which now included a little boy they had all come to love, though he was not her own. She smiled as she watched Nicholas's face and listened to his chatter as he sat between the two elder ladies on the long settee, still exclaiming about his presents. Her Aunt Eliza looked ecstatic when the child turned to her to explain—for the fourth

time—exactly how he would place his new army of tin soldiers
to win the battle of Waterloo. Lady Midland was also absorbed
in the boy's chatter; her head at a slight angle, she regarded
him with a strange little smile on her lips.

"Nicholas seems to be having the time of his life,"
Carrington remarked, and Samantha saw that his eyes were soft
as they regarded the child. "I have you to thank for that,
Samantha. The lad has not had much of a family life with me
these past four years. He misses India, of course, and is not yet
accustomed to the severity of the English climate."

"My aunt is dotty about him," she remarked. "To say
nothing of Felicity, who has always wanted a brother, anyway." She glanced at her husband and observed him carefully
as she added, "And even Mama is growing to love him. She
told me the other day that Nicholas reminds her of somebody,
but she couldn't think who."

Carrington, who had been regarding the family scene with a
lazy smile, turned to stare at her, his smile gone. "What did she
mean by that, do you suppose?" he inquired, after a lengthy
pause.

"I could not say," Samantha replied. She regarded him
speculatively for as moment before adding daringly, "Perhaps
she recognizes the boy's father."

Philip's face became very still, and Samantha could have
sworn that she saw a flicker of alarm in his eyes. It was gone
before she could pin it down, however, but she was sure the
idea had given her husband a shock.

"You did say he was well known here in England, Philip, so it
is entirely possible that my mother knows him. It would not
surprise me at all. The Ashleys are fairly prominent themselves,
you know." And so are the Silverdales, she added to herself. At
the last minute, she had not been able to bring herself to say it
aloud. She was not yet ready to come right out and let her husband
know that she had guessed his guilty secret.

He looked at her for several minutes, but his mind was
obviously elsewhere. "I trust you are wrong," he said at last,
gazing across the room at the happy tableau on the settee. "Let
us hope, for all our sakes, that you are wrong."

"What a strange thing to say, my lord," she said lightly.
"What difference could it possibly make to my mother, or to
me for that matter, who the boy's father is?"

He made no response, and Samantha felt that the chasm of mistrust between them, which the family gathering had momentarily bridged, had opened up again, as wide as ever.

It was almost one o'clock when the Marquess of Carrington and his lady returned to their house on Cavendish Square. Little had been said during the short ride, and Samantha felt as though the passionate moment they had shared earlier that evening in her bedchamber had happened to another couple.

Sally was waiting for her when she got upstairs and had laid out her nightclothes on the huge bed. The room was slightly chilly in spite of the fire still burning in the grate, and Samantha was glad to get out of her satin finery and into the lacy nightrail and warm robe. She sat at the dresser to have her hair brushed, and removed the sapphire necklace, remembering the warmth of her husband's hands as he had placed it round her neck.

She sighed at her own perfidy. How was it that she could harbour such tender feelings towards a man who kept guilty secrets from her? she wondered, not for the first time. Why else had he refused to name the father of the child? Didn't he trust her to forgive him for a sin of passion, committed in a faraway place by a lonely man? She loved the boy, couldn't he see that? They all did, even Mama, who held the key to the mystery, if only she could remember who Nicholas reminded her of.

She was willing to believe that Gerald had been wrong about Lady Sylvia Towers. Seeing the two of them together in Hatchard's yesterday had made her realize that she had tormented herself for days about their possible romantic liaison without a shred of proof, aside from Gerald's malicious accusation. She was even more willing to believe that Gerald had lied about Carrington's gambling debts. It seemed unlikely that a man with pockets to let would give his wife an extravagant sapphire and diamond necklace as a Christmas present.

And the ring. She looked down at the faceted blue stone on her finger and moved it gently to catch the candlelight. It was not as large as the traditional Silverdale Emerald, that was true enough; but it was by no means small, either. It must have cost a packet, and she smiled as she relived, in every sensuous detail, the thanks that her husband had extracted from her. He had wanted more, she knew. He had wanted all of her. And if they had not been committed to the Christmas Eve party at her aunt's, she might well have . . .

She dragged her mind back from these indelicate thoughts. What good would it do to daydream like a silly wet-goose? she told herself. It was not going to happen while there were still so many unanswered questions between them. Even if she were willing to believe in his innocence regarding Lady Sylvia and the gambling debts—the latter would be easily refuted by Mr. Mac-Intyre's response to her note—what about Nicholas? How could she overlook Carrington's odd reaction to her deliberate comment regarding her Mama's possible recognition of the boy's father?

She sighed again. Men were nowhere near as simple as Mrs. Radcliffe's novels made them out to be. They did not fall at one's feet, hopelessly besotted, and swear everlasting love and passion, hands clutched together in supplication, eyes filled with adoration.

A small chuckle escaped her at this bizarre picture. She couldn't for the life of her imagine Philip in such an ignominious posture. And, if truth be told, she wouldn't want him there.

"Will you be wanting anything else, milady?" Sally, who had finished putting away her mistress's clothes, wanted to know. "A little glass of warm milk to help you sleep, like in the old days, perhaps?"

Sally had developed the habit of referring nostalgically to the days of her single life at Ashley Hall as if they lay in the remote past, instead of having been barely two weeks ago. Samantha considered her abigail's suggestion.

"That does sound nice, Sally. But Cook is probably in bed by now."

"I shall get it for you meself, milady," Sally replied and made for the door. Before she could open it, there was a tap, and Samantha heard Turner's voice in consultation with the abigail.

"I'll tell her ladyship," Sally said and turned back into the room. "Turner here says that he left a message for you in the Silver-Room, milady. Forgot to mention it when you got home, he did. Silly old noddlehead that he is," she murmured under her breath.

"A message?"

"Yes, from the City, he says. Shall I fetch it for you, milady?"

"No, thank you, Sally. I think I'll have my bedtime toddy in the Silver-Room before the fire. Bring it to me in there, will you?"

When Sally had gone off to get the warm milk for her mistress, Samantha rose, adjusted her robe more closely around her slim figure, and opened the door to the master suite sitting-room next door. No sooner had she stepped across the threshold, however, than she realized that she was not alone. Carrington lay sprawled in an easy chair beside the fire, a glass of brandy on the table beside him.

"Oh, excuse me," she murmured self-consciously. "I didn't know you were here, Philip." She hesitated, wondering how she could retrace her steps without appearing to be avoiding him.

"Don't run away, my dear. I was just having a nightcap and warming my toes before turning in." He had risen as he spoke, and Samantha realized with a shock that he was indeed dressed for retiring. He was wearing a frogged dressing-gown of brightly patterned brocade silk that reached just below his knees and a pair of red Morocco slippers. She noticed with a jolt of shock that his legs were bare. His nightshirt—she assumed he had one on under his dressing-gown—was not visible.

Samantha swallowed hard. She wrenched her gaze away from the strong line of her husband's bare throat and the thatch of black hair that covered his exposed chest and nervously looked about the room for Mr. MacIntyre's note.

"Turner said he left a note for me in here," she stammered. "Have you seen it?"

"Is this it?" He plucked a folded sheet of paper from the mantelpiece and glanced at it casually. "From MacIntyre, it seems." He held it out to her.

She approached cautiously, took the folded paper from his outstretched hand, and saw that it was indeed from Mr. MacIntyre. Her heart lifted. Perhaps now another of the barriers between them would disappear when the truth came to light. She tore open the letter and read it quickly. When she got to the end, she read it through once again, more slowly this time. She sighed and crumpled the offending note in her fingers. Mr. MacIntyre had given her the truth, but it was not the truth she had expected.

For a moment Samantha wished she had never asked him if Carrington had claimed the sum offered by the estate if he fulfilled the conditions of the will. She gazed blindly into the fire and wondered why her husband had never mentioned that on December the tenth—the very day after they were married—he had received from MacIntyre and Hamilton a draft on the Ashley estate for ten thousand pounds.

"Is there anything wrong, my dear?"

Samantha looked at him and saw that he was smiling that lazy smile of his that threatened to turn her into a jelly. Resolutely she turned her eyes back to the fire. *Is there anything wrong?* he wanted to know. Didn't he *know* what was wrong? She may not have any proof of an illicit connexion with Lady Sylvia Towers, but he had not been honest with her about Nicholas, had he? And now, here was irrefutable proof that he had not been honest about the ten thousand pounds received from the estate. Why, she asked herself in despair, had he kept the transaction a secret? There was no need; after all, he was entitled to claim the money if he chose to do so. It was in the will, not as a condition, but as an option. Why, indeed, unless he had no wish to divulge what he had done with it?

"Come, my love. You can tell me, you know. I'm your husband." He tried to put his arms about her, but she shook him off, and the smile died in his eyes.

"That is an unfortunate fact I shall endeavour to live with," she replied, her heart shrivelling at the coldness in her own voice. "And you, my lord, can tell me about this, if you please." She held the letter out to him defiantly.

He read it in silence, then looked up at her with a suggestion of a smile tugging at his mouth. "What about it, my love? It seems perfectly clear to me. What more do you wish to know?"

Samantha could not believe what she was hearing. He intends to bluff his way out of it, she thought furiously. A little voice in her heart tried to tell her she was being unreasonable, but she plunged on, determined to pull aside the veil of half-truths and secrecy behind which her husband seemed to be hiding.

"I wish to know why I was not informed of this transaction."

"Oh, but you obviously have been informed, my dear," he said softly, his dark eyes observing her with a remoteness that chilled her soul.

Samantha gave a moue of disgust. "Do not try my patience, my lord. You know very well what I mean. Why did you not inform me that you had taken this . . . this . . ." Words failed her. "This *bribe*," she spat out at last.

A dead silence followed this outburst during which Samantha was only aware of the pounding in her ears.

When he finally spoke, it was with such sadness that she felt her heart would break. "I am sorry you feel that way about it, Samantha. I truly am. It was nothing of the kind, of course. Please take my word for it."

She gazed into the fathomless depths of his eyes and restrained herself with an effort from making an absolute cake of herself by bursting into tears. She swallowed hard.

"Why didn't you tell me?"

"I hardly thought it was necessary. It was stated in the will, my dear."

"Yes, but only as an option. You did not have to take it. I never thought you would, actually," she added, hoping she could end this terrible interview before she collapsed. "But then, perhaps you did not want me to know why you did accept it, my lord. Is that it?"

A shadow passed across his face, and Samantha felt her heart sink into the very soles of her slippers. When he made no reply, she forced herself to continue.

"Why did you?"

Instead of answering, he turned to the fire and stood gazing down at it, his face a hard mask.

"I had a very good reason, Samantha. Believe me."

"Gambling debts, no doubt," she stormed at him in a sudden burst of frustration.

He glanced at her quickly, surprise on his face. "No, that's not it at all."

"What then?" she insisted.

"I don't see that it really matters," he said slowly.

"I see," she said with a finality which sounded ominous even to her own ears. "You do not intend to tell me, my lord. That will make at least two secrets you are keeping from me. Very well." She walked over to the door and turned back, one hand on the knob. "I shall have to learn to live with that, too, I suppose."

She went through the door and closed it softly behind her.

17 * The Miniature

THE TURMOIL OF EMOTIONS THAT WRACKED HER AFTER HER LATEST brangle with Carrington had so distressed Samantha that she was certain she would not sleep a wink all night. She was mistaken. After a short bout of tears, she fell into a deep, dreamless slumber which lasted until Sally threw open the shutters at ten o'clock the next morning to let in the weak winter sunlight.

"I would have let ye sleep till noon, milady, but Mrs. Collins is fit to be tied. Claims that Cook is upset with one of the kitchen-maids because she let the goose dry out. Everything is at sixes and sevens belowstairs this morning," she grumbled, setting a cup of hot chocolate on the spindle-legged table by her mistress's bed and plumping up the pillows for her.

"Never seen the likes of it meself. The whole place is in an uproar. That old codger Turner's running around like a lost sheep, bleating about the holly boughs all over the hall."

Samantha sat up and reached for her chocolate. Her head ached abominably, and she wondered where she would find the strength to live through the day. It was, after all, Christmas Day, and her family was invited for dinner and an evening of holiday cheer. She had never felt less cheerful, she thought, watching Sally flit around the room laying out a warm morning gown of russet wool trimmed with blond lace. She did not know how she was going to face Carrington after their dust-up last night. And the thought of having to put on a show of conjugal harmony was almost more than she could bear.

"Mrs. Collins particularly wished me to ask you, milady, if the party this evening is still going forward, even if his lordship ain't here. Rare cut up about it she was, the silly twit."

Samantha set her cup down sharply. "What are you talking about, Sally? His lordship *is* here."

"Oh, no, 'e ain't, m'dear," Sally responded, lasping into her country brogue. "Left this morning at the crack of dawn, 'e did." She paused, apparently satisfied with the effect her announcement had made on her mistress. "Called for 'is curricle before five this morning and went off without 'is breakfast, 'e did, too. Turner was sore cut up about it, I can tell you, milady. Appears the old geezer was not up yet. Enjoys 'is sleep-in, that man does, and no mistake."

"I am not interested in the butler's sleeping habits," Samantha cut into this recital sharply. "Kindly find out at what time his lordship will be back."

"Oh, 'e won't be back," Sally answered. "At least, not any time soon, I reckon. Said 'e was going down to 'is country estate, the one in Hampshire, that is. Silverdale something or other it's called, I believe, milady."

"Silverdale Grange." Samantha said mechanically. She could not believe her ears. What was Philip about, to abandon her at a time like this?

"Did Mr. Dalton accompany his lordship?" she asked.

"No, milady. But Mr. Dalton ain't 'ere, either. Gone over with Master Nicholas to pay a morning call on our Miss Felicity, if I'm not mistaken. Fair taken with our lass, is that gentleman. Wouldn't surprise me if we was to 'ear wedding bells before long."

At least Tony was still here, Samantha told herself. That was something. But Carrington's desertion was monstrous. The deuce take the man, she thought angrily, swinging her legs out of bed and reaching for her gown. There must be some mistake. Surely he wouldn't do this to her.

But apparently he had.

When Tony Dalton walked into the drawing-room with Nicholas in tow at a quarter past the hour of two, Samantha had become resigned to the fact that her husband had truly taken himself off. She had settled the quarrels among the household staff and invented an emergency which had necessitated Lord Carrington's immediate presence in the country. But her own spirits were so low that she seriously considered retiring to her bed for the rest of the afternoon.

Samantha waited until Nurse Hudson had bustled Nicholas up to the nursery for his tea, and then she turned a harried face to Dalton. "You have heard, no doubt, that your cousin has gone down to Silverdale Grange. Rather precipitously, I might add."

"So Turner informed me," Dalton replied. "Deucedly odd thing to do, if you don't mind me saying so, Samantha." He eyed her cautiously. "Didn't come to cuffs with him by any chance, did you, m'dear?"

Samantha glared at him, too mortified to answer.

"Well, it sounds like a hum to me. It's not the sort of thing Phil would do. 'Tain't like him at all to sherry off without so much as a by-your-leave to anyone. Dash it, Samantha, you must have done something to put his back up." His blue eyes regarded her speculatively.

"We had a small tiff last night," she confessed reluctantly. "But not enough to send him off in a pelter like this."

"Sounds like a rapper to me, my girl. Just how small was this tiff, anyway?"

Remembering some of the hurtful things she had flung at Carrington's head during the course of their brangle, all of which she now bitterly regretted, Samantha had the grace to blush.

"Ah, I thought as much," Dalton said grimly. "The two of you had a regular set-to, I'll wager. Don't blame the man for making himself scarce until the dust settles. Only sensible thing to do, if you ask me."

"I have told the staff that there was an emergency at Silverdale Grange," Samantha explained. "What else could I do, Tony?"

"Nothing much you could do if Phil took it into his head to go off in a pucker. All I can say, Samantha, is that if you wanted to break squares with him, you couldn't have chosen a worse time. Dash it all, girl, this is Christmas Day."

"Oh, I know it, Tony," she wailed, tears sparkling on her long lashes. "I'll never forgive myself if anything happens to him."

"What could possibly happen to him?" Dalton asked in surprise.

"He's gone off in his curricle, which is not exactly the warmest way to travel in winter, you know. He might even get caught in a snowstorm and freeze to death."

"Fiddle! Phil ain't one of your Bond Street fribbles with more hair than wit, Samantha. Besides," he added practically, "if it snows, there are plenty of posting houses between here and Hampshire. Stands to reason he won't freeze. And Crofts is with him. Good head on his shoulders, Crofts."

And with that, Samantha had to be content.

Her first Christmas Day as the Marchioness of Carrington had to be the very worst she had ever experienced, Samantha reflected, lying awake in the cold predawn hours the next day, listening to the rain and sleet lashing at her window-pane. The one thought that consoled her was that Philip would be safely at the Grange by now, warm and dry. She wondered whether he regretted his impulsive flight as much as she did her hasty words. Small comfort, she thought. But at least she had lived through the day without him.

The Fathingtons and Lady Midland had accepted her explanation of Carrington's absence with regret but without hesitation, but Felicity had no scruples in ferreting out the real reason.

"Lovers' quarrel, I'll be bound," she teased as soon as the sisters had a moment together in private. "Poor White Knight, what have you done to him, Sam?"

"Nonsense! I haven't done anything to him." Samantha tried to keep up the pretense, but she had never been a match for Felicity, who knew her sister far too well. And before she knew it, she had been bullied into admitting that she and Carrington had had a falling out.

"Only a small one, Felicity," she insisted.

"Philip obviously did not consider it small, you silly peagoose," Felicity scolded. "How you could bear to pull caps with him after he gave you that scrumptious necklace, I'll never know," she added. "I would have been in alt over such a gift, and rewarded him accordingly." She glanced slyly at her sister, but Samantha did not take the bait.

"I had meant to, Felicity," Samantha said. "Truly I had." And she had, she thought, remembering the tender insistence of her husband's kisses the previous evening. If only she had not questioned his acceptance of that money her father had, for some obscure reason, thought fit to include in his will for

Carrington. But what good would it do to cry over spilt milk? she thought miserably. He was gone, and she would have to face the fact that she had driven him away.

She sighed. In spite of the absence of the host, the party had been a great success, thanks mainly to Felicity, Tony, and Nicholas, who had obviously enjoyed themselves. When the conversation turned to her mother's imminent removal to Hampshire, however, Samantha wondered what she would do all by herself in London. Carrington had talked of their own removal to Silverdale Grange, it is true, but what kind of a welcome would she get from him now if she appeared on his doorstep? The thought of having to endure a chilly reception from him daunted her. So when her mother suggested she come down to Hampshire with them, Samantha gratefully accepted.

"Dalton is to accompany us, my dear," Lady Midland explained, evidently pleased with this arrangement.

"My father's estate is a bare thirty miles from Ashley Hall, so it is practically on my way." Tony regarded her for a moment, then added, "I would be happy to escort you to Silverdale Grange, Samantha. For I presume you intend to join Philip there for the New Year."

Samantha smiled. Actually, she had made no plans to do anything of the sort, but she would cross that bridge when she came to it. Perhaps by that time Philip would be glad to see her, she thought wistfully.

"And Carrington has promised to let me keep Nicholas with us at Ashley Hall for a few days," said Lady Midland. "The boy tells me you have promised to show him the hunters, dear. He can talk of nothing else."

And so it had been agreed. She would be going home again with her mother and Felicity. Somehow, the idea of going home to Ashley Hall did not appeal to her as it might have done only a week ago. Had two weeks of marriage changed her so much? she asked herself. If she were honest, she would have to say that it had. She had other duties now, other loyalties. She had a husband whom she missed and a little boy who depended on her for love and affection. Yes, she had changed, and the sooner she put aside her missishness and started behaving like a real wife to Carrington, the better it would be for all of them, she decided.

Having come to this momentous decision, she reached for the bellpull to summon Sally with her morning chocolate.

Once Samantha had made up her mind to make the best of her situation, the day flew by in a bustle of activity. She had packing to do, Nicholas to get ready for the journey tomorrow, arrangements to make with the housekeeper, and a dozen other tasks that would not get done if she remained lolling about in bed.

By two o'clock she was pleasantly tired but satisfied that all was in readiness for the morrow, when Lady Midland would come for her and Nicholas in the travelling chaise. She had ordered a solitary tea-tray for herself in the drawing room and was about to pour a cup when Dalton came strolling in, waving *The Gazette.*

"Have you seen the news, Samantha?" he exclaimed, obviously in high good humour.

"I have not had time even to glance at a newspaper, Tony. Why don't you sit down and tell me what has put you in such high gig."

"Lady Sylvia Towers has just announced her betrothal to Hugh Davenport," he replied. "Philip and I have known the wind was in that quarter for some time, of course, but now it's official. They plan to have a spring wedding in St. George's, I gather."

Samantha gave a gasp of surprise. So it was true, she thought. The Incomparable Sylvia was to marry the handsome Sir Hugh. What a relief to know that at least one of her suspicions about Carrington had been completely unfounded. She felt as though a weight had been lifted from her heart. "I wish them luck," she said, and meant it.

Dalton grinned. "I expect it will be my turn next," he said with a rueful laugh. "That is, if I can work myself up to the sticking point. Seems to be catching."

Samantha had to smile. "Then I wish you luck, too, Tony," she said, pouring him a cup of tea. "I know that whichever lucky lady you choose will be fortunate indeed."

At that moment Turner came silently into the room with a note for his mistress. Samantha's heart jumped up into her throat at the possibility that the missive might be from her

husband. She was disappointed, however, for the paper bore
the name of her agent, Mr. MacIntyre.

The contents were brief and to the point, and they caused
Samantha's heart to sink again. He thought it his duty to inform
her ladyship, Mr. MacIntyre wrote in his dry style, that his
lordship, the Marquess of Carrington, had recently set up a
Trust Fund with his own man of business in the City, in the
sum of ten thousand pounds. The fund was to be administered
by himself, as trustee, and was registered in the name of a
minor, one Nicholas A. Sloughcum.

Samantha sighed. At the very least, she consoled herself, this
proves that Philip has no pressing gambling debts. But why
would he put that large a sum in trust for Nicholas if he were
not the child's father?

With this new revelation, two of Gerald's accusations had
been proved false. Now it seemed that the third one had to be
true. Could she learn to accept Nicholas into her heart if he
indeed proved to be Carrington's love-child? Samantha looked
deeply into her soul and found the answer. Impulsively, she
excused herself and ran upstairs to the nursery. She wanted to
hug a little boy who needed her love, regardless of whose son
he was.

"Are we going to see your hunters, Aunty Sam?" Nicholas
demanded excitedly as the coach wound its way slowly out of
London.

"We certainly are," Samantha replied. "And if the weather
is good, I shall take you out for a ride on my favourite,
Raspberry Treat."

"Raspberry?" he repeated. "Why do you call him that?"

"Because he's raspberry-coloured, dear." Samantha laughed,
happy to be on her way, at last, to Hampshire, where Philip
was.

Lady Midland had arrived at Carrington Court promptly at
nine o'clock that morning to pick up her daughter and
Nicholas. And Samantha, who had spent a restless night
wondering what she could possibly say to her husband to mend
the breach between them, was anxious to be on her way.

She had discovered, during the past two days, that life
without Philip was unthinkable. It had taken this unexpected

separation from him to find out that he was the one man she wanted to spend the rest of her life with. He had somehow wormed his way into her heart. Samantha could not explain how this had happened. She had been prepared to be a dutiful wife, but now she also wanted to be a loving one. And she wanted to be loved in return. Whether this was possible or not, she did not dare ask herself; but she would do everything in her power to recover the affection, if not the love, of the husband she had doubted so unjustly.

Such was her impatience to be near her husband again that Samantha found the journey tedious beyond bearing. Felicity was in high gig at the prospect of returning home and had brought a book of fairy-tales to read to Nicholas during the trip. Samantha envied her this carefree happiness, much of which, she knew, was due to Tony Dalton's presence on horseback beside their carriage. Every adoring glance Felicity received from the besotted Dalton during their frequent stops made Samantha feel more keenly her own loneliness.

Lady Midland insisted on spending the night at the Red Angel in Basingstoke, since the condition of the roads had made progress slow. As a result they did not reach Ashley Hall until midafternoon on the second day. By this time, Samantha was no nearer to solving her dilemma of how to win back her husband's regard than she had been the day before.

"Welcome home, milady," a beaming Biddle greeted her as she entered the front hall with Nicholas at her heels.

"Let us have a tea-tray in the drawing-room, Biddle," Lady Midland requested, as soon as they had assembled in the hall. "And this is Master Nicholas Sloughcum, Biddle. Please ask Mrs. Biddle if she will get the nursery-suite ready for him. His nurse will be arriving shortly with the other servants."

Later that evening, after she had pleaded fatigue and retired early to her room, Samantha sat before her dressing table, wondering how it was possible that the calm, beautiful face that stared back at her did not betray, by so much as a hint, the despair that raged in her breast.

She had found no relief from her longing for Carrington at Ashley Hall. Quite the contrary, in fact. His remembered presence was everywhere. In the dining-room, where she had toyed with her food last night; in the library, where he had first

kissed her; in the stables, where the admiration in his dark eyes
had made her heart pound. But most of all, in the bed-chamber
next door, where he had lain with a bullet wound in his
shoulder; where they had been wed in that crazy midnight
ceremony; and where he had kissed her a second time. Really
kissed her, she thought, remembering every movement, every
caress, every touch of his warm hand on her breast.

She sighed. You've got to stop this immediately, she told
herself sternly. You're behaving like a silly chit mooning over
a calf-love. Tomorrow she would have a long talk with her
mother, she thought. It was time to make a decisive push if she
ever wanted to have her husband back again. And even if he
rejected her, which he had every right to do, she thought
miserably, at least she could let him know how mistaken she
had been in doubting his loyalty. As for Nicholas, that had all
happened in the past, over six years ago, to be exact, before
Carrington had even met her, much less discovered he was
betrothed to her. No, she was determined not to let Nicholas
come between them. If necessary, she would adopt the child
herself.

Her mother would know how to advise her, Samantha
reasoned, as she climbed into bed and pulled the covers up to
her chin. Tonight was four nights since she had quarreled with
the marquess. Four nights and four long days of being without
him. Mama would help her find a way to undo the wrong she
had done him. She might even be persuaded to accompany her
daughter to Silverdale Grange. The prospect of seeing Carrington again made her smile. Perhaps, Samantha thought
sleepily, tomorrow would not be so painful after all.

Samantha awoke to the sound of the curtains being drawn
and a cup set down on her bedside table. Strange that Sally was
so silent, she thought drowsily, unwilling to open her eyes to
the new day. Stranger still when the bedsprings creaked, and
someone sat down on the bed beside her.

Her eyes flew open. "Mama!" she cried, suddenly wide
awake. "Oh, Mama. I'm so glad to see you." Even to her own
ears, her voice sounded teary.

"I rather thought you might be, my love," Lady Midland
replied calmly, stroking the red-gold curls back from her

daughter's brow. "Sit up and drink your chocolate, dearest. And I will have a cup with you, even if it is past ten o'clock."

Samantha rubbed her eyes and glanced around the room. "It doesn't seem that late, Mama," she replied. "It's still so dark."

Lady Midland laughed. "That's because it is snowing, my dear. We had a snowstorm last night, and it shows no sign of wanting to let up."

"Oh, dear," Samantha wailed. "This cannot be happening to me. I had planned to go out today."

"There is no way you will be going anywhere today, Samantha," her ladyship said gently. "Now, I think it is high time you told me just what is going on between you and Carrington, my love."

Samantha sighed and reached for her mother's hand. "Oh, Mama. You have no idea how bad things are. I've been such a silly widgeon, you wouldn't believe."

"I think I can guess, dear. You had a falling out, is that it?"

"It's much, much worse than that, Mama," Samantha murmured. "I have harboured the most dreadful suspicions about him, and now they have turned out to be false. Most of them, anyway," she added.

"I gather you did not consider voicing these suspicions to Carrington, my love?"

Samantha regarded her mother in horror. "How could I possibly ask him to his face if Lady Sylvia Towers was his mistress, Mama? Surely you would not have wanted me to do anything so . . . so unbecoming."

Lady Midland only smiled. "I gather she was not, dear?"

"No. She is betrothed to another. A love-match, from what I hear."

"She is to be envied, then," her ladyship remarked. "But I fail to see how this mere suspicion could cause you to fall out with Carrington."

"It didn't, Mama. You see, I also accused him of having gambling debts," Samantha confessed.

"Oh, dear. That is more serious, dear. No man likes to be called to brook for losing at cards, you know. Men have such an inflated sense of their own worth, Samantha. It never serves any useful purpose to deflate it, as you will find out before you are much older. And it's not as though Carrington has pockets to let. Actually, from what MacIntyre told me, he's as rich as Croesus."

"I thought so, too, until Gerald told me about his addiction to gambling."

"Gerald told you this? You should have had more sense than to listen to that noddlehead, my dear. You must know he has always resented you and tried to cut you out with your father. Even as a lad, he was devious to a fault. Why, I could tell you stories . . . but that is neither here nor there."

"I know that now, Mama, and am heartily sorry I was so taken in. Mr. MacIntyre tells me that Philip set up a trust with the money he got from Papa's will. And to think I accused him of accepting it as a bribe. I was never more mortified when I found out. He must think me the veriest shrew."

Samantha paused when she noticed that her mother was staring at her with an arrested expression in her eyes. "A trust, you say. For you, my dear?"

"No, for Nicholas."

"Ah." Her mother let out her breath in a long sigh. "Then I was right." She got up and moved quickly to the door. "Stay here, dearest, I will be right back. I have something to show you."

Samantha did not have long to wait. In less than a minute Lady Midland was back, carrying something in her closed fist.

"Here, my love. Take a look at this and tell me what you think." She placed an old-fashioned gold locket in Samantha's hand.

Intrigued, Samantha put her thumbnail in the groove, and the locket snapped open. She found herself gazing down at a delicate portrait of a young boy with dark, trusting eyes and a shock of unruly black curls making a halo around his small head.

"Oh, Nicholas!" she exclaimed in delight. "Mama, wherever did you get this likeness of him?" Then she sobered and glanced at her mother. "That's another thing I haven't told you, Mama. Nicholas is Philip's son, you know."

Lady Midland regarded her daughter for a long moment, and Samantha wondered why her mother appeared so pale.

"No need for you to fly into a pucker, Mama. It really does

not signify. I am quite determined not to regard it. The child so obviously needs a mother, you see. 'Twould be selfish of me to deny him that.''

"Yes, dear. And very proper of you to feel that way, my love. Or it would be if Nicholas were indeed Philip's son." She took the locket from Samantha's hand and gazed at it with a curious little smile on her lips. "Which he isn't, of course."

"He's not?"

"No, he is not."

"But he looks just like him," Samantha insisted, wondering what maggot had got into her mother's head.

"The nose is quite different, dear. Noticed it right away. Oh, I'll admit there is a superficial likeness, but the nose is not a Silverdale nose at all. I knew I had seen it somewhere before, and I was right. Just look at that portrait. I remembered it last night as I was getting ready for bed."

Samantha felt a sudden premonition of disaster, but she was not yet ready to admit that she had been wrong about the child.

"But that is Nicholas in the portrait, Mama, so of course the nose is the same."

"Oh, no, dear," Lady Midland murmured. "Your grandmother gave me this locket over twenty-five years ago, when I became betrothed to your Papa." She paused and gazed again at the portrait of the young child. "This is definitely not Nicholas."

An overwhelming wave of panic washed over Samantha, and she found it hard to draw breath. She could not take her eyes off her mother, and when Lady Midland raised her own from the incriminating locket, mother and daughter stared deeply into each other's eyes for what seemed like an eternity.

"Are you trying to tell me, Mama, that Nicholas is my . . . my brother?" she managed to ask in a strangled voice.

"I'm afraid so, my love," replied Lady Midland with infinite sadness. "I'm very much afraid so."

18 * The Return of the White Knight

THE MARQUESS OF CARRINGTON HAD BEEN IN A FOUL MOOD FOR SIX whole days, ever since Christmas Day, when he had descended unexpectedly on his family seat in Hampshire. The staff tiptoed about and tried to be as unobstrusive as possible, and even the butler, who had known Philip Silverdale since early childhood, nearly got his head bitten off for enquiring when they might expect to welcome the new marchioness at the Grange.

The truth was, Philip thought as he paced to and fro before the library fire, he had made a muff of the whole affair. What maggot had inspired him to leave London in such a helter-skelter manner, he wondered, dashing off in a bang like some Johnny Raw when Samantha had ripped up at him on Christmas Eve.

The sound of her voice still rang in his ears. Indeed, it had rung there all the way down from London during that long, cold drive. He remembered springing his cattle mercilessly, behaving like a madman, the veriest whipster, and so unlike his usual self that his valet had several times cautioned him about the risk of breaking their legs. All Crofts had gained for his advice was a snarled command to keep his tongue between his teeth if he didn't want to be set down at the next posting house. It was a wonder they had all survived.

The worst part of this whole affair was that before they were even halfway down to Hampshire, he had begun to regret his hasty flight. Pride had kept him from turning right about and rushing back to Cavendish Square and his wife. Pride, and a deep-seated reluctance to admit that he was partially to blame for the accusations she had thrown so cavalierly at his head during that dreadful brangle in the wee hours of Christmas Day.

He had hoped that night to break down Samantha's defences at last and claim, not just his rights as her husband, but a share of that tender fire he suspected burned beneath her calm exterior. She had returned his kisses that evening, hadn't she? It's true she had been dazzled by his gift of sapphires, but that alone could not account for the sweet way she had pressed herself against him while he kissed her. Her arms had reached around his neck, and she had trembled, perhaps with awakening desire, he thought hopefully, when he had caressed her body with his eager hands.

Carrington groaned aloud and kicked impatiently at a log in the fireplace until it sent up a shower of sparks. Had he been too passionate, he wondered, and given her a disgust for him? Well-bred young ladies of the *ton* were often ill-prepared for the physical realities of married life, and he had heard that some even took an intense dislike to any contact at all with their husbands. Samantha did not seem to be one of them, however, and he had been charmed by her warm response to his embrace.

By God, he thought, what kind of a fool was he to be kicking his heels here in Hampshire when the woman he wanted beyond endurance was in London? How much longer would he pretend to himself that he enjoyed taking his gun out into the Home Wood every afternoon to try for a brace of pigeons? And every afternoon he had come back empty-handed, his gun not even fired. The servants had long since ceased to be taken in by such farradiddle and now kept out of his way whenever possible.

If he had any sense at all, he thought, he would get on the fastest horse in his stables and ride back to London without any further shilly-shallying around. He would take his delectable wife in his arms and kiss her until she begged for mercy. Then he would tell her everything about that confounded bequest of ten thousand pounds in Midland's will, why he had been forced to take it, and what he had done with it. How could he justify allowing his promise to a dead man to destroy not only his own happiness, but the happiness of the woman he loved?

He paused in his nervous pacing, and a smile twitched at his lips, the first in many days. And there you have it, he thought. He had been moping around here like a love-lorn jackstraw without recognizing what was ailing him. What a sap-skull he had been, not to have realized that he had finally met his nemesis, a woman who could lift him into transports of joy or cast him into the deepest pits of despair.

Carrington ran his fingers through his hair until the dark curls stood up in disorder. Dashed if I'm not in love, he thought ruefully. Call me a monkey's uncle if it ain't so. I'm in love with my own wife. The realization of this phenomenon made him heave a sigh of relief. At least now he knew what he had to do. He would leave immediately for London to tell Samantha. With pleasant visions of the repercussions of this delicious scene evolving in his mind, he strode purposefully towards the door.

He opened it to find his butler advancing towards him, bearing a letter on a silver tray.

"Have Ajax saddled immediately, Jenkins, I'm off to London."

The butler gaped at him. "If I may say so, milord," he murmured nervously, "there's a regular blanket of snow out there, and more to come from what I hear. Been coming down for the past hour, it has, milord."

The marquess swore under his breath and stalked to the library window. A quick glance confirmed that Jenkins was right. He had been so absorbed with thoughts of his wife that he had failed to notice the silent snowfall. Should he make a bolt for it and trust his horse to get him through, or should he wait for the morrow and hope that the storm would have ceased by then? With a sigh, he turned from the window. Although he ached to be on his way, the latter choice seemed advisable.

"What have you got there, Jenkins?"

"A letter, milord. One of Mr. Dalton's grooms just delivered it. Seems as though the storm is coming from that direction, milord. The groom had a hard time getting through."

Carrington picked up the missive and opened it. His face brightened, and he astonished his butler by grinning at him. "Seems as though we won't be going to London after all, Jenkins. Her ladyship is safe with her mother at Ashley Hall." He glanced again at the window, which was darkening ominously. "I shall leave in the morning. Ask Crofts to have Ajax ready at first light."

* * *

Her mother's revelation had left Samantha utterly speechless. As the monstrosity of what she had heard penetrated her paralyzed mind, she choked back a sob and threw herself into Lady Midland's arms.

"Oh, Mama," she sobbed disconsolately. "How could Papa do such a thing? How *could* he?"

"There, there, my love, don't overset yourself. What's done is done, and there's no mending it. We must bear up, my dear." She patted her daughter's shaking shoulders and smoothed her riotous curls with a hand that trembled only slightly.

"But how positively lowering for you, dearest," Samantha moaned. "You must be devastated beyond bearing. I almost wish the boy had been Carrington's after all. I can't bear to have you hurt like this; it's simply not fair. How could Papa do this to you? I'll never forgive him. Never!"

Lady Midland hugged her daughter tightly and rocked her as if she were a child. "Females sometimes fail to understand the pressures gentlemen have to endure, my dear. They are beset by passions that gently bred females can only guess at, my love. Do not be so harsh on your father. I fear I am partly to blame for what happened."

"You?" Samantha gazed at her through tear-filled eyes. "How can you possibly be blamed for Papa's perfidy? You cannot be serious, Mama."

"Oh, yes, dear. I am serious. Many times your father begged me to accompany him to India, but I could not see exposing you and Felicity to the rigours of a foreign climate, my love. And I always found excuses not to go. So I cannot lay the blame entirely at his door. I can even find it in my heart to pity him, Samantha. Just think on it a moment. He finally had the son he wanted so much but could not acknowledge him as his own. That must have been punishment enough, dear."

Samantha was not entirely convinced. "No more than he deserved, surely," she said reluctantly.

"Let us be generous, Samantha. I know how much you adored your father, but, for my sake, forgive him this weakness and help me to raise his son as he would have wished. Please, dear."

Samantha looked at her mother tenderly. "You are wonderful, Mama. Of course I will help you. Nicholas is my brother, after all.'' She smiled, savouring the new idea. ''I wonder what Philip will say when he finds out we know all about his secret?''

Lady Midland rose briskly and went over to the window. ''We will go to Carrington together as soon as it stops snowing, my love. But I fear we may have to wait a day or two. 'Tis monstrously thick out there.''

When Samantha came downstairs for breakfast she found little solace in the soused herrings, buttered eggs, and York ham which Mrs. Biddle had set out to tempt her appetite. She poured herself a cup of tea from the silver pot and moodily spread a thick layer of raspberry jam on a slice of toast.

She spent most of the morning flitting restlessly about from window to window, watching a seemingly unending fall of snowflakes blanket the grounds of Ashley Hall. Just before noon, during a lull in the storm, she had the stable-boys and gardeners dig out a pathway between the house and the stables so she could take Nicholas to visit the horses. Samantha was thus able to while away several hours that afternoon introducing her eager half-brother to the delights of riding.

But Philip was never far from her mind. His remembered presence in the stables made her all the more eager to go to him. There were so many things she had to get off her mind. She could hardly wait to tell him that her quarrel with him had been a terrible mistake, brought on by groundless suspicions planted in her head by her malicious Cousin Gerald. None of Gerald's accusations had been true at all, she realized. And she cursed herself for being so taken in by his lies that she had imagined her husband guilty without any proof at all. Would he ever forgive her? she wondered miserably. Or had she forfeited her chance at happiness with Philip through her naive stupidity?

That evening as she sat in the nursery with Lady Midland, listening to her mother read a bedtime story to Nicholas, she realized how much Philip had changed their lives. Ever since his arrival at Ashley Hall in the middle of a snowstorm over three weeks ago, he had affected all of them in different ways. She herself had found a husband she could love. Never mind that it had taken her so long to recognize what she felt for Carrington as love that she may have lost it forever. Philip had also brought Tony Dalton into Felicity's world; Samantha had little doubt, having observed them together during the past three days of snowbound confinement to Ashley Hall, that the two would make a match of it.

And then there was Nicholas. Her face softened as she watched her mother listening attentively to the child's questions about the story she was reading to him. Against all reason, Mama seems to be enchanted with her husband's child, Samantha thought, amazed at her mother's courage and capacity for love. It was almost as if Papa had come back to her again. The idea was absurd, of course, she told herself; but Nicholas has given Mama a new reason to live.

None of this would have happened had it not been for Philip, she thought. The three of them would have been on their way to the moors of Northumberland by now but for the miraculous arrival of the White Knight. She sighed. Felicity had teased her about her romantical fantasies, but they had come true. Except that she had not lived happily ever after, of course. She had driven her knight away with her foolishness. And if he refused to take her back, she would have only herself to blame.

This mood of despondency stayed with her when she went upstairs to dress for dinner. She could not seem to find joy in anything anymore. Even the choice of a gown to wear on this New Year's Eve failed to rouse her from the dismals.

Only when Sally took out the blue satin she had worn that last night with Philip did she find the energy to protest.

"Not that one, Sally. I don't feel like wearing that one tonight."

"It's the prettiest one you have, milady," Sally replied placidly. "And it looks so well with the necklace his lordship gave you for Christmas. Stunning is what it is, milady. No doubt about it. His lordship couldn't take his eyes off you, if I remember rightly."

Samantha gave up and allowed her abigail to slip the smooth material over her head. Memories flooded back as she sat down at the dresser to have her hair arranged and the sapphires clasped around her neck.

"You're a mite pale tonight, milady. Shall I rub a little colour on you cheeks perhaps?"

Samantha shook her head. If her husband had been here to

kiss her as he had the last time she had worn this dress, there would be no need for potted creams, she thought. But he wasn't here, and she would have to get through this evening somehow, pretending to a gaiety she did not feel.

There was a tap on her door, and Felicity burst in with her usual lighthearted banter. It seems as though everyone but me is looking forward to the New Year and what it will bring them, Samantha mused.

"You look like a fairy princess in that dress, Samantha!" her sister exclaimed jubilantly. "All we need is your Prince Charming to come along and wake you with a kiss."

Samantha could not help laughing at this farradiddle. "You are being nonsensical, darling. I am wide awake, thank you. And you have your fantasies mixed up. Prince Charming is waiting downstairs for you, dear, and no doubt he will kiss you before the year is ended." She was surprised and pleased to see her sister blush shyly.

"As for me," she continued with an attempt at levity, "I would much prefer a dark stranger masquerading as the White Knight to come knocking on my door as the clock strikes twelve."

"Crawling on his hands and knees through the snow, no doubt." Felicity laughed as the two made their way down to the drawing-room. "Well, at least we have plenty of snow, Sam." She glanced at her tall sister with a gleam of compassion in her blue eyes. "Have faith in him, dearest. Have faith. I know he will come for you again."

Felicity's words, absurd though they were, filled Samantha's head with pleasant thoughts, and she was able to enjoy her sister's banter at the dinner table and watch with amusement as Felicity charmed Tony Dalton with her saucy repartee.

As the only gentleman present, Tony did not sit over his port after dinner, but joined the ladies in the drawing-room, where Felicity persuaded her sister to play some rollicking folk songs for them. Try as she could, however, she could not persuade Samantha to sit up until midnight with them to welcome in the New Year. So it was not long after the tea-tray had been brought in at ten o'clock that Samantha decided to say her good-nights and slip up to her room.

She had hardly crossed the hall towards the stairs, however, when she was waylaid by Biddle, who announced, in an agitated voice, that her ladyship had a visitor.

"A visitor? At this hour?" Her first thought was that her mother's butler had been tippling rather too liberally on account of the New Year celebrations in the kitchen.

"Yes, milady. Most insistent he was to see you, milady. Most anxious indeed."

Samantha stared at him. "Who is he?" she said. Her voice sounded oddly breathless.

Biddle looked apologetic. "He wouldn't say, milady."

"Where is he? In the library?"

"No, milady." Biddle cleared his throat with a discreet cough. "I put him upstairs in your ladyship's sitting-room. He insisted, milady."

"My sitting-room?" Samantha's eyes opened wide in disbelief. Then sudden light dawned, and a delicate flush stained her cheeks. "Oh, thank you, Biddle," she gasped and ran up the stairs as lightly as a thistledown.

Samantha did not allow herself to doubt for an instant that her White Knight had done it again. Holding up her skirts, she ran along the hall and flung open the door to her small sitting-room.

And there he was, leaning easily against the mantelpiece and smiling that lazy, caressing smile she remembered so well,

"Philip!" she exclaimed breathlessly. "You've come!"

"So it would seem, my love," came the amused reply.

"Felicity said you would." She longed to throw herself into his arms, but she was suddenly afraid that this tall man who was regarding her with hooded eyes would reject her.

"Your sister is infinitely wise, my dear." He regarded her for a moment, and then smiled. "You are even lovelier than I remembered, Samantha." His smile faded as his eyes slowly raked her from head to foot until her cheeks became hot.

"Philip," she began nervously, taking a few steps into the room. "There's something I must tell you." She stopped abruptly, suddenly aware that her husband was dressed in his brocade silk dressing-gown. How had she not noticed his state of undress before? she wondered. Was she losing her sense of decorum?

"What happened to your clothes?" she asked without thinking, and then blushed furiously at her indiscretion.

Carrington laughed. "Wet," he replied. "Biddle insisted I change into something dry before I caught a congestion of the lungs. I must have given the old boy a bad start, for he wanted to tuck me into bed with a hot brick." His eyes gleamed with amusement. "I managed to convince him that I had other plans, my love."

Samantha dropped her gaze. She would not permit herself to wonder what her husband's plans might be. Casting around for a change of subject, she noticed the remains of a meal on a nearby table. "You have had dinner, I see," she remarked unnecessarily. "How long have you been here, then?"

"Over an hour."

"Why didn't you come into the drawing-room, or at least let me know you were here?" Samantha could have kicked herself. Why could she not stop asking inane questions when what she wanted from Philip was a sign that he had forgiven her.

"I was not presentable. And besides, my business was with you, my dear."

"Business?" Her voice quavered slightly. The word sounded ominous. Was he going to disown her? Have their marriage annulled, perhaps? Samantha felt her face go pale. This was worse than she had imagined.

"In a manner of speaking, yes. We do have some unfinished business between us, Lady Carrington." His glance ran over her satin gown again, and he grinned. "I suggest you take that off, my love. We wouldn't want to crush it, would we? Since it did cost a king's ransom, I believe."

"But I have something important to discuss with you, Philip. Something you should know."

Carrington walked over and took both her hands in his. Samantha felt a tremor run through her as he kissed her fingers lightly.

"Later, my love. I have some things to tell you, too, Samantha. Things I should have told you sooner, perhaps." He looked deeply into her amber eyes and smiled tenderly. He could lose himself in her eyes, he thought, and wondered how he had refrained from snatching his delectable wife into his arms and holding her against him as he longed to do. No, he told himself sternly. There were certain confessions he must make before he could risk that ultimate confession of love that, even now, trembled on his lips.

"Go," he ordered. "But come back soon, or I swear I will come and fetch you, my sweet."

His eyes followed his wife hungrily as she fairly ran out of the room.

Sally awaited her in her bed-chamber, and Samantha was uncomfortably aware that every domestic in the house probably knew by now that Lord Carrington had arrived to claim his lady. Sally most certainly had guessed that something momentous was afoot, for she had laid out a lacy confection that Felicity had brought home one day in London as a belated wedding gift for her sister. Samantha had been mildly shocked that her little sister had chosen such an outrageously seductive garment and so obviously had expected Samantha to wear it. She never had, of course. Until tonight, there had been no excuse to do so.

Now she allowed Sally to slip the provocative nightgown over her head without a murmur of protest. She was quite determined not to give Philip the slightest occasion to call her an unwilling wife. Quite the contrary, she thought, with a thrill of excitement. If the aching sensation she was feeling now, at the mere thought of him waiting for her in the next room, was any indication of her readiness to be his wife, then she might surprise him.

She blushed faintly at the immodesty of this thought and quickly wrapped herself in the warm woolen robe Sally was holding out for her. After Sally had let down her hair and brushed it vigorously until the gold highlights shone among the auburn curls, Samantha knew she could delay no longer.

"I won't need you any more tonight, Sally," she said quietly. When the abigail had left, Samantha opened a brightly enamelled box on her dresser and took out her mother's locket. The time had come to break down that last barrier between them.

Philip still stood before the fire, one arm on the mantel, and as Samantha came towards him, he smiled and held out a hand invitingly.

"Was that soon enough for you, my lord?" Samantha enquired, glancing up at him through her long lashes.

"No, you minx!" He laughed, taking her hand and drawing her close. "But it is much sooner than I had any right to expect."

She had expected him to kiss her, but when he didn't, she looked up and saw that his eyes held that predatory expression she had seen in them before.

"Samantha, love . . ." he murmured, his voice strangely husky.

"Before you say anything, Philip," Samantha cut in hastily, her heart moved by an unexpected hint of pleading in his tone, "I want you to see this." She opened her left hand and showed him the locket lying in her palm.

Carrington looked down, momentarily distracted. "What is it, my dear?"

"A locket, Philip."

"I can see that, my sweet." He raised an eyebrow at her.

Without another word, Samantha flicked the locket open to reveal the miniature. "There," she said. "A surprise. What do you think of that, my lord?"

Philip regarded it for several seconds. "It is a wonderful likeness, my dear. But when did you manage to get a miniature painted of Nicholas?"

Samantha sighed. "It is not Nicholas."

Philip took up the locket and examined the tiny portrait more closely. "Of course it's Nicholas," he repeated. "Who else could it be?"

Samantha took the miniature from his fingers. "It certainly appears to be Nicholas, that I will admit," she replied. "However, it cannot be. You see, this portrait must be fifty years old." She paused and looked up into her husband's eyes. "Mama has had it for at least twenty-five."

He stared at her in silence for a long moment, and she saw dawning comprehension in the depths of his dark eyes.

"Yes," she said at last. "It's a portrait of my father as a young boy. I confess it fooled me, too, Philip."

"So Lady Midland has guessed?"

Samantha nodded. "It is true, then?"

Philip turned to gaze down into the flames, his face troubled.

"Yes, it's true. I had thought to save you both this embarrassment. I could not very well abandon the child at Christmas, Samantha. He has not adapted well to living at the Grange. There are no other children there for him to play with, and I have no sisters who might take him in." He looked at her, as if searching her face for something.

"I promised your father I would protect him, Samantha, and I cannot fail to do so. You do understand that, don't you?"

Her smile encouraged him to continue.

"The bequest in the will was meant for Nicholas, my dear. It was not for me at all."

"I know that now, Philip. Mama guessed it must have been Papa's way of providing for his son."

"Your father knew I wouldn't need any bribe to marry you, my love. I will send Nicholas back to India. You need have nothing to do with him if it pains you."

"No!" Samantha spoke sharply, and her eyes took on a determined expression. "I will not allow you to do anything so shabby to my brother, sir. Neither will Mama, as you will very soon find out." She laughed up into his surprised face. "She loves him dearly, you know, and I doubt she will take kindly to losing him, my lord."

"And you?" Philip enquired softly, slipping an arm around her waist and finding no resistance "Whom do you love, my pet?"

"Oh, I love him, too. He takes after Papa in his love of horses, you know. He is quite unafraid of them, just as I was at his age. Matt is already teaching him to ride and—"

Philip stopped this torrent of words with a kiss. "That is not precisely what I meant," he murmured against the curve of his wife's neck.

"Oh," Samantha gasped, snuggling closer into his embrace. "I loved him even when I was sure he was yours, Philip," she confessed, glad of the chance to get that guilty burden off her mind.

"You did what?" Philip's head snapped up, and he frowned at her. "What are you saying, madam?"

Samantha looked contrite. "I know it was foolish of me, Philip. But you were so reluctant to tell me his father's name that I naturally assumed it must be you.'' She glanced up at him through her lashes. ''Please say you forgive me.''

If he could only forgive her for this breach of faith, she thought, she would make it up to him in a million different ways. At least he had not taken his arms from around her. He was still holding her quite breathlessly close, so close, she realized with a sudden shock, that she could feel the hardness and warmth of him through both their robes. She coloured at the thought of what little actually lay between them. Tentatively, she eased herself closer into the lean curve of his body.

''Baggage!'' Philip groaned, and a shudder shook his entire frame. This saucy minx was going to be everything he had dreamed she would be, he thought, sliding his hand down from her slender waist and cupping her more firmly against him. He raised his head for a moment and gazed into her eyes. Aside from a faint rosy blush on her cheeks, his wife seemed quite unperturbed by this tantalizing intimacy which was making his own blood fairly sing. She returned his gaze with a limpid innocence that made him pause, uncertain of himself, until she dropped her lashes, and a shadow of a teasing smile touched her lips. The naughty minx was flirting with him!

Samantha caught his astonished expression, and a gurgle of laughter escaped her. She had, after all, succeeded in surprising him with her daring. And pleasing him, too, she thought. There was no mistaking that gleam of delight in his eyes. If only it were love, she wished. Perhaps, in time, he would learn to love her, but in the meantime she must be content with her power to make him happy. That would have to be enough.

''Am I to understand that I am forgiven?'' She smiled at him, slipping an arm around his neck. Knowledge of her power to seduce him had given her courage.

''You're a sad tease, my lady. And when you flirt with me like that, I can deny you nothing. I will probably come to regret that admission some day, but yes, you adorable creature, you are forgiven.'' To prove his point, Philip lowered his head and captured his wife's lips in a kiss that progressed, during several minutes, from the gentlest of caresses to the most shattering of experiences that left them both breathless and trembling.

''Yes, my love,'' he murmured against her lips. ''You are completely forgiven, on the condition that—''

"No conditions, my lord," Samantha interrupted, pulling her lips away and looking up at him seriously. "I want no conditions and no secrets between us ever again, my lord. Do you understand?" Her face was flushed, but she held his gaze steadily.

He grinned, and she could tell what he was thinking before he spoke. "No conditions at all, Samantha? I think I can go along with that. But do you realize that you are putting yourself entirely into my hands, my sweet?"

"Yes," she said.

He regarded her for a moment, his eyes unreadable. "Is this what you really want, Samantha? We both know what I want, my dear. But is it what you want, too?"

"Yes," she whispered, lowering her lashes so he would not see the love in her eyes. And it was true, she told herself. It was definitely true. But there was something missing that would make the moment of surrender perfect. He had not mentioned a single word of love, and perhaps she had been foolish to expect it. Love was for the characters in romantical novels, for White Knights and damsels in distress. To think of Philip Silverdale, the Marquess of Carrington, as her own White Knight had been fanciful in the extreme. What if he had saved her from a distressful situation? This was real life, and no knight could be expected to crawl on hands and knees through the snow to carry her off to live happily ever after.

Samantha signed and gazed up at the real man who had just ridden nearly fifty miles in a snowstorm to be with her. Perhaps this was better than novels after all, she thought, and smiled at him tenderly.

"That disposes of all the conditions, dear heart," he was saying as he tightened his hold on her again. "And as for the secrets, you already know all of mine, Samantha. Do I know all of yours?"

"Of course you do, Philip."

"All of them?"

She looked at him with a startled expression. Could he have guessed the secret she was determined to carry in her heart forever?

"Come on, confess it, dearest. There's one you haven't told me, isn't there?"

"How did you know?" Her voice was so low he had to bend his head to catch her words.

"Because there's one I haven't told you either, you silly goose. And if you haven't guessed it, you must be singularly unobservant, my little love."

"Tell me, Philip!" she cried, an odd surge of hope making her giddy. "I want to know this instant. Please tell me."

He grinned at her then, a lopsided, whimsical grin so full of affection that it made her heart turn over.

"I love you, you sly little minx. As if you didn't know it. I've just spent six of the worst days of my entire life. When I finally realized I was miserable because you were not there with me, I had to do something about it, snow or no snow." Suddenly he picked her up in his arms and held her cradled close to his heart. "And now I intend to do something else about it, my girl," he said huskily, looking at her with that hungry gaze she had been waiting for. "Come hell or high water."

"Oh, Philip." She giggled. "There's no need to look so fierce about it, my love. I'm not going to insist that you wade through hell or high water, or even crawl through the snow, for that matter. I'm quite resigned to the fact that you are not a knight, after all. But I love you just the same," she added close to his ear and so softly that he wondered if he had heard aright.

"Of course I'm not a knight, you peagoose. I'm a marquess. Thought you knew that." He leaned down to nuzzle her mouth possessively. "And what was the other thing you said, dearest?"

Samantha gazed up at her marquess and wondered how she could ever have been so foolish as to wish for a knight. "I love you, Lord Carrington, sir," she said clearly, her amber eyes reflecting the truth of her words.

With a satisfied smile on his lean face, the Marquess of Carrington carried his wife into her bedchamber and kicked the door firmly shut behind them.